The Broken Hearts Honeymoon

Lucy Dickens is the pseudonym for Lisa Dickenson. Lisa lives by the Devon seaside with her husband and one very boisterous Bernese Mountain Dog.

LUCY DICKENS

The Broken Hearts Honeymoon

arrow books

2 4 6 8 10 9 7 5 3 1

Arrow Books
20 Vauxhall Bridge Road
London SW1V 2SA

Arrow Books is part of the Penguin Random House group
of companies whose addresses can be found at
global.penguinrandomhouse.com

Penguin
Random House
UK

First published in Great Britain in 2020 by Arrow Books

www.penguin.co.uk

A CIP catalogue record for this book is available from
the British Library.

ISBN 9781787466159

Typeset in 11/17 pt Palatino
by Integra Software Services Pvt. Ltd, Pondicherry

Printed and bound in Great Britain by Clays Ltd, Elcograf S.p.A.

Penguin Random House is committed to a
sustainable future for our business, our readers
and our planet. This book is made from Forest
Stewardship Council® certified paper.

Dedicated to
anybody in need of an armchair adventure

Chapter 1

We had a whole plan
Dream wedding, dream job, dream life
Then shit hit the fan

Has my fiancé always been this much of a wet wipe? The question won't leave me alone, that question of all things, as if focusing on that, instead of his face and his words and the noise around me, will somehow bring me answers to what is happening.

What *is* happening? Is he seriously saying this? *Now?*

For ten years Matt and I have been each other's everything, and for him to drop this bombshell makes me wonder if he's changed at some point without me noticing, or if he was like this all along.

Let me set the scene for you.

It's Saturday evening and Matt and I are sitting on the floor in front of our coffee table. We share a boxy little flat near to where we both grew up, with none of our own furnishings or decor, but it doesn't matter because new beginnings are peeking out at us over the horizon. We've been working hard and saving the pennies ever since we left university.

It's early spring. The sun has journeyed south for the day and outside the cracked window, the sky is a denim blue. A cool breeze is trickling in and making the flames on the two lit candles flicker. The table is lightly peppered with crumbs of cheese and nearly finished bowls of crisps. There's an empty bottle of red between us, and Billie Eilish is playing on a low volume in the background.

All feels right with our world. It's comfy and familiar but also exciting because the whispers of adventure are becoming louder by the day, and those new beginnings are woven with absolute security because our wedding is three weeks today.

'This time in three weeks we'll be chowing down on our wedding cake,' I marvel, smiling at his face. 'This time in *four* weeks we'll be in Tokyo. Or will we have left on the honeymoon tour yet ... ? No, still Tokyo, I think. Which reminds me: we should check if we need to book at that robot restaurant I heard about.'

He smiles back at me, that ol' familiar smile that tells me he's thinking about something, trying to settle on what he wants to say. I know this expression well.

'Charlotte. I have a proposal for you.'

'Another one?' I joke, reaching for more cheese, but somewhere in the outer depths of my universe where I can barely even feel it right now, a tiny black hole of foreboding has opened up. And it's all because of the way he pauses before he says:

'We've been together since school, which is a really long time, and we're planning to be together for the rest of our lives, right?'

I stuff in a lump of Stilton. 'That's the plan, unless a Hemsworth brother moves to town.'

'So I've been thinking a bit. Well, a lot, actually. I'm not sure what you're going to think of this so here goes: how about we take a week off, just some time to put the breaks on and have some space, a pre-wedding break?'

'You need a holiday *before* our wedding?'

I mean, I get what he's saying. Between the endless phone calls from my mother about the wedding, and the constant updates from my siblings' WhatsApp group screenshotting Japanese cat cafes that they have seen online and insist I have to visit, Matt and I haven't had much couple-time together, but that is what the honeymoon is for, and not forgetting the little thing of spending the rest of our lives together. It's sweet that Matt wants to do this, but we don't have the time or, quite frankly, the money to go away three weeks before the wedding.

I'm thinking of the right way to let Matt down gently when he suddenly blurts out, 'Not a holiday together, a holiday from each other. A week off from our relationship, to sow some wild oats, to *make sure* that we're doing the right thing.'

Suddenly, the Stilton feels like chalk in my mouth.

He smiles at me like he's suggesting we buy blue-top instead of green-top milk for a change, though I can see a little shake in his hands, a nervous flicker to his eyelashes. Meanwhile, I have started choking on the cheese.

Just to make sure.

We're doing the right thing.

Matt and I were each other's first kiss. We lost our virginities to each other. We stayed together through school, sixth form and university. Sure, once or twice we both probably wondered what it would be like to try going out with someone else. But to do something about it was never more than a flitter of a thought passing by on the breeze. We grew up together and we stayed together.

And now, *now*, he decides it's a great idea to sow some wild oats, right before our wedding?

Do you ever have those dreams where someone has crushed your soul but you seem to be invisible no matter how much you scream and cry at them? That's how this feels. Only I'm not at the screaming and crying stage yet because I'm consumed with the feeling of not knowing the person I had thought I knew most in the world, who I thought would never hurt me, who said he wanted to marry me, who I thought was equally excited about the plans we'd made together, but is now backing out, finding excuses, giving up. And I stare at him, with my seemingly all-important question: has he always been this much of a wet wipe?

Let's go back to the beginning ...

4 December 2009
Friday night, 11.38pm

'Shh, come in here but don't wake up Mum,' I whispered to my siblings, ushering all four of them into my room one by one. I unravelled my skinny scarf and threw it on my Twilight duvet cover, and hoiked up my favourite shimmery low-rise bootcut jeans before taking a seat centre stage.

I was fourteen and had just got home from my first ever proper party, a sparkly Christmas disco the school had put on in an attempt to stop us growing kids from throwing house parties at the snifter of an absent parent. I say 'us kids', but I'd not actually been to one of those affairs yet, still, I could feel it like the tremor before an earthquake – the promise of late nights, sips of alcohol, snogging. At this school disco, the year nines had been allowed to stay until eleven o'clock with the year tens and elevens. I'd just got home, and it had been the best night of my whole life, but I had a conundrum, and I needed my brothers' and sisters' advice.

My sister Mara, the oldest of all five of us, who was finishing sixth form next year and heading straight to uni, sat upon my bed. Her reading glasses were pushed up onto her head, and she was still dressed, so I knew she'd probably been pouring over data for her coursework, unable to give it a break even on a Friday night.

Graham is my older brother. We've always called him 'Gray', and when later, when Fifty Shades was released I think he milked it, if I'm honest. He was in year eleven but he was too cool for the school disco so he'd spent the evening at one of his mates' houses. He sauntered into my room with a bare chest and PJ bottoms, and collapsed onto my moon chair and closed his eyes.

I'm the middle child, so Marissa is my younger sister, and she was freshly into her first term of secondary school. She was wide-eyed with excitement for being up so late but a yawn gave her away as she curled into Mara on the edge of my bed.

And finally Benny, the little brother to all of us, just ten years old. He really should have been fast asleep but heard

Marissa get out of her bunk and had to follow. He plopped himself on the floor.

'So what's the problem, Charlie?' Mara asked, beginning the board meeting like she was already the company director she was planning to be one day. Ten years from now, Mara would be exactly that – she'd always been a girl to stick to a goal.

'I kissed a boy tonight,' I declared, full of dramatic emphasis. Marissa gasped, Gray groaned, Benny scrunched his nose and Mara just smiled.

'You woke us up for that?' said Gray.

'You were not asleep, I heard you on the phone to your girlfriend,' replied Mara.

'Shut up!'

'Believe me, you are the one that needs to shut up, these walls are thin,' she murmured, and stuck a middle finger up at him.

'Who did you kiss?' asked Marissa, the idea of kissing boys being a far-away dream. Though to be fair, if she was anything like me it would be, somewhat. Tonight was my first kiss. Sort of. Not counting when Craig Emmens and I touched the tip of our tongues for a dare in year seven and then he cried and moved tutor groups.

'Matt Bulverton.' I declared this climactically, like I was the queen bee in one of my favourite high school movies, treating my siblings to the juiciest of gossip.

Matt Bulverton. He was my dream boy. Or at least, a boy who I had made eye contact with several times over the past few weeks and had subsequently scribed epic paragraphs about in my diary, imagining the heady day he would ask me to the cinema and how I would ask him if he wanted to share a bag of Maltesers just so our hands could meet when we both reached for one and it would cement our LOVE.

'Matt Bulverton is a twat,' said Graham.

'He is not a twat! You're a twat!' I flared, pink with rage, and Graham smirked, scratched his balls and closed his eyes for a nap in my moon chair. 'He's really nice, and he has hair like Justin Bieber,' I told the others. Marissa swooned.

Mara, practical Mara, said, 'Don't let a floppy fringe fool you. Every boy in your year has hair like Justin Bieber. Is he a nice boy and do you want to kiss him again?'

I've never told Matt that the first time I ever heard Graham say his name was to call him a twat. And at the time I'm sure my brother never expected to be asked to be his groomsman one day.

'This is why I've called you in here tonight,' I said. 'He asked me out. Like, to be his girlfriend. So now it's more than a kiss, it's a whole lifestyle decision.'

'Why do you want a boyfriend?' asked Benny.

'Because when you're more grown up,' I answered my little brother, sounding like a pretentious know-it-all, 'sometimes it's nice to share your life with someone. Also, I really like him, I quite liked kissing him, and he told some of my friends at school that he was more Team Jacob, which I think might be because he knows I am too.'

'So why wouldn't you go out with him, he sounds so dreamy,' teased my big brother and Mara reached over and thumped him right in the crotch.

'Because I'm just a bit ...'

'Scared?' Marissa piped up.

'Well, you've never had a boyfriend before,' Mara coaxed.

'But what if I don't go out with him and he tells everyone I'm frigid?'

Don't judge me – I was a young girl and I know better now. Thank God.

'Believe me,' said Mara, 'when you're older you'll see how that is not a good reason to go out with someone.'

She was right.

I continued, 'But I don't think he would do that, he's really nice. He's not one of the cool boys or anything but everyone really likes him. He's so funny, like this time in maths when *we were in the middle of a test and he got hiccups and they were so loud so he tried to hide it by humming the national anthem. He's just really funny like that because he, like, never has good timing.' And I trailed off, my heart a flutter with the hope and nervousness that I might be on the brink of having my first ever boyfriend. Imagine if fourteen-year-old me knew Matt Bulverton, the boy with the nice hair and bad timing, would become my husband.*

Well, maybe she would have laughed in my face.

But I went out with Matt Bulverton and we kissed some more, and he was ingratiated into my gaggle of girlfriends to the point that by the time we reached sixth form and were still together, they confided in him as much as they confided in me. We were best friends, unbreakable as a couple, and everyone liked his funny, dorky, charming attitude, including me. Every first from aged fourteen was a first for both of us, together, and we fumbled and giggled our way through our teenage years. We opted to go to the same university together, despite advice from our friends and family that maybe we should give ourselves a little more freedom, and we fumbled and giggled our way through that too, making new friends together, doing everything as part of a group. I was never alone.

And no, thinking back on it, Matt hadn't been a wet wipe. He'd been confident and sure of himself and sure of us, and his sureness felt safe and heady and intoxicating all at once. It was always Charlotte and Matt on the path together and I still can't pinpoint where we took different forks in the road. Were we still stuck in that teenage dream? Should I have done more to pull him towards adulthood with me? Or did I pull too hard, and he wasn't ready?

Back to the living room, present day. Where were we ... ? Right, I was talking about how excited I was to be finally married to my Matt, and he was talking about how exciting it would be to see if there was anything better out there first.

Now, let me widen the scene for you. Oh, did you think it was just Matt and I having this incredibly intimate, life-altering discussion? Were you picturing us alone, in our home, somewhere we could really thrash it out and I could cry and he could pour his commitment-phobic heart out? I think I've missed out one very important detail about this man of mine, probably the thing that most defines him: Matt is completely, laughably, incapable of picking his moments. He doesn't mean to, but without fail he will always pick the worst possible moment to take any kind of action. For example:

Matt's Top 5 Worst Timings

1. **The not-quite proposal**. Matt asked me to marry him three times before I actually heard him. The first time I was in the bath, and he was hanging about reading his book on the loo (don't judge us – he wasn't *going* to the loo, just sitting on its closed lid). I'd dunked my head back and he chose to look up and make some declaration that sounded like nothing more than distant whale noises to my submerged ears, and asked me to marry him. He was very quiet with me for the rest of the day, which I later found out was because he thought I was taking my time and not giving him an answer. The second time was at a restaurant and Matt had planned to ask me just before the starters arrived. He then choked on his prosecco and tried to wheeze the words out anyway, but I thought he was saying 'will you carry me' and so I escorted him from the restaurant and tried to Heimlich manoeuvre him on the street.

2. **The sound of second-hand mortification**. In the sixth form, Matt took part in the school play of *The Sound of Music*, playing lead-baddie, Hans Zeller. Moments before one of his big, intensely Nazi scenes, Matt tried to make his mates backstage laugh by

pulling a length of shirt out through his trouser fly. Then got it stuck. And so what should have been an uncomfortably dark but necessary moment of the show became just plain uncomfortable, for Matt, and for every parent in the audience.

3. **The foot-in-mouth disease**. We went to a wedding a year ago for two of our uni friends. Among the guests were a campus golden couple, together from the first year and Hallmark-perfect. Until they split up just before the wedding because she'd cheated on him. The bride warned us all in a group WhatsApp to please not mention it as they were trying to keep it civil. Matt promptly forgot this and before we'd even all sat down for the meal, managed to steer both of them into him and declare to the table, 'It'll be these two next!' I dragged Matt to his place, hissing that they'd broken up, and he tried to lighten the mood by saying, 'Whoopsie daisy, sorry mate, did she realise there were better fish in the sea?' He growled that yes, she had. Matt said, 'Could be worse, at least it wasn't with that good-looking brother of yours,' at which point I kicked him in the shin and the guy lunged for him.

4. **The funeral**. Ah yes. Matt had to give a eulogy at his grandad's funeral, and to try and calm his nerves

and sadness watched an episode of *The Inbetweeners* just before leaving for the church. He couldn't stop himself thinking about it, and couldn't stop chuckling from the pulpit.

5. **The 'we were on a break?'.** Right now. When he asked me for permission to knob other people three weeks before our wedding, in front of all our friends.

It's endearing, usually, something everyone jokes about, but I'm not in the mood to laugh right now.

So here's the wide-angle version for you.

It's Saturday evening, early spring, sun dipped, window open, cheese on the table, yada yada. Matt and I are sitting on the floor, and around us are *seven* of our friends. There's Daisy, Alex and Dev who we went to university with, their partners Will, Carter and Dylan, and Brienne who we went to school with and who is one of my bridesmaids. We're a close group, even though Dev and Dylan live further up country, and we're south, but within the next few months all of us will have moved to London, and it's going to be so nice to finally start our careers in the capital with a ready-made group of friends. In fact, we'll be neighbours with Daisy and Will, and Brienne is just a short tube journey from our new flat, which has a river view at the Docklands.

'What are you most excited about after the wedding?' Brienne is asking, topping up her wine. 'Honeymoon or moving to London?'

'All of it,' I enthuse. 'But if I had to pick it would be London. I just can't wait to start the whole rest-of-our-lives bit. It's going to feel like we're real grown-ups.' We all laugh because being grown-up still seems a million years away.

'Did I tell you the gym in the building is nearly open?' Daisy says.

'That's so cool,' I look at Matt. 'How lucky are we to be able to live in a building with its own gym?' He nods through a gobful of cheese.

The reality is, we truly are lucky. Neither of us could afford to live in that flat solo, especially since I'm going to be on a barely there internship wage for the first few months. It might seem crazy to pack in a stable job copy-editing at the small local paper to move to the pricy capital for an internship straight after forking out for a wedding and honeymoon, but the internship is with *Adventure Awaits* magazine in their digital content department, and my dream is to combine travel and writing. I nearly turned it down out of financial fear but Matt and my family convinced me we could make it work. And so I've worked two jobs for the past nine months, at the paper and picking up bar work, and will be supplementing the internship by working evenings in a trendy all-day breakfast cafe a walk from where we're going to live. And hopefully, if all the stars align, I'll be able to bag a paid job at the magazine after I've proved myself.

'That said,' I continue, 'I can't wait to spend some time in Japan away from the main cities, exploring the zen gardens and getting a bit of peace and quiet before we come back here and everything goes mad-busy again.'

Matt nods. 'Agreed. Some time alone to think sounds perfect right about now.' I think he's agreeing with me but it sounds a little morose.

And that's when I say, '*This time in three weeks we'll be married ...*' and everything crumbles, like a cookie dipped too long in tea that falls apart and is lost, never to be whole again.

'... a week off from our relationship, to sow some wild oats, to *make sure.*'

When Matt has said these words there's a stunned silence in the room, and then Dylan lets out a nervous giggle, thinking this must be one of Matt's inappropriate jokes he's heard so much about.

'Matt, you're bonkers to joke about that in front of your bride-to-be,' Brienne says with both a chuckle and a tiny sliver of warning in her voice.

'It's not a joke, I'm serious,' Matt protests, and everyone looks at me, holding their breath.

'You're not serious,' I shake my head, and a giddy giggle escapes from my lips so I guzzle some more wine. But as I look at him over the rim of my glass and see the pain in his eyes that don't match the confident smile on his face, I can see that he means it.

'Hear me out, everybody,' he says.

Everybody. Of course. Growing up with four siblings, a boyfriend since school and a group of close friends means every life decision of mine feels like it has to be made by committee, but even this? Really, Matt? 'I think it would be a good test of our relationship, like a final safety test before a car is sent out, to make sure everything is ... up to spec.'

'What are you talking about?' I bristle.

'I mean, we've been together since year nine, all we've known is each other. I don't want you to have any resentment further down the line or for us to end up doing something unforgivable once we're married.'

'So this is for me, to avoid me having resentment?'

'You, and me ...' He's getting a little uncomfortable now.

'So, let me get this straight,' the volume of my voice is gradually creeping up. 'If I don't want you to cheat on me once we're married, I have to let you cheat on me now?'

There is a silence and I'm aware of the other people in the room, each holding their breath.

Matt clears his throat. 'It wouldn't be cheating, though; it would be like a hall pass. Like a get-out-of-jail-free card.'

There is a collective gasp and I smash the wine bottle on the table and hold the jagged weapon to his neck.

No, I don't, *of course I don't*, but I do think about it for a second.

'No, no, I don't mean like that, I don't want to get out, more like a, um, day release. That you would be fully on board with. Paperwork signed. I'll behave, officer, but not too much.' He salutes and Brienne murmurs, 'Oooh, he's making it worse.'

I close my eyes. This is a bad dream, it's got to be, because comprehending what is really happening will break me. So I decide to play along, firmly gripping my wine, which, in the time it has taken to open my eyes, someone had poured into a pint glass and topped up. 'So after your day release,' I seethe, 'when you come back to the prison that is our loving relationship, what then?'

'Then we get married and nothing changes. If we still feel that's the best thing to do.'

'Okay, okay,' I whisper, and I see the others lean forward so as not to miss a syllable. 'So you've had your break, you didn't find a better option, and then you just stroll back in and we forget all about it? Lucky me.'

'But you'd be allowed to take a break too; it would be a mutual thing.'

'Oh, *thank you so much.*'

He shuffles closer to me and gives me that smile again, which now seems false and patronising. 'It's not about finding a better option, I promise. It's about not being so hard on ourselves to fit into this strict social norm of "once you're with the one, you can never be with someone else ever again". Because you and I have been a couple for nearly all our lives, we never gave ourselves a chance to experience anything else.'

I stare at him, at my Matt, and my anger slips a little. Not because I'm not mad any more – because I am, I'm fuming – but because mostly I feel sad: I never realised what different pages – different *books* – we were on. And everything I thought I knew about my life and my future is floating away and I can't catch it.

Matt turns to our friends. 'What do you guys think?'

'I think this is kind of a private matter,' says Dylan, but Dev shushes him, keen to join the debate.

Daisy offers her opinion first, clearing her throat and addressing me, or at least the shell of me that is swaying under the weight of what's happening. 'Well, to be honest, Charlotte, I don't think I could marry Will if I knew he'd been with someone else, even if I gave my permission. I just wouldn't be able to stop wondering who she was and what she was like.'

'Well—' Matt starts but Daisy cuts him off, and I vaguely wonder what he was going to say.

'But I do see your point, Matt. Do you think this could just be bog-standard cold feet?'

'It doesn't sound like that to me,' says Alex. 'He seems to want to get married, just wants her permission to experience being a single adult for a moment. I mean, I think it's good that you're discussing it and it didn't happen behind anyone's back.'

Matt looks horrified. 'Absolutely – I'd never cheat on her, I wanted this to all be really open and I was hoping we could keep it, um ...' he trails off.

'What?' I ask.

'Well, not a big deal. Like it wouldn't mean anything, it would just be an experience.'

Daisy turns back to me. What an interesting debate this was. 'Charlotte, has the thought ever crossed your mind that you're missing out by never having kissed-or-whatever anyone else?'

'No!' I splutter.

Well, that isn't strictly true ...

It was just a quiet freak-out, an internal one, you couldn't even hear it above the low-volume love songs playing inside the bridal boutique. I stood in a changing room the size of a Kardashian's walk-in closet, looking at myself in this beautiful dress. Its white organza flowers scattered the gown like cherry blossom in full bloom and I held a prop champagne flute, wondering if I was making a huge mistake.

My mum's voice called through the curtain. 'Do you need any help in there, honey?'

'No!' I called in my chirpiest voice, but my mum could hear the crack and slipped straight in.

'What's wrong?' she asked softly, removing the glass from my hands and sitting us both down on the floor to stop my legs shaking. I looked like Maya Rudolph in that infamous *Bridesmaids* scene, which I found funny for a moment before I remembered what a huge, massive mistake was about to happen.

'Nothing, everything is just perfect,' I said, the very vision of someone having the most perfect moment.

'I think something is on your mind. Is it because I brought up shapewear? I'm sorry, darling, I didn't mean a thing by it, it was just a question about what kind of underwear we needed to factor in under this dress.'

21

'It's not the shapewear, or any underwear. Underwear isn't the problem.' The black and pink bra straps jutting out the top of this gown would disagree with that, but that's my bad – my strapless was in the wash. 'I'm fine.'

Mum stroked my arm. 'Then why are we sitting on the floor like a couple of dropped marshmallows?'

'What if this is all wrong?' I whispered.

'That's okay, we'll just go a little further afield on the next trip, there are plenty more dress shops around that we haven't tried yet. Just … outside a thirty-mile radius.'

'Not the dress, this, how do I know Matt is the one? He's the only boyfriend I've ever had. What am I thinking?'

'I think you're thinking that you love him and you know him, and he makes you happy.'

I couldn't breathe, the dress was squeezing my organs and my skin felt hot. This is a mistake; marriage is a mistake. 'But Dad made you happy and look what happened.'

Mum took a pause, and I felt awful for bringing up bad memories. I quickly added, 'I'm sorry. I'm just tired from all the hours I've been doing at work, and it's raining outside, again, and it's probably just wedding dress shopping blues.'

'What happened between me and your dad was just something that sometimes happens. But I hope you know I certainly wouldn't have had it any other way. Because everything that happened before he left was so wonderful. It was you, and Mara, and Graham, and Marissa, and

Benny. Enjoy your life, honey, don't waste it worrying about what ifs.'

I tried to remember what my GP had told me about dealing with anxious thoughts. *This isn't a real worry, it's a hypothetical one. I mustn't let it overwhelm me. Acknowledge and move on.* I sniffed and took out my phone, finding a recent photo of Matt and I being silly in mouse ears at Disneyland Paris. I did enjoy my life with Matt, I did. I just needed reminding that marriage is still worthwhile.

So no, I'm not perfect. Matt's not perfect. We both had pre-wedding jitters, but I got over them and I certainly didn't react even close to how Matt is reacting now. How did he think I would react? How did he want me to react? How sad that we're in such different places after seeming to be so in sync for so long.

'I can't do this.' I stand up, for once not wanting everybody's input in my life.

Matt stands with me. 'Would it help if you met her?'

I freeze.

Dev and Dylan clutch each other and Dylan whispers, 'He did not just say that.'

'There's a her already?' Brienne asks tentatively and with a side-eye on me. No, please no.

'Nothing's happened, there's just a woman at the leisure centre where we use the gym who seems to smile at me a lot and I think she'd be up for going on a date or two. She's called Katie.'

'The blond girl who wears a lot of Jack Wills?' I ask.

'Yes, that's her!' He catches himself beaming at the thought of her, and yes, I know her, with her friendly banter and her pert bum on the spin bikes and her *fuckinggggggg* pretty hair.

Brienne leaps up and pushes Matt back towards the sofa. 'Shall we take a breather outside, Charlie?' she asks, steering me towards the door.

We're out the front of my building, and I pace on the steps, unable to process, unable to talk.

'I think we should go,' says Brienne. 'You and Matt need to be alone, he's an arsehole for doing this in front of other people.'

I nod, numb, just wanting time to go backwards.

'I'm going to get the others and I'll call you tomorrow, but Charlie?' I meet her eye. 'Don't agree to anything you don't want just because you don't want to upset any plans. Screw the plans.'

The others leave, pitying shoulder taps on their way past, awkward glances, and I sit on the steps for a long time in the cold, staring into the darkness. I'm not debating what to do, I know what to do, I'm just processing.

Eventually, I return indoors to where Matt is quietly packing dishes into the dishwasher, the living room cleared up neatly and the music and candles extinguished. We silently turn the lights off and walk to our bedroom, undressing without looking at each other, and climb into bed, letting the darkness lie over us like a blanket.

'If you don't want to do this, or you don't want me to, I won't,' he says, and I feel him turn onto his side to face me while I remain on my back, eyes wide open, looking towards the ceiling above that I can't see.

'What I want is for you not to *want* to be with anyone else.' It comes out as a croak; I've been breathing in cold night air for so long. 'But you want out. So I've had the decision made for me.'

'I don't want to break up,' he says quietly. 'Charlotte, we've always been together, it's always been the two of us, and I love you so much.'

Tears are falling from my face onto the pillow, quiet streams. 'This isn't just cold feet, is it?'

He pauses and then whispers, 'No.'

'I've got to call off the wedding.'

'Don't do that.' He sounds shocked, panicked, talking quickly. 'Let's talk about it. Do you want to call your mum or your bridesmaids or someone?'

'No, I'm making this decision. It's not a debate.'

Matt's crying now, which makes my own tears flow, because I can hear that these aren't tears of regret at what he's said but tears of acknowledgement that it really might be over. 'I can't imagine being without you.'

'I can't imagine being without you either.' My breathing is deep, drawing in and letting go of the air we've so long shared in our bedroom. I know what I need to say but how cruel life is to make me say these words instead of simply letting me say *I Do*. 'But the difference is,' I whisper, which is all I can manage, 'that I can't imagine being without you because you're part of me, and I want to tell you things and show you things and see your face light up when you laugh.' I turn my head to look for his face in the dark, my Matt's face. 'You can't imagine being without me because you're scared to make the jump.'

'You're putting words in my mouth.'

'I know, but it's words you're too scared to say. You said it yourself, this is more than cold feet. I think this is an escape plan. And I get it,' I sigh. 'I get it but I don't feel the same, we're in completely different places. There is no way for us to move forward with our plans and our life together. And I'm going to be mad at you for a long time for holding on to this and only telling me now.'

He's silent for a while and then says, 'I'm so sorry.'

'Me too,' I whisper back.

He's been a part of my life, my identity, my heartbeat for so long that I can't imagine how to function without him. And I know life doesn't stop at a break-up, I know that after some heartache and healing I will move on – I know because my mum did it, even after five kids. Matt was my first boyfriend, my only love, he got to know me as I was getting to know myself during those teenage and university years. And it seems so alien to me to know who I am without him.

We don't speak again but lie together for what we both know is the last time and eventually his breathing slows and he shuffles into the deep sleep of someone who has finally released something heavy that was weighing him down.

In turn, after I've memorised the feel of his skin and the sound of his breathing so I can hold them with me, I release myself from under his arm, which was weighing me down, and I walk away.

Chapter 2

All threads to unpick
Rewinding our decisions
Everyone, shut up.

I brace myself. 'Blurghurghurghurgh,' I say, in that way that actors and singers do when they're readying themselves for a performance. I shake out my shoulders and roll my neck and place a sisterly hand on my Michelle Obama print above my desk. Then I click the 'dial into meeting' link.

I am the last to join the call, and when the audio and video connect I'm hit with a wall of my siblings in their individual thumbnails, all talking over one another.

'Hello, everyone,' I say.

'Heeeey!' cries Marissa, the first to notice me, her face floury from whatever delicate morsel she'd been whipping up over the course of the morning. Having recently returned from an advanced patisserie course in Paris (yes, really, I know) she's on track to become one of the youngest dessert chefs at the London hotel she works at.

Benny is scraggly haired and shirtless, sitting on his bed during his final year of university, the sun glinting off his face from a window beside him.

'Benny, did you just wake up?' I ask.

'Yep, last night was sick, everyone's gonna start revising like, all day every day soon so we had this epic night out.'

'Please don't tell me we're about to see any other nipples rise out of that bed, B,' Mara comments, and in his thumbnail Gray lifts his head from his phone to look at his computer screen lest he miss anything. Mara continues, 'Hi, Charlie, what's on your agenda to talk to us about today? The invite wasn't very clear.'

This makes Mara sound sarcastic, but she really isn't. She had this probably genius, definitely anally retentive, idea a few years back that any time we all needed to discuss something important we should do it via a video conference during working hours. And we all need to get creative with the meeting subject lines so they sound too boring and realistic for anyone else to want to join, should they get wind of it. That way, in spite of our various busy jobs and lives, it's blocked out in our calendars, everybody knows they need to attend, and 'nobody can lie and say they have something better to do'.

'Okay,' I start. But I don't quite know where to start.

'You said it was about the wedding, is there something we can do?' Mara prompts, using the camera as a mirror and adjusting her suit jacket.

Marissa starts singing Bruno Mars' 'Marry You' and I know I need to do what I always do with my family: blurt it out like a big cowpat and see how they all think it should be cleaned up.

And so I say, 'I've cancelled my wedding. Matt and I aren't going to get married any more. At all. Now or never. To each other, anyway. We've broken up.' My voice cracks at the end, just a little, worsened by the stunned silence from the others.

They're all agape for so many seconds I begin to think my connection has frozen and start muttering curse words at my Wi-Fi until Gray growls in true big brother fashion, 'What did he do?'

'Nothing, really, well something. Well, it's more what he *wanted* to do.'

'Oh Charlie,' Mara waves her hand around. 'Don't worry about that, all guys want to do that at some point, just say no if you're not into it. No need to be so dramatic.'

'I don't think we're talking about the same thing,' I clarify quickly.

'What happened?' Benny asks, pulling a T-shirt on.

'He ...' My voice wobbles, my eyes mist, and that lump wiggles up my throat. I really thought I was cried-out but seems not. I put my face in my hands, breathing through it, wanting to have a clear conversation with my family. I can feel them all watching me, but when I look up I see compassion and patience. Even Mara doesn't seem to be getting twitchy about keeping the meeting to schedule. Marissa's put her fingers near the camera lens like she's reaching out to touch me.

I can do this. 'He told me – well, actually, he told me and all of our friends at the same time – that he wanted to sow some wild oats before we got married.'

They all gasp.

'He wanted a break, to make sure he wasn't missing out on anything,' I continue. 'He said we've never been with anyone else and maybe we should make sure first.'

'Told you he was a twat all along. I've always said it, haven't I?' says Gray.

'*Graham!*' Mara scolds. 'So what did you say?'

'I said that I already was sure and if he wasn't then we clearly aren't on the same page any more.'

'I'm so sorry, Charlie,' says Marissa. 'Do you think it's just cold feet? Last-minute nerves? Shall I give him a ring?'

'He didn't seem nervous, in fact, he seemed quite pleased with his great idea.'

'When did this happen?' asks Benny.

'The day before yesterday.'

I slept on the sofa that night, it hurt too much to lie next to him. We spent twenty-four hours walking around in a daze, avoiding phones and emails and the outside world. One of us would switch on the TV and the other would watch next to them for a while before wandering off to another room. It's like we both hoped the other would change their mind and we clung to this self-inflicted cooling off period before we took any steps towards cancelling the wedding. To be honest, though, as much as part of me wanted Matt to realise he was an idiot who'd made a mistake, the damage was done. He wasn't all in, and I was; you can't come back from that.

'So anyway,' I conclude, 'that's my news. Wedding's off, and I just wanted to let you all know first.'

There is silence for a moment more before Graham pipes up and asks, 'Out of interest, had you already paid for the hog roast, and if so, what were you planning to do with it now?'

That opens up the floodgates for all four siblings to start throwing in their thoughts and opinions and questions.

'You should be happy. You realised this about your relationship before it was too late. I know it hurts now but ultimately you should be happy.'

'Are you kidding? She wasted so much time on him, she should be furious right now.'

'I think you should make him do all the cancelling of the wedding plans.'

'Anything that can be refunded make sure you're the one who is getting the cash.'

I let them go on for a while, everything they're saying is what I've already had rattling about in my own head since we broke up. I love my family, but it can be exhausting listening to all of that noise. I say my goodbyes and promise to call them all again very soon to let them know what's going on, and then close the lid of my laptop.

Almost immediately, Benny calls my mobile. 'Hi, bro.'

'Hi, sis. Just wondered how you were really doing?'

My little brother and I are the closest, funnily enough, both quieter than our other siblings but happy to be enveloped in big crowds and go with the flow. 'Honestly … I feel like I've been punched in the stomach, and the head and the fanny, and like it keeps happening again and again every time I think about it or think about him with … but anyway, I'll be okay. You know what though? I'd love to talk about something else. Tell me about this epic night, did you kiss any girls?'

'No,' he says shyly, and I settle down to listen to him talk all about uni life, and for an hour I don't think about heartbreaks or honeymoons.

A few days pass and I'm at my mum's house, which I've moved back into while I figure out what the heck I'm going to do next. She fixes me a tea while I hover around the kitchen table where all my wedding planning bumph is spread out.

I hang up the phone. 'Bollocks.'

'No luck?' Mum asks.

'The flowers themselves I can cancel, but they say they can't take back the vases because they've been painted.' I look at the corner of the room where a stack of fifteen mottled vases, each two-foot-high, are piled on top of each other. Months and months ago I was shopping with Brienne and we passed the florist in town, who were selling a bulk load of these vases on the cheap as part of a clearance. Brienne had convinced me they would make spectacular centrepieces and we could paint them whatever my colour scheme was going to be closer to the time. We staggered home with fifteen of the things, probably too many for the number of tables, but better to be safe than sorry. Now I was sorry.

I hurumph as I flick through a stack of magazine cut-outs of table arrangements, everything from rustic countryside casual to dripping diamante *Real House-wives*-style bling. 'I don't think half of these were even cut out by me. I mean look at this one, I would never have done an all-white minimalist table, that's totally more Mara's style than mine. What's it even doing here among all this crap?' As you can tell, I am delightful company right now.

'Your sister was probably just keen to share her ideas,' Mum says, diplomatically. 'At the end of the day, the things you went for were what you and Matt wanted, weren't they?'

'I don't know,' I sigh, looking back over at the vases, painted a sultry purple. They weren't really my style, if I'm honest. But do I feel that now because they're tainted with the wedding that never happened? I get up from the table and wander over, picking one up. 'How would our guests have even seen each other across the table with these things in the way? They're the worst vases in the entire world.'

'Okay,' Mum says and starts making me another cup of tea.

With every scrap of paper I find, every entry in my wedding planning notebook I've written, every phone call I have to make, the gravitas of cancelling The Big Day grows. The break-up is something that stings from within its own little compartment, but separated from that is my wedding, which took a long time to plan. So many details and arrangements and decisions over the course of the past year, which are now having to be knocked down one brick at a time, but rapidly, and I'm trying to beat the deadlines and read the fine print to the point that it feels like I've locked myself in an escape room. If I don't get out of every commitment, I might end up standing in a hotel conference room in a wedding dress, on my own except for a couple of guests who didn't get the memo in time, and a chocolate fountain. And these pissing vases.

'What do you reckon I could get for these vases on eBay?' I ask Mum. 'Some other bride and groom might want a job-lot of them, mightn't they?'

Mum takes the vase out of my hand and pulls her glasses down from the top of her head to look at it. 'I think you'd have to specify that they've been painted ... was it washable paint?'

'It was glass paint.'

'Hmm. So not wash-offable?'

'No,' I take the vase back off her. 'What are you saying? Don't you think they look good?'

'Somebody might love them.'

I stand up and grab my coat. 'Right. I'm heading over to the hotel.'

'The Crumble?' Mum asks. The Crumble is – was – my wedding venue.

'Yep, I need to speak to Cecily in person and find out what the options are.'

'Do you want me to come? Or call Matt for you and ask him to meet you there?'

I shake my head. 'No, I'll go on my own. Thank you, though.' Cecily is – *was* – my wedding coordinator at the Crumble. She hasn't been answering her phone to me often in the last couple of weeks, which is irking in itself, but more than that I need to get out on my own for a while and get some fresh air.

Mum gets a big kiss plopped on her cheek from me before I go, though. 'Thanks for being brill, Mum. I'll pick us up some doughnuts on the way home.'

It's surreal to be standing in the lobby of the Crumble. I've been here many times in the last year, but with less than three weeks to go before the wedding, the next time I expected to be here was the afternoon before, when we were going to be allowed to start decorating the conference room.

I can almost picture how it would have played out. The sofas to the right of the reception desk would have been straining under the weight of boxes being unloaded from cars in front of the hotel. Bridesmaids and groomsmen would be deployed to move them into the conference room. Matt's parents and my mum would have been coordinating because Matt and I would keep being distracted by the familiar faces of our guests arriving to check in for the weekend. I'd be in jeans and trainers and joking about how I was so shattered that 'I might just wear this tomorrow'. Matt would be forgetting everybody's name, instead calling each person 'mate' or 'm'dear'.

But today it's quiet, a drizzly Tuesday at the beginning of April not being an enticing time for a flurry of tourists. I head to the sofas and take a seat, remembering the time I came here and decided it would be my wedding venue. Well, *we* decided.

And by 'we', I don't mean Matt and me.

2 June, last year
Sunday morning, 10.20am

'*How did this turn into the social gathering of the year?*' *I asked with a laugh, shutting the car door behind me. Matt was driving, using his dad's car, while his parents locked up their house behind them. While we waited for them to finish faffing in and out, remembering that they needed tissues, did the cat have enough food, were the windows closed, I looked out of the* back windscreen. The car behind ours was my mum's, which contained her, Mara and Benny. Gray was on a work trip in Germany, and Marissa in Paris, but the others had trailed home for a few days around work and university, so had invited themselves along for a day of wedding venue viewings with Matt and me.

Mum had then suggested we involve Matt's parents.

Matt's parents had got their neighbour Evie over when I called, so now she was in the backseat too, his folks not wanting to be rude.

Brienne was also home with no real plans, and wanted to come for a nosey, and that meant she was also joining the convoy. Daisy got wind of this and jumped on an early-morning train from London, and Brienne's brother Calvin had a massive crush on Daisy since he saw her in one of my Instagram posts, so he came too, for ogling purposes.

So that was eleven of us heading to four different venues today. I was already looking forward to takeout pizza with just Matt later on that evening!

'Where are we going?' asked Evie as Matt pulled away in the car, the others behind us.

'We're going to look at wedding venues,' Matt's father Paul explained, in a loud voice.

'For who?'

'For Matthew and Charlotte. They're getting married next year.'

'Oh, are they? Where?'

Matt's mum Fay changed the subject (slightly). 'What's the first stop, kids?' she asked me.

I looked at my notepad, though it was all in my head if I'm honest, like a million other ideas and thoughts that had been swimming about since Matt proposed a couple of months ago. 'We're heading to the furthest away one to begin with – the barn conversion I was telling you about.'

The place looked lovely in the pictures, but also bloody expensive and we'd need to put on transport for everyone since there was nowhere to stay for miles around. We were also viewing a stately home, a field, and a hotel.

Arriving at the barn we were met with problem number one: parking. There was space for two cars beside the barn, the third needing to park a ten-minute walk away, downhill. We got over this now by squeezing in and double parking, but already I saw Mara's eyebrows raised.

The owner appeared in snazzy Joules wellies and a headscarf. 'Morning ... everyone! The Bulverton wedding?'

Matt and I stepped forward. 'Yep, I'm Charlotte, this is Matt.'

'Fab, let me take you into the main attraction.' She led us, all of us, along a gravelly track lined with loops of fairy lights, towards an imposing barn. 'We had a wedding here yesterday, actually, and the party aren't coming to take away their things for another couple of hours. The cleaning team – which is

included in the price – have done their bit so it's not messy, just lived in.'

She stood in front of the high double doors, the wood stained a dark brown, and gave us all a smile like she knew she was about to hear a chorus of gasps.

Opening both doors at the same time and standing aside, she was right. Inside it looked like a wedding venue you'd see in a magazine – pretty string lighting accenting the beams in the high ceiling, long oak tables decorated with lines of white candles and lilac petals, white swathes of fabric floating beside the windows, wildflower bouquets hanging down from the ceiling and a chandelier made of antlers lighting up the whole room with a soft amber glow. Boxes sat neatly on the white tablecloths containing stacked place settings and leftover party favours, and cleaned champagne flutes sparkled in a group on the wooden bar.

The owner said, 'We offer a complete package with catering, cleaning, loos, post-wedding accommodation for the bride and groom, and can add on a photographer and decorating assistance for an extra fee. I think you have the prices in the email, and they'll vary a little depending on your total guest count. I'll leave you to have a look around but will be outside if you have any questions.'

The woman left, and Fay said, 'It's very beautiful, isn't it?'

'Very pricey too,' answered Matt.

'Matt ...' I said. 'We did know that before we came and we said we'd keep an open mind.'

He was right though. It was way too expensive and we shouldn't have even been looking at it, but when we'd first got engaged Brienne wouldn't stop going on about this place because she'd worked here once when she was a waitress at school. It had stuck in her mind and she thought I'd love it.

'What do you reckon?' she said, gripping my arm.

'It's lovely,' I agreed. 'But, I don't know, it's a long drive and I hadn't really thought about long tables instead of round ones ...'

'The long tables are great,' said Daisy, joining us.

'Do you think? I'm not sure about this place,' said Mara and Daisy shook her head. She's always been a little intimidated by my big sister, always acting like Mara is the general manager and she's a lowly temp who feels she should agree with everything Mara says.

'Testing!' Matt's dad found a microphone on the other end of the barn. 'Good sound system!' he boomed.

'Mum, what do you think of this place?' I asked, sidling over to her.

'It's certainly charming.' She looked at me, puzzled for a moment. 'Is it you though?'

'I don't know,' I replied, and turned to Matt, but I could see he wasn't keen because he was studying the woodwork like he wanted to think of something to say about it.

'What did she say about toilets?' he said, instead.

'They're included in the price,' I answered. 'I assume they have those fancy Portaloos.'

'I wonder if we could get a discount if we went for non-fancy Portaloos. I'll ask her.'

'No, Matt—'

'Excuse me,' he called, and the owner popped back in. 'If we brought our own Portaloos, like the ones they have on building sites, would we be able to get a discount?'

She explained that no, we'd have to use their state-of-the-art mobile facilities but I saw that her confident assurance that we would snap the place up had faded just a little.

'I really like it,' I said to her. 'Thanks ever so much for letting us pop in for a look. We'll have a think and let you know.'

Back we all went to the cars and it was on to the next venue, the stately home, which had a Cluedo vibe that Matt loved, and he started banging on about how we could have a murder-mystery themed wedding. This place, with the stone walls and rich mahogany fabrics, got a nod of approval from Mara, Benny, Matt's parents and Calvin, before Daisy said it gave her the creeps and Calvin defected to being on the 'no' side.

I liked it, it was a good price, and it was interesting, but there was a downside in that the room we would have the use of was very small. We weren't planning a massive wedding, but in all likelihood people would spill out of this room once the meal was over, and the bar area of the home was open to the public. None of this was a huge problem, but it kept the venue as a 'maybe' and not a definite 'yes'.

'This feels perfect,' I shouted over the wind to Matt at venue number three as the eleven of us stood in the middle of an empty field. The wind whipped my hair in front of my eyes, and we were all huddled together and exposed, but the view was outstanding. You could see for miles, even on an overcast day, over hills and forest and woodland. It was wild and exciting, and I could picture us being able to do whatever the hell we fancied because the farmer wanted just a few hundred for use of the field, plus a little extra for two neighbouring fields if we wanted to add camping and parking.

'Don't you think this could be perfect?' I called to Matt again. 'We could have yurts dotted about, and a marquee, and however many Portaloos you want! Benny, don't you think this is cool?'

'It's definitely cold,' he replied, but he flashed me a quick grin.

Matt's parents didn't look too comfortable, and Daisy was trying to wipe cowpat from her shoe.

'Do you think you'd rather do everything ourselves rather than a package?' Matt asked.

Hmm. People don't phrase things in that way unless they want the opposite to you. 'Let's chat about it more tonight, when we're out of the cold,' I said.

On to our fourth venue.

The Crumble hotel was in the middle of town, with a private car park and a pretty, photogenic entranceway. Inside the lobby we were met with two sweeping staircases on either side of the reception, sparkling spotlights high above, and pistachio and cream furnishings. Our party all visibly warmed up following the windy field, and spent a few unsubtle minutes shaking off their coats and untangling their hair.

'Afternoon, all. I'm Cecily, the wedding coordinator. Can I assume you two are Charlotte and Matt?' she addressed Calvin and Daisy, and Calvin blushed furiously and stepped away from where he'd been hovering, gazing at her.

I spotted Cecily darting a knowing glance at me and smiled, and I stepped forward.

'That's actually us, thanks for meeting with us today. We've brought a few people along.'

'Not a problem,' smiled Cecily. 'Come on through to the Elizabeth suite and you can see where your wedding and reception could be held. I've already laid out some tea and coffee in there, and I'll bring some extra cups and biscuits through.'

She tap-tap-tapped ahead of us down the corridor while we all followed, Matt and I leading. Behind me I could hear chatter about how nice the place was, how nice Cecily was, ooo tea and coffee, ooo biscuits.

The Elizabeth suite was large but not too large, warm but airy, sparse but with 'great scope to decorate however you'd like'. Prices were fair, as fair as weddings go, and could be tailored according to requirements, from exclusive use to simple room-only. Cecily was kind, sweet, accommodating, and got more chocolate Hobnobs without even being asked after Evie scoffed the lot. It was the obvious choice.

For everyone else.

For me, I couldn't help but think about that wild and windy field, with all its potential and the view for miles. I stood on that hill and felt like, on my wedding day, I would be taking the first step into married life. London life. Into a wonderful adventure with Matt.

I don't think I need to hit you with a spoiler alert, because as you know, we didn't pick the field. There was a lot of discussion among all of us, and everybody threw in their two-pence worth, and there was overwhelming favour for the Crumble hotel. It ticked all the boxes, it suited young and old and mobile and immobile. It was sensible while still being romantic. At one point we all voted, even Evie, who thought she was voting for more chocolate Hobnobs.

First up was the barn. Only Brienne put her hand up for that one, though we all agreed that if Matt or I found a richer partner second time around we'd revisit.

The stately home, aka 'murder-mystery house', got Matt and Benny's vote.

I was the only one who put my hand high in the air for the field.

And everybody else put their hand up for the Crumble hotel.

Matt and I faced each other, and I said, 'Well, if you want Murder House and I don't, and I want Deserted Field and you don't, I think we have to shove both of them off the list.'

He nodded. 'Are you okay with that?'

'Yeah,' I shrugged. 'It's the fair thing to do. I want us both to be happy with where we get married.'

'Would you be happy doing it here?'

I looked around at the room, at the big windows and soft lighting, and pictured my wedding day playing out. It was a lovely hotel, spacious but still boutique-feeling. I even remembered having a cream tea here with Dad, oh, many years ago. It was a nice memory.

'You don't have to pick any of these places if you aren't sure,' said Benny, echoing the words I'd said to him two years before when he was struggling to pick a university. 'You don't have to decide right now.'

But the decision was made, by all of us, and we handed over the deposit on that very afternoon, agreeing to marry the following April.

Matt and I left the hotel arm in arm, content and excited, and he whispered to me, 'Now that's out the way, let's start planning the honeymoon.'

I smiled but held my finger to my lips. 'Let's wait until we're on our own, because I expect everybody here will want to tell us where we should go. And I have an idea I want to run by you that I've been thinking about for a really long time ...'

'Hello, Charlotte!' smiles Cecily, joining me on the sofa with her ring binder. She looks around. 'No other family members today? Not even Matt?'

It is true that Matt is usually with me, but the rest of my family haven't seen Cecily since we booked. Except for when Mara came along to help us negotiate the package. Oh, and when Gray and Mum tagged along to chat about discounted rooms for guests. Ah yes, there was also the time Brienne wanted to take measurements of the Elizabeth suite.

'I think I know why you're here and I must apologise,' Cecily continues before I can speak. 'I haven't been able to take as many calls as I would have liked over the past few weeks from your wedding party; it's just that I do have other weddings occurring this spring. I will be more careful to pick up from now on.'

I'm confused. 'From my wedding party? You mean from me or Matt?'

She looks uncomfortable. 'Or from your sister or bridesmaids. Matt's parents ring me several times, um, a week, just to ask little things to do with the day or their room or whatever. Your mum has been in once or twice.'

I shake my head. I swear everybody in my extended family can't keep it in their bloody heads that this was my wedding, not all of theirs. Anyway. It's none of ours any more so I'd better break the news to Cecily.

'Well, if it's any consolation, you probably won't hear from them again for a while. Or ever. At least to do with this wedding.'

Cecily is mystified and then shock crosses her face. 'Are you going to try and get me fired?'

'No, no, it's not that bad, well, not for you. It's me. And Matt. The wedding is off.'

'Off?'

'Cancelled. Kaput. Dead.'

'Matt's dead?!'

'No,' I'm rubbish at this, apparently. 'It's just cancelled, we won't be getting married now. Or ever.'

Cecily sits back into the sofa and the ring binder slides on to the floor. 'Well, that's a big shame.' She shakes her head and looks genuinely surprised. 'I'm so sorry. Are you okay?'

'Yes, I'm fine, I'm just taking mountains of cocaine to get me through it all!' *Why* would I joke about that? Cecily must think I'm a right headcase! 'Just kidding, ahem, yes, I'm okay, as well as can be expected. Anyway, I just wanted to let you know to, you know, not expect us to be here in two and a half weeks.'

'Right,' she says quietly, and mulls for a minute. 'Charlotte, I'm afraid we aren't able to return your money so close to the wedding. We won't be able to give the slot to anyone else. At anything under six weeks a cancellation is non-refundable.'

'I know,' I sigh. I did know this, but still, any money we can get back would be amazing. 'Is there anything we can get back, like the food and drink, or the rooms?'

'Any guests of yours that no longer want to make use of rooms they've booked can cancel up to forty-eight hours in advance with no charge, so that's something. The five rooms your party had booked along with the package, I can release those and refund you for them, but obviously you did get a discounted rate for them which will be what I can return to you.' She thinks for a moment more. 'I'll check the food and drinks packages because we may be able to return the wine and prosecco to our supplier, and the kitchen can cancel the fresh food, which they won't have ordered yet. But it won't be the full amount back because of course the chef has spent time and money on your menu.'

'Complicated, isn't it?' I put my chin in my hands.

'It is a bit. I am sorry, Charlotte. I hope nothing too serious has happened.'

'Bleeeeeeuuurgh, just that Matt wanted to "sow some wild oats" before the wedding.'

'Oh, what a fucking twat!' she exclaims and then claps a hand over her mouth. 'I'm so sorry, Charlotte, that was unforgivably unprofessional.'

I laugh. "S'all right. My brother said something similar.'

'I always thought Gray seemed like a clever man.' Cecily blushes but I like that I'm seeing this unmasked version. I bet she's a right laugh to go for a drink with. 'Anyway, I'll get back whatever I can for you, Charlotte, I'm just sorry in advance that it won't be all that much.'

I thank Cecily and leave her to it, and when I step from the hotel I look back up the entrance one last time, just in time to see the door slowly close.

Back at home, I tell Mum everything while I make her a spag bol she didn't ask for.

'So that's venue, flowers and cake all cancelled, which are some of the main things, but I can't find the info about the cars or suits. I might just ask Matt to take care of those.'

At the mention of his name, Mum raises her eyebrows. 'Yes, I think you should. No reason you should have to do all of this.'

'I want to,' I said, squinting at some fine print on our wedding ring receipts as I stir the sauce. 'Because if I don't keep busy, I have to think about how humiliating all of this is.'

My phone bleep-bleeps with another 'OMG!' message, and I swipe to clear it and then put my phone on silent. I've asked my family and my bridesmaids to help get the word out to all the guests. But though I'm grateful for the sympathy messages and calls that have started coming through, along with a wave of opinions, for the first time in my life I want to be left in peace.

'How are you doing, Mum?'

'How am I? I'm all right.'

'I'm sorry for the money you helped put towards this. And for all that wasted time spent shopping for wedding dresses and mother-of-the-bride outfits.'

'Wasted time? It wasn't wasted, it was time with my daughter. And let's not worry about money for the moment.'

'I'll work super hard so I can pay back all the non-refundable things.'

'That reminds me,' Mum begins, while I dish up a big fat plate of pasta. 'I wondered what your plans were about London, if you know.'

London. Our 'new beginning'.

'We've given up the flat. There's no way either of us could afford to live there alone, and I can't face the thought of living there with Matt as just a roommate. It momentarily crossed my mind before I realised that I was being nuts. Luckily, it's still enough in advance that they've given us our security deposit and first month's rent back. It's only the estate agent fees we've lost now.'

'Are you still going to go to London and do the internship?'

I shrugged. 'I haven't got that far in my thinking yet.'

What I meant was, it's on my mind all the time but I have no idea what to do. At the moment, I don't even want to go to London. I was so excited about it but it has a dark cloud over it and now I'm struggling to muster the enthusiasm. Maybe it was never really there. That's the problem with shared dreams, isn't it, knowing just how much of yourself is wrapped up in them, and how much was never really part of your dream in the first place.

The magazine though … that was me, right? I remember being right here in this kitchen when I got the call …

17 January
Friday evening, 7.05pm

'I got the job.' I'm shaking as I stand in front of Matt and my family. My mum was just serving up the lasagne she'd made for us all that Friday evening when it had just become late enough that all hope I'd had of being chosen had drifted away on the cold January breeze. 'They said we'd hear by the end of the week – I thought they mustn't have picked me.'

Mara walked into our kitchen from washing her hands. 'Wait, you heard about the internship?'

I faced my big sister, surprise still painted across the freckles on my face. 'I did. I got it.'

Mara threw her arms around me which prompted everyone else into action and my siblings – all home for the weekend from their various parts of the country for Mum's birthday – crowded me, asking questions, singing congratulations. I looked past them at Matt, because this affected him too. If I took this internship it meant uprooting our lives and moving to London. 'What do you think?' I asked him.

It was unfair of me to put him on the spot like that in front of everyone, but I was so taken by surprise that Adventure Awaits *magazine, one of the biggest travel magazines in the country and whose pages I'd thumbed through since my mum subscribed after my dad left, wanted me.*

'You've got to take it,' Marissa said. 'Remember that game where we'd make each other choose a page and—'

'—And then we'd say, "You've won a trip to Cuba!"' Benny interjected.

'"Do you want to keep it or gamble it for Graham's prize?"' Marissa finished, with a laugh.

I pulled myself from their arms and their memories, though I could have stayed wrapped in them for ever, and took Matt aside, trying to read his face like I usually could. 'What do you think? Be honest.'

He smiled at me. Damn, he can still melt me with a smile, I thought. I can't wait to marry him.

'I think this is going to be big, and you have to go for it.'

I blinked back tears of relief. 'But it would mean we'd have to move to London.'

'Weren't we planning to anyway at some point?'

'But this is forcing our hand. It hasn't given you time to look for a new job.'

'We've been talking about moving there since finishing uni. Now is the right time.'

'I won't be making any money, and right off the back of our wedding and honeymoon ...'

'Well, if you don't want to,' he shrugged and picked a piece of garlic bread from the bowl on the table while my family watched on and Mara was rolling up her sleeves to kill him.

'I do want to!' I yelp.

'Good. Then it's happening.' He grinned, chowing down on the garlic bread.

At that point, my mum swept me into her arms and breathed in my hair, the same chocolate-brown colour as hers. 'I'm so proud of you,' she said. 'Don't ever let anything stand in the way of making this life what you want from it.'

Mum cuts through my thoughts, saying, 'You can move back in here, you know, properly, and take as long as you like to figure out the next steps.'

The newspaper I'd just left have said I can come back to working for them any time.

I'm a train wreck, derailed from my own tracks, and I don't know which is the safe way home.

'Sooo, what we can do is cancel the flights and you can get some of your money back for those, but the tour is non-refundable,' the travel agent says to us, with the awkward 'sorry' face that anyone in his position would put on when a couple comes in to cancel a honeymoon. I look at Matt, at his unshaven face and tired eyes. I'm glad to see him looking a similar level of dishevelled as me because at least it seems that this has been hard for him too. He must be allowing himself a mourning period before chasing after pretty, preppy Katie. I snort through my nostrils at the memory and turn back to the agent.

'And our travel insurance won't cover it?'

'Not in this instance. Because this counts as you changing your mind, not like, a horrific accident or something, so all you can get back is what the airline and tour company are offering.' He swallows, clearly hating this part of his job. 'One moment, let me just check something.' The agent scurries off, but whether he's checking something or begging somebody else to take over is to be seen.

Matt turns to me. 'Maybe we should just go.'

'Maybe you should take Katie,' I retort, and he looks a little chastised. I soften. 'I don't think a Honeymoon Highlights tour is what either of us need right now.'

'You were so looking forward to it, though.'

'So were you, weren't you? Don't tell me this is something else you didn't really want to do?'

'Of course I was, but Japan was an adventure you'd always really wanted to take. You've always been more adventurous than I have, Charlie. You spent hours, days, weeks, months researching this trip.'

We lapse into silence again and the agent returns. Before he speaks, I ask him, 'Is there any way of transferring the places on the tour to a different time? Like, could one of us go now and the other in a couple of months?'

'To be honest, you'd have to pay such a premium for a single supplement to go at another time it wouldn't really make sense to stick with the, um, honeymoon tour. You'd be better off just paying again for a, um, solo traveller expedition. However,' he brightens. 'I just spoke to the company and they said that because some of the hotels are paid by the tour guide on arrival, as a gesture of goodwill they're willing to refund you the cost of those if you decide not to go. So that's something.'

'If one of us went now, would we have to pay the single supplement?' I ask the agent.

'No, because you've already paid for two people. If only one of you goes you just get a nice double bed to yourself everywhere.'

The cogs are turning in my head. I have a month before I'm due to start the internship in London. I'd wanted to be able to impress them, and perhaps Japan could provide me with some inspiration to do just that. It might even reignite that thing inside me that still, somewhere, wants this. It's all paid for. It's all planned. All my life people have been telling me, you should do this, you should feel like this. I think it's time I pull up my big-girl pants and listen to my own opinion, for a change. Make a decision by myself.

Do I have the balls to go on my honeymoon ... alone?

Chapter 3

Those Tokyo lights
Keep me awake all night, am
I ready for this?

Tap-tap-tap-tap-tap-tap-tap-tap-tap-tap.

I'm in a coffee shop at Heathrow Terminal 5, perched on a stool that's too high for my dangling legs. To my right are holidaymakers, tax-free bargain hunters and business travellers strolling through the concourse, and to my left ginormous glass windows overlook the planes gliding along on the runways.

Tap-tap-tap-tap-tap; I bounce the biro in my hand off my paper coffee cup. Amid the tangled anxieties about the upcoming flight, the new country, the different language, all of which I'm about to explore on my own, I wonder who I stole this biro from.

Draining the last of my coffee I pull my phone out, opening up the Duolingo app to cram a few last-minute words into my vocabulary, and use my napkin to try and scribe from memory the hiragana script for Hello – こんにちは. I whisper it out loud, with the careful precision of someone who really *really* wants to at least try. 'Konnichiwa.'

A small boy wandering past with a Trunki looks up at me and replies, '*Konnichiwa!*'

I must have said it right! He understood me! I am flush with pride and confidence, so I say back to him again '*Konnichiwa!*' with more gusto, and his mother looks over and I think I'd better shut up.

There's one thing left to do, that I've been putting off all this time, but I think, *I think*, I'm ready to admit it. I can't go ahead with this internship. I know that part of my reason for coming on this trip was so I'd fill up with material to be able to impress them with at the magazine, and maybe I could still use it in the future, and I'm *sure* I could at least persuade my local paper to let me write a travel guide to Japan or something. That would be exciting. And much more realistic than trying to get something published at an international magazine. The more I've been thinking about it over the past couple of weeks, the more uncertain about it I've become. I can't go and live in London on my own to do a job that won't even be paying me. I should stay put, where I can take my time and figure everything out.

Now I just need to tell them.

Adventure Awaits won't care if I pull out. There were loads of candidates at the recruitment day I went to, I bet they could fill my place within a matter of hours. It's ages – a whole month – away.

So ... why don't I send the email now?

Well, perhaps now isn't the best time because I need to think about wording and tone and really I'd better vacate this seat because I've finished my coffee. I could compose something on the plane. One more day isn't going to hurt.

To be honest, I'm not sure what to do with myself. Usually, when Matt and I took trips we'd get to the airport super early and loll about for a couple of hours until boarding time, safely through security without anyone planting a wheelie-suitcase full of drugs on us, and abuzz with pre-holiday excitement. I'd always find a reason to buy some essential extra mini-toiletries from Boots and a duty-free sarong from Accessorize, and Matt would linger around the confectionary stands trying to blag us some free Toblerone samples. We'd have a big meal and then window shop at Gucci and Tiffany's and the Harrods store and eventually part with our final British change at WHSmith on a magazine or three bars of chocolate and one of those delicious Graze pots we'd probably end up having to chuck because we wouldn't get around to eating it on the plane and I'd be worrying about taking nuts through customs.

But now ... I miss him by my side. I know I shouldn't and I can't think too much about what he might be doing now, but that's how it is. So I get up, chuck my coffee cup, leave my (not my) biro for the next fidgety-fingered soul and take a walk. Because I still have a good hour and thirty minutes before I need to head to the gate.

'Good morning,' says a smiling lady as I enter World of Duty Free. 'Would you like to try some whisky?'

'Well, it is ten in the morning after all,' I say in way of reply, and she pours me a thimble of caramel-hued liquid that I knock back like I'm an extra in *Westworld*. 'Very nice,' I choke.

'It's on a special offer today for just seventy-nine pounds for the litre bottle. Would you like to buy some?'

'Maybe later ...' I reply, thinking of my already fairly wiped-out bank account.

I'm going to Japan, I think as I try on a pair of Ray-Bans.

I'm going to Japan, I think as I dab a little Mac sample blusher on my cheeks before running away from the approaching sales assistant.

I'm going to Japan, on my own, I think as I stand in the queue clutching a heavily discounted Britney Spears perfume and a massive bottle of Smart Water.

I then walk over to Tiffany's and just for a minute allow myself to be the girl in the romance movie who stares at the engagement rings while a slow song by Adele plays in my head and a single tear rolls down my cheek. It isn't easy, knowing I should be married by now, remembering this was supposed to be my honeymoon. It sucks and, like I said, I miss him, I miss *us*. I miss the plans we'd made and the scenarios I'd played out in my head of how every minute of this trip would go.

But then I see the sales assistant behind the glass looking at me with a half-sorrowful, half-please-move-away-you're-depressing-our-customers look on her face and I decide to move on. Literally, not figuratively; not yet.

I ate all my plane snacks. All of them. I'm still at the gate, but I think the nerves have started to creep in, just slowly, like a conga line that isn't sure if it can pass through this way yet so is staying on the outskirts, picking up recruits.

Boarding should open in about twenty minutes, which isn't really enough time to go and get more … is it …? I crane my neck around, just in case there's a stray WHSmith loitering next to the loos.

It's okay to be a little bit on edge, I guess. I am flying to the other side of the world, on my own, and at this point in the game it feels unlikely I'm going to be offered an unexpected upgrade to business class. It's just such a long flight, to such a new place; if I was jetting to the Italian lakes for a week, I'm sure I'd be fine. And then it dawns on me how true that is, at least in this moment. I'm sure I'll have a multitude of anxieties over travelling alone, missing Matt, being in a foreign land, but it's the destination that's got my knickers in a twist right now, not any of the other bumph.

It's Japan. It's because visiting the Land of the Rising Sun has been a goal of mine since, oh, before I'd even heard the name Matt Bulverton. I've read about it, dreamt about it, because of that country I have indirectly and through a series of events plotted out the first decades of my life.

15 August 2011
Saturday afternoon, 1.50pm

The wooden chair was creaking under my constant fidgeting. I looked around me at the floor-to-ceiling bookshelves, maps and travel journals clustered in twirling racks, world globes with brass stands upon tables also piled with guidebooks and non-fiction titles with covers showing dirty walking boots, postcard-perfect scenery, written by people like Bill Bryson. It was a hot day in London, and the other members of the audience, including Matt, were fanning themselves with their handouts while they waited for the speaker. But I didn't care about the heat; to me it just added to the tropical atmosphere and it felt like the perfect environment for what we were here to witness.

I saw this event advertised inside Adventure Awaits, of course, way back in the spring. 'Meet Adventure Awaits' own Ariel Cortez at Stanfords map and travel bookshop for a lively talk on How to be a Travel Writer, Saturday 15 August, 2pm. Tickets £15, includes a drink.' A photo of Ariel Cortez was displayed alongside the advert, a larger version of the thumbnail portrait that had been running alongside her articles ever since I first started reading the magazine. It's like she was speaking to me, telling me: come on, Charlotte, you say you want to be a travel writer like me, and you're sixteen now which means you'll need to start making some decisions soon. Come and hear me out.

I told my mum this is what it felt like Ariel was saying, and my mum smiled and said that if I could pay for my ticket, and if Matt would go with me, she'd cover my train fare to and from London for the day.

My watch said we'd be starting in just a few minutes. I pulled my five-year-old copy of Adventure Awaits from my bag, the first copy I ever bought, which I pored over, reading the articles again and again, and wishing I could jump on a plane or ship or train and travel to these faraway lands, away *from a place where my home had broken in two and my dad had been the one to run away instead.*

I flipped to Ariel's article about Japan. Six pages long, with dazzling photos and light, funny, delicate wording, this had been my favourite piece in the whole magazine. I'd marvelled at Ariel's writing style and how she could make me feel like I was journeying through Japan beside her, there on the trains, visiting temples, seeing monkeys bathing in the hot springs. She'd fast become my favourite columnist, the first stories I read in each edition I purchased.

'Do you think she'll mind signing this for me?' I whispered to Matt for the zillionth time.

He flipped his hair to the side, which he'd grown out from Justin Bieber to a Harry Styles style, and pulled me in for a one-arm hug. 'You're such a fangirl. No, she won't mind, she'll probably love that you've been holding on to that battered old thing for so long.' 'Ladies and gentlemen,' said a man in a pinstripe shirt rolled up at the sleeves, and a tie that he'd already loosened in the heat. 'Thank you for coming to our event inside Stanfords this hot afternoon, and for anyone visiting London, welcome. I'm sure our special guest today has visited places far more sweltering than this during her career as a travel writer, and may I say, "adventurer," so, without further ado, let's give a hand for Adventure Awaits *magazine's Ariel Cortez!'*

I clap my hands off and sit up super straight, wanting to show respect for my idol, uncaring whether I looked like a fangirl. I was a fangirl.

Ariel walked in and waved at the rows of chairs, taking a seat on a tall stool next to the announcer, who would be moderating the talk and asking her questions. She looked so great, effortless in a white T-shirt and loose jeans rolled up at the hem, studded gladiator sandals on her feet, black hair pulled into a casual top-knot, simple yet beautiful jewellery that made the whole look presentable and put-together despite its casual feel. Her smile was wide and her fingernails polished.

'Wow, there's a lot of you here,' she smiled at the audience of twenty-, thirty-, forty-, and fifty-somethings. 'Are you all going to steal my job?'

'HA HA HA,' I laughed loudly along with the others, and as Ariel's eyes swept the room she caught my eye, the youngest there, and smiled wider.

As Ariel gave her talk, I soaked in everything she had to say. How she became a writer, what choices led her to travelling for a living, her top tips for those that want to do the same, and when it came time for audience questions I shot my hand straight up, even though I hadn't fully formed what I was going to ask.

'Yes, the girl in the beautiful blue blouse, what's your question?'

I blushed and fumbled my words. 'Um, hello, um, thank you. My question is ... well, I have this copy of an article ...' I paused and took a breath. Calm down, Charlotte. 'I first read your writing about five years ago when you did a big article about Japan, and I loved it. The way you described the hike up Mount Fuji and the food, and the night you spent inside a temple, it was so other-worldly that it made me feel like ... it made me realise I wanted to do that, to travel to places, and write about them in a way that people like me, who can't be there, feel like they can be. If that makes sense. So my question is, I guess, if you were giving advice to your sixteen-year-old self right now about how to be brave enough to follow this path, what would you say?'

'What's your name?' Ariel asks in return.

'Charlotte.'

'Firstly, Charlotte, thank you so much for your kind words, and for bringing that copy of the magazine, and letting me relive that memory. If you ever go to Japan you'll have to let me know what you think.' I nod at Ariel. I will go to Japan one day, I know it. She continues, 'My advice to you, Charlotte, would be to take any opportunity to have an adventure. Anything at all, even if you're scared, or it's new, or even if it's something close to home, as long as it feels safe, then catch that adventure and live it. And then write about it, write down your thoughts on how it felt, and how it sounded and tasted and what it smelt like. Oh and make sure they're your thoughts.'

The confusion must have shown in my face, because Ariel added, 'Tell your story of how the adventure feels to you. Don't just write a timeline of events, make it authentic, and tell your story.'

'Okay,' I say, thoughts tumbling around my mind faster than I can process. 'Thank you.'

Ariel looked at me a moment longer, as if she was remembering all the journeys she'd taken. 'You never know what can come of having an adventure. It might be something big. So catch every adventure you can.'

I took Ariel's advice and wrote down everything about every adventure I, and usually Matt, took. I started that evening, on the train back home, using a map-covered journal I'd purchased in Stanfords that afternoon. I went on to take journalism at university. I lost myself in books by Michael Palin, Elizabeth Gilbert, Jack Kerouac, Cheryl Strayed and, of course, Bill Bryson. I had 'me-time' in my calendar for the first Sunday afternoon of every month, where I'd read my new issue of *Adventure Awaits* from cover to cover. Anything with a travel-theme, I devoured.

Now, here in the airport, where I'll soon be boarding my flight to Japan, I pull that same tatty old copy of the magazine out of my bag, which I'd dug out of storage at

Mum's a couple of days before I left. I flip to Ariel's article, where her face smiles out beside her signature that she signed for me that day in 2011.

So no, I'm not at this point nervous about getting on that plane solo or forgetting my etiquette when I get to the other side. I'm afraid because this journey is important to me, and it's been a long time coming, and I don't want anything else to risk it being taken away from me. I want, desperately, for the sake of the person I think I am, to love every second of it.

'Hmm ...' I say out loud, scanning over the movie choices in the in-flight magazine. I have a nice seat by a window, with a middle-aged woman and her partner next to me, and a fully functioning entertainment system (yay!). I'm a nice distance from the nearest emergency exit where, in the event of a forced landing, I'd be unlikely to have to haul the door out of the gap myself but would almost certainly make it out of the plane.

'Lots of good movie choices,' I say to the woman, who looks up from the duty-free magazine and smiles.

I look at the other passengers still filtering on and finding their seats and grumbling at the ways other people have stored their belongings in the overhead lockers.

'Never seems to be enough room in those things, does there?' I say to the woman.

'No ...' she replies, smiling again and then flipping her page.

'Are you two just going to Japan for a holiday?' I ask and then realise something I never knew about myself. I've always travelled in groups or as part of a couple. Now I'm travelling on my own – it turns out *I'm* the annoying person who wants to chat to strangers!

I decide to leave her in peace and move my attention to the food and drink section of the in-flight magazine and as soon as I can I order one of those little complimentary bottles of Jack Daniels and some Coke. If Matt and I were here we would have probably popped a couple of those mini prosecco bottles, but I guess that Charlotte-on-her-own is a whisky kind of person.

The plane starts to taxi and shudder lightly around in a huge arc to face the runway. This is it. I can do this.

What am I thinking? I can't do this. It's not just going to Japan that's making me nervous, I'm going to be so far away, so many hours and miles and time zones away from my family and my friends, and yes, from Matt. I can't do it. I'm scared.

I'm scared of being out of my depth and I'm scared of getting lost and not being able to speak the language. I'm scared of something happening to someone back home and me not being there. Or something happening to me or to this plane. Nobody on this plane cares about me. Without Matt here, if we go down, who will protect my teeth so the police know it's me? I suppose Matt would have been protecting his own teeth and not mine, though, regardless. Thanks for nothing, Matt.

I close my eyes and breathe, and let the aeroplane sweep me and my tangled thoughts and loss of self up into the clouds, leaving the noise of everybody else in my life back in England, and trying instead to focus on listening to myself.

It then occurs to me: I'm not alone. I'm – what do they call it? – self-partnered. And in the Land of the Rising Sun I'm looking forward to getting to know the real me, myself and I. I down the rest of the whisky in my plastic cup and wince. I'm not sure I even like whisky.

Five hours into the nearly twelve-hour flight, I take the battered travel brochure out of my handbag and flip to the page showing the tour we booked on to. The 'Japan Honeymooners Highlights' trip. Little faded biro markings showed price quotes jotted down, and where

Matt has starred the things he was most looking forward to. A tea-stained mug ring partially covers the white of Mount Fuji in the main picture, which had happened when we'd both squealed with excitement after finally booking it and I'd knocked into the brochure causing the tea to break a wave over the rim of the mug.

It had taken us ages to come to a decision about how to handle our trip in Japan. Both of us wanted to see as much as we could within the month we planned to be away. Both of us wanted to travel by rail rather than on an escorted coach. Both of us wanted to spend some time in Tokyo to kick things off. Beyond that, we wanted to immerse ourselves as much as we could in the Japanese lifestyle and culture.

I was keen to buy a twenty-one-day rail pass and do our own thing, exploring the Big Sights but also the smaller, beautiful intricacies and places, the natural beauties away from the tourist trails. The kind of places I could write about and maybe impress my manager at *Adventure Awaits* with. Matt was more on the side of playing it safe and being on a structured tour. He wanted someone to explain everything to us, and make sure he could tick off all the main attractions and not miss out on anything. Hmm ... where had I heard that before?

14 September, last year
Saturday afternoon, 4.30pm

'Don't you want the easy option, though, considering it's our honeymoon?' Matt asked, pushing the group tour page closer again.

'It's just that we may only ever go to Japan once in our lifetimes, and I don't want to miss anything out.' I looked at the tour page again. 'I do like that this tour includes loads of activities and experiences, and they do sound fun ...'

'Shall we call Alex again?'

'No,' I shook my head. We'd already chatted to our friend about this trip three times. He was the only person we knew who had been to Japan, but ever since we'd asked him what his 'must-do' tips were he'd wanted to be involved in everything, from picking the hotels to suggesting flights. It was helpful, but it was really down to me and Matt to buckle down and choose what we wanted to do.

'I know you want to go to every one of the nearly seven thousand islands that make up Japan, but we can't fit all of it into four weeks. Let yourself relax a little while we're there, too.'

He was right. Everybody (except Alex) was quick to tell us how shattered we'd be following the wedding and how a poolside week might be a more suitable option. But looking at the brochure, the page filled with details that made my happy heart sing, I knew it was a winning compromise.

'Let's do it,' I said. 'Let's book it right now.'

'This one?' Matt pointed at the Honeymoon Highlights tour. 'Are you sure?'

'Yes, it sounds perfect. And we can add on a day or two in Tokyo, right? Just to have a little freedom before it all starts?'

'Definitely. Shall I call and book it?'

'Call and book it.'

I watched my future husband fumble his way through a call with the travel agents, reading out credit card numbers, making stupid jokes about requesting separate rooms or asking if they could swing a free honeymoon upgrade on the flight for him but not me.

When he was done, I squealed, leaping up to squeeze him and knocking my tea on route, which splashed on our brochure. But we didn't mind.

I love him so much, I thought. *He's my best friend. Always has been, and now always will be.* I tried to imagine us in Japan, seeing the world, bonded together and I wondered where we would be in ten years' time. *What kind of adventures will we have taken by then?*

I feel stupid remembering this now.

The Honeymoon Highlights tour ticked most of the boxes, with a little compromise. It would be an intimate group of three couples and one guide, a little over three weeks long and starting from Tokyo, using the Japanese rail network (including the bullet train) and promised both 'the security and serenity of group travel with plenty of opportunity to tailor your own experience at each of our stopping locations'.

Well, now it was going to be two couples and me. And the guide. Oh gee, I was going to have to partner with the guide for everything, like when your teacher takes pity on you in PE and says you can practise relays with her because nobody else wants your short, slow legs holding them back.

I exhale louder than intended, and the woman next to me looks over. She seems to see something different from when she looked at me last time, perhaps glancing the name of the tour and wondering to herself why I was travelling alone. 'Are you okay?' she asks.

I smile at her. 'Yes, thank you. Just a little nervous about taking a trip on my own.'

'Is this the tour you're doing?'

'Yep. Only I'm going to be the only one not honeymooning.'

The woman looks like she doesn't know what to say, so to stop her thinking the worst happened, I add, 'We called off the wedding, it was for the best, but I decided I could still do with a trip away to clear my head, and this was already booked and paid for.'

'Well, I'm sorry to hear that. I can understand why you'd be a little sad. Would you like the rest of my Jack Daniels?'

I shake my head but thank her. I settle back in my seat and look out the window at the clouds below me, slivers of sunset appearing on my horizon, and my eyelids droop.

When I wake up it's dark, and I'm face-down on a hotel bed, fully clothed, my suitcase unopened beside me. The curtains are open, framing a vast cityscape beyond the glass windows that looks like the opening shot of a film noir, only with futuristic towers stretching into the inky sky and neon lights like Christmas bulbs.

'Dammit,' I mutter. I didn't mean to fall asleep. I had so little kip on the plane that by the time I arrived at Tokyo's Haneda Airport I was so bleary that I barely remember the jostle of passport control, the bustle of baggage collection, the hubbub of the arrivals lounge and the shuffle of the shuttle bus journey to my hotel, nestled on the outskirts of the Harajuku neighbourhood.

I sit up. The room is pristine and quiet, the double bed lower than I'm used to and an opaque screen separates the sleeping area from the bathroom. Decorated in plums and browns it doesn't give away the location, and I could nearly be in AnyHotel, Anywhere, if it wasn't for the tiny details that pop out at me. Intricate calligraphy stencilled onto the wallpaper. The postcard-sized Manga print above the kettle. And when I go for a wee – I had my bladder to thank for waking me up – an array of electric buttons along the side of the loo lead me to experience a surprise water spurt.

My brain is still foggy, still desperate for more sleep, but if I close my eyes now I'll never adjust to the time zone. Besides, *grrrrrowl*, my tummy tells me it's dinner time. Or lunch time. Or breakfast time. I shoot a quick message off to my family to let them know I'm here and then freshen up in the shower before heading out into the early evening.

Warm air hits the bare skin of my face as soon as I step outside, and my ears fill with a thousand different noises that had been masked from within my glass sanctuary. Cars, distant trains, chatter in a language almost alien to my ears, apart from the odd recognisable word that I catch on the breeze. But all the careful preparation, the print-outs of hiragana characters I'd stuck to my fridge, the hours spent googling and YouTubing our destinations, hadn't prepared me for how much of a complete novice I would feel. I don't even know what the shops are called that I pass, or what the road signs say, and I wish I had someone else here to figure it out with me.

Luckily, I do have trusty Google Maps, which I've cached on my phone so that I can use areas I've downloaded offline, and I navigate my way towards the central hub of Harajuku. I don't have a plan (which is a little unusual for me) but my weary body and mind seem to want to just take me for a wander.

There's laughter from passers-by which tinkles alongside pop music. I can't quite tell if it's coming from the shops or from speakers above them but it seems to be the same song. I turn onto Takeshita Street and am met with a candy-crush dreamscape that sounds like Disneyland after dark and looks like multicoloured sequins have been thrown in the air and are floating in front of me to light my way. The long, shop-lined strip has a bokeh effect on my still weary eyes; the rainbow of illuminations out of focus. I follow the trail past stores spilling out with cute stuffed cartoon animals, Hello Kitty merchandise, vintage clothing and much, much more. I move with the crowd and keep having my eye caught by the sight of young women dressed in powder-puff pinks and mint greens, sunshine yellows and bold turquoise stripes, mermaid-toned hairstyles woven into plaits and bunches. They walk with a confidence and individuality, showing themselves and their outfits off, and they're mesmerising.

I should write about this. All of this, I need to capture the *kawaii* culture in all its cutesy Technicolor glory. It's so much to take in that I switch my phone screen away from the map and start videoing everything from the anime-print socks to rainbow candy floss. Maybe during the lonelier nights here in Japan I can write a few pieces, maybe blog posts, maybe articles, to show *Adventure Awaits* when I get home.

'I'm in Tokyo,' I narrate from behind the camera, feeling a bit silly talking to myself but too sleepy to care. 'Just arrived into Harajuku and the jet lag is pretty outstanding, but so is this street. Check out all of this swag. I think I'm the dullest-looking person in the whole district right now.' I turn the camera around and pan it down my body, showing my muted jumper and jeans and coat. Maybe I should start wearing more colour.

My stomach gives off such a loud howl that for a second I'm not sure if it's that or one of the moggies inside the cat cafe that I'm passing, so I take it as a sign to refocus my search for food. I hover beside a crêpe stand on the street for a moment, deliberating between sweet and savoury, but I'm kidding myself: there's only one crêpe I'm going for.

'*Konbanwa*,' I say to the woman behind the counter, and give a bow. So far so good. Thank you, Duolingo app, for giving me little Japanese lessons daily for the past couple of months. I then notice that all the crêpes have the English translation under them and my tired brain takes the opportunity to shut off and forget all of its carefully learnt phrases, so instead I stand like a fool pointing at the crêpe, a dopey, hopeful expression on my face and say slowly, 'Custard caramel cheesecake special?' I loathe myself and swear that I'll do better after tomorrow.

I'm yawning again. After this I'm going to give in and go back to the hotel, call it a night. But for now, once I'm handed my crêpe-wrapped cheesecake slab, I stand to the side and munch it with the hunger of someone who last ate aeroplane bread rolls. Me in a sea of people. It's so busy here, and the streets of Harajuku, Tokyo, only seem to be filling up more as the night unfolds. In crowds this big a solo traveller could start to feel lonely, but for me it feels freeing to get a little lost in translation.

Chapter 4

Loneliness follows
The happiest place on earth
When the curtain falls

'Good morning, Tokyo!' I say out loud, my heart bursting with a sense of happiness and freedom as I fling open the curtains to sunrise over the city. It's early, but already the streets are bathed in a warm, spring yellow glow the colour of Easter chicks. Looking down from my window, I see some of the capital's 9 million residents already beginning their day, or ending their nights, with a jog, a coffee, a moment of zen.

I'm moving accommodation today, away from Harajuku cute and into high-rise chic, to the Park Hyatt Tokyo, the hotel made famous in *Lost in Translation*. If it hadn't been a non-refundable part of the tour I probably would have cancelled and stayed put here, not because I don't want to visit the hotel but because it's a bit of three-night luxury I can't afford now.

Technically, the tour starts tomorrow. An arrival night was included today, then a free day tomorrow, and tomorrow evening I'll meet the other couples and the guide for dinner. We then have one more day and night in Tokyo before heading on the bullet train to Kyoto together.

But today is *freeeeeeee* and I'm feeling so well rested and giddy from the immersive *kawaii* cuteness of Harajuku that there's just one thing I want to do. It wasn't on the itinerary for Matt and me, but bugger Matt, I can do whatever I want now. And I'm going to spend the day at Tokyo Disneyland!

After a pleasant half hour on the toilet experiencing all the exciting settings, I'm ready to pack my things back into my hefty great suitcase and make tracks. I think I'll walk! A lovely morning stroll will take me right past the Meiji Jingū shrine, protected from the lively hum of the city by a large tree-filled park, and out the other side to the Park Hyatt within forty minutes or so. There I can hopefully leave my clobber, and jump on a train to Disneyland.

Leaving the hotel, I swing by my new favourite crêpe stand for another sugar hit for breakfast (*promise* I'll start eating all that beautiful, fresh, healthy Japanese food really soon, but also, my trip my rules, right?) and this time opt for an early-morning-friendly option of blueberry jam and cream cheese.

Ah, spring days in Tokyo. I could be an extra in *La La Land*, just on the wrong continent, the way I'm promenading along with a spring in my step. My suitcase bump bump bumps along the pavement behind me and I have to switch arms every few minutes because it is a little heavy, but thankfully it doesn't take long to reach the entrance to the park and the path widens, and there are fewer businesspeople around. Early-morning sunshine dapples through the trees and the forest thickens, leading me towards the Meiji Jingū shrine, which is one of the places Ariel Cortez visited in her Japan article. The 'eye of the tornado', she called it, referring to how calm the shrine was among the wonderful rush of Tokyo.

Bow twice, clap hands twice, make a wish, bow again, I chant to myself as I walk along. I read that on the website this morning as I was packing up – it's the correct way to show respect once you've got to the shrine itself. And I do not want to be that kind of tourist who looks like they stepped off the plane and expects everything to be catered for them.

I reach the *torii*, the giant, angular, wooden archway that signifies the pathway changes from the everyday to the spiritual and leads towards the shrine. I'm the only one around right now, me and my suitcase, and I stop for a minute to take in the quiet magnificence of the arch above me.

I wonder where I'll be in a month's time. Not physically: physically, I'll be back in Tokyo about to fly back to the UK. Physically, I shall be ten pounds lighter because of all the delicate, light Japanese cuisine and my treks up and down Mount Fuji. Providing that I honour my vow to stop eating dessert for breakfast, my skin will be clear and glowing from the vitamin D bestowed upon me by being outdoors for a month, and the break from working hunched over a copy-editing desk. Physically, I feel very confident that I'll be returning as Gigi Hadid's twin from this adventure. But emotionally, where will I be? Hmm.

Like all good spiritual soul-searching in the twenty-first century, my thoughts are supplemented with the tinkle of bells from my mobile phone. Even though I'm standing on my lonesome, a little lost tourist unsure if I'm allowed beyond the archway, I feel guilty at the noise and scrabble for my phone in my bum bag.

Yes, bum bag. I saw loads of people wearing really cool ones in Harajuku so don't 'Coachella 2015 called …' me.

Hey sis, are you up? It's Benny on our siblings' WhatsApp group.

I am, I'm off to a shrine! I tap back.

Disneyland?

No, a real shrine! I say.

Very cultured, Charlie, thought you'd be hitting Disneyland for sure, chimes in Mara.

They think they know me so well ... *No*, I write. *That's AFTER the shrine.*

Noooo, you're not serious! You can't go all the way to Tokyo to spend your first day in Disneyland!

I bloody well can, I tell my big sister. I can almost feel Mara shivering at my tackiness. *And there's piss all you can do about it.*

Marissa has started typing, and shortly after a message pops up. *Hi, C! I was talking to one of the chefs at work and his sister married a guy whose boss lived in Japan for a year and he said you HAVE to go to something called ...*

... Marissa is typing ...

I'd like to carry on towards the shrine but don't feel I should text and drive this suitcase within the gate, so I wait.

... Marissa is typing ...

I write, *So how are you lot? Isn't it 11 pm-ish at home? Or is it morning already because Marissa's been typing for so long?*

Izakara Alleys! She eventually sends. *They're these tiny little drinking taverns and they sound really cool. Nightlife in Japan sounds epic – go for a big night out if you really want to live a little.*

Does Tokyo Disneyland have the same rides as the Paris one? Benny asks.

I'll let you know! Thanks for the tip, Marissa, I might look into that, though I'm not sure if a lone gal on a heartbreak honeymoon should start drinking sake alone in a Tokyo backstreet.

All right, sis? Gray has come online. *Yep, it's late here, I was in bed dropping off to sleep.*

As if you were, replies Mara.

You guys, I need to get going – I'm switching hotels via this shrine and want to get to Disney before the queues are huge. Text you all later?

Send pics! Benny replies.

Have a good day, adds Mara.

Later, says Gray.

… Marissa is typing …

I press on towards the shrine, a few other early-morning visitors passing me and my suitcase along the route. Reaching the font, I falter. Now I remember there was some particular etiquette for this part of the shrine too but I'd been so busy repeating the other mantra to myself this part is foggy. Do you rinse your left hand and then your right hand, or was it *raise* your left hand then your right hand? But why would you raise your hand? Unless it's because you aren't supposed to touch the water with your hands at all. But no, there was definitely instruction to bring water to your mouth to rinse it.

To be on the safe side, I do an exaggerated raise-to-rinse motion, like someone pressing a buzzer on a gameshow in slow motion, first with my left hand and then my right. I put a little water up to my mouth and rinse my hands again, do a little bow for good measure, and vow to be much more careful with swotting up on my instructions at the next spiritual site I visit.

And finally my vista opens up and I'm at the shrine itself, a large, peaceful courtyard surrounded on three sides by humble, low buildings in dark woods, with sweeping roofs and one structure taller and more prominent than the other.

The sounds of Tokyo have been tucked out of earshot by the congregation of trees, and the world is quiet. Yet I feel incredibly *within* Japan, centred, like my real journey starts here.

I watch no more than a handful of other visitors, a small amount, I guess, due to the time of day, as they stand noiselessly and pay their respects prior to continuing with their busy days. I, too, pay mine, just as I'd practised, and into the quiet seeps a word, soft like a whisper caught on a breeze. *Matt* …

I let it float away, but I help it on its way with a gentle nudge in case it comes back. I'm so tranquil that I could stay here for hours, but before my thoughts can circle back around I remember that I have a plan for today. A plan with a very *kawaii* mouse.

The Park Hyatt Tokyo stood tall and glinting in the morning sunshine. Three connecting towers of concrete and glass known as the Shinjuku Park Tower due to the other shops and offices that occupy the first thirty-eight floors. This district feels miles rather than minutes from the tranquil forests of the shrine, or the sequin-coloured cuteness of Harajuku.

I stride into the lower lobby and hop in the elevator. I love hotels. Always have and I expect I always will. There is just something so romantic and exciting about their promise of adventure, their temporariness. In fact, a hotel stay in Paris first gave me my chronic and incurable travel bug …

29 July 2004
Tuesday afternoon, 3.05pm

I stared down the never-ending corridor, a tunnel of quiet doorways and spotlights, a blue carpet and a series of watercolour prints of Parisian scenes at perfectly uniform placement upon the walls. I turned to face the other way and saw the exact same thing. The ice bucket felt too full and kinda heavy in my skinny, nine-year-old's arms. Hmm.

'MUM,' I shouted. Silence.

What was our room number? Was it 16? I tried the door but nothing, so I tried 19 though I was pretty sure there wasn't a nine in it because I would have remembered that, being nine (and a half) and all. 'MUM?' I shouted again.

I didn't want them to go to the Eiffel Tower without me, and a little pebble formed in my chest because I wanted to cry. 'Mummy?' I said quietly to door 21, where I could hear the sound of a TV in another language.

And then Gray appeared, his scruffy head sticking out of door 26. 'Told you you'd get lost,' and then Mara shoved past him to hold the door open for me.

'I wasn't lost,' I was indignant and embarrassed.

'Were so.'

'Shut up, idiot.'

'Charlotte,' Mum warned, weary from the travel and trying to do something with a room key and the light switch.

'He started it,' I sulked. 'I got the ice.'

'That's lovely, honey,' said Mum. Perhaps she was right that we hadn't needed ice as soon as we arrived since we were going to head into Paris from our large hotel soon anyway.

When I was safe with my family again, I couldn't help but think back to the corridor. How could there have been so many doors, all with rooms and people and families like us in them, *all with completely different lives and even speaking completely different languages? All these people who were visiting and finding their rooms and trying out the cool ice machine. I thought: I'd like to explore some more hotels.*

I bow a greeting to the friendly reception staff who don't bat an eyelid at my less-than-immaculate appearance that some of the other guests at the Park Hyatt Tokyo are sporting. They check me in with discreet confusion: 'Just one, Miss Charlotte? Not two guests?'

'No, just me, the other guest couldn't make it,' I reply and we hold eye contact for half a second before the receptionist smiles, tinkers on her computer and then points me in the direction of a secondary set of elevators that shoot me up to my bedroom.

Not only was I not expecting to be allowed into my room this early, but inside I find she's upgraded me! And if I didn't expect it might be some kind of social faux pas, I'd run back down and give her a kiss. I was expecting a regular double but this is definitely what the website describes as a deluxe. I wonder ... did the receptionist connect the dots?

I have a view out across the city, high above the other skyscrapers, a glittering circuit board of grey and morning yellow. I have two chairs and a squidgy foot stool in soft beige to match the curtains, walls and carpet. A big, dark-wood sideboard houses a television, some books, the minibar and a little teapot and cups. And in the bathroom there is a fat, deep, soaking tub and a standalone shower, plus *two* robes – two! – so maybe I'll bloody well wear them both at the same time if the mood takes me!

My mind wanders, remembering all the times Matt rushed for the hotel-room robe the second we checked in. He had a thing about stripping off and walking around the room in the robe; it got him into vacation-mode instantly. Give him a hotel robe, a room balcony with a view, and some complimentary sparkling water and he would be in seventh heaven for at least thirty minutes until he wanted to get dressed again and go out and explore.

I shake away this memory and sit on the bed to look at the view, my eyes trailing down to the windowsill. I wonder if I can recreate that famous shot from the movie where Scarlett Johansson is sitting on the windowsill looking out across the city in her knickers. In reality, that windowsill doesn't look very wide, unlike my bottom ... Still, I expect that I'll give it a try at some point this evening. Sneaking a look in the minibar, I see some jolly interesting cans and bottles, but although my stomach hasn't caught up with my time zone, there's no need to show up to Disneyland smashed so I'll leave those for now. In fact, I'll leave everything for now, all the unpacking and exploring and button-pushing, because there's a mouse to say *konnichiwa* to.

After an eventful train journey that took me on a merry wiggle through Tokyo, I step back out into the sunshine, now higher in the sky, and am greeted by the unmistakable sweeping curves of colourful exteriors that is Disney around the world. Familiar childhood anthems tinkle out of speakers and guide me and the troop of other merrymakers across a gas lamp-lined bridge towards the entrance of the park, past eateries and coffee shops all with surprisingly English names.

I queue for my ticket, already glimpsing a vast, flowerbed Mickey just beyond the security checks and a ripple of excitement shimmies its way around me. *I'm in Disneyland, bitch*, I tell Matt in my head.

Distracted by a gaggle of Japanese teenage girls wearing cute Minnie-inspired matching dresses and carrying cuddly Winnie the Poohs, I nearly miss my place at the front of the line.

'*Konnichiwa,*' I bow to the ticket seller. '*Chiketto ichi-mai, kudasai.*' One ticket, please. I don't say this with confidence, because it feels like every bit of Japanese I carefully learnt has fallen on the floor like a dropped ice cream and I'm staring at the poor ticket seller like a constipated koala. The words come out slowly and apologetically, like I've actually said 'one thumb in my nose, now' or some such thing. And aren't there two different words for 'please'? Did I use the wrong one?

'*Ohayo*,' the ticket seller replies, kindly, and, 'One ticket for both parks?'

I nod with the enthusiasm of a puppy and place the money on the counter rather than handing it directly to the employee, like I'd read in my guidebook. Tokyo Disneyland is made up of two parks, the main shebang and a place called Disney Sea. I don't know what that one's all about but I'll find out later. I'm going to try and squeeze in as much as I can.

As the seller sorts out my tickets and begins stacking up some maps and leaflets for me, she says gently, '*Konnichiwa* is more for the afternoon; *ohayo* is how you say "good morning".'

'Oh!' I blush. 'I forgot, thank you. *Arigato*.'

She smiles at me and hands over my Disney swag. 'It is no problem, have a very happy day.'

'And you.' Off I trot through security and into the park and yes, I know that maybe, on some level, it's a little off-piste for me, Ms Billie-No-Mates, to have chosen to come to a theme park that caters almost exclusively for families and children. I also know that my eldest sister will be thinking that my decision indicates some unconscious desire to regress to my childhood or exist in a state of arrested development. And she may be right, but right now I'm happily having fun in a Disney park, and why the hell not? Everyone else is here to have fun, to forget the difficulties of the world, and to have their hardest decision be 'Space Mountain next or Tower of Terror?'

It's so familiar here, but with sprinkles of differences, and I walk through what would be 'Main Street USA' in the other parks I've been to, here I'm in the World Bazaar, a covered area (presumably in case of those naughty rainstorms I keep hearing that Tokyo has, not that I've seen any sign of a drop yet) with beautiful shops and cafes showcasing the best of Japanese Disney memorabilia. I'll hit this area later, but first I think I'm ready for a ride.

En route to something called Monsters Inc. Ride and Go Seek! I stop by a popcorn stand selling soy-sauce-butter-flavour corn. Since I've pretty much only eaten sugar since arriving in Japan, I think it would be *sensible* to purchase some of this. After paying, I walk off with my scrummy, savoury popcorn inside a large, plastic Lightening McQueen from *Cars* bucket, which I must have agreed to accidentally. I see that others have hung these popcorn tubs around their necks like big nose bags, so when in Rome ...

Shuffling along in the queue I make friends with an elderly Japanese man who is being dragged around by his large family, judging by all of their matching T-shirts. We take it in turns to 'ooo' and point out details to each other of interesting things on the walls and ceiling and at characters popping out behind doorways, even though we can see them for themselves. But I like this chap, and when his massive entourage fills up five of the two-seater tram cars and he's left on his own in the back one, I'm happy to sit beside him when he beckons me in.

Once we're seated, my friend's face lights up and he explains to me in Japanese how the ride works, shoving one of the two big plastic flashlights in front of us into my hands, and gesturing to his forehead. I turn the torch on him thinking this was an odd way to start a ride and he laughs, his whole face crinkling with amusement, before pointing my torch for me at the characters we're beginning to pass, and as my torch beam hits the 'M' on a cartoon construction hat there's a piercing DING and a monster pops out of a fire hydrant.

My friend cheers and I cheer and now we're all systems go. So the point seems to be that you have to find the hidden monsters as the little cars wiggle their way around a series of *Monsters, Inc.* scenes. I pull my phone out to take a tiny bit of video, which is probably very shaky since I'm also one-handedly still flapping my torch around, determined that me and my pal are going to find all those damn monsters. I turn the camera on him and he beams at me, holding the torch up to his forehead again and laughing, before whipping back around to a big bank of 'M' hats and standing up in his seat shouting, '*Hai, hai, hai!*' until all his family members start yelling back at him from their separate carts and he sits back down.

I love that the characters are speaking Japanese throughout the ride. I mean, of course they are, but I'm still pleased, even if I don't have the foggiest what they're saying. I also love that there are Japanese touches scattered among the scenes we pass, including a Japanese restaurant with *shoji* translucent paper walls. The ride is beautiful and I could ride on it a hundred times and still not spot everything.

But alas, we're at the end, and my friend and I climb out and bow at each other, laughing, and then I take a photo with him and all of his family and he takes one of me, and all of his family, and then I give him some of my carful of popcorn and we go our separate ways.

My day is spent queueing and riding and laughing and marvelling and I don't feel lonely or out of place once, and I flitter back and forth between the two parks, refilling my popcorn car three times and making sure I take a turn on all the major attractions on my must-do list (I'd never get around everything in one day).

'*Ichi, kudasai!*' I say, spotting a stand selling little pots of green blobs. Pretty sure these are mochi: squidgy, chewy little dumplings filled with a flavoured bean paste, usually. The woman hands me a plastic cup filled with these green blobs, and I spot they have eyes painted on them so they look like a little cup of those aliens from Toy Story. And when I bite into one of their little heads *ohhhhmygod*. Japanese food is just the best and I'm never going home. In fact, I might never leave Disneyland. The filling is strawberry and creamy and I gobble it down in one and then THE NEXT ONE IS CHOCOLATE. I am definitely going to throw up on Tower of Terror, with its sudden stomach-lurching drops, but it's worth it.

For the rest of the afternoon I walk around, capturing the sights on video, listening to the claps and the music from the parade from where I sit on a wall gobbling another cup full of mochi aliens, joining some single-rider queues and waltzing straight onto the rides, and feeling on top of the world. I need this. I need a day to be childlike and unafraid and distracted, in a place that is comfortingly familiar while laced with gentle reminders that this country is where I'm calling home for the next month.

I'm tired by the time I leave the parks, the sun having set and the lights of the Tokyo Skytree lit up and towering above the city in the distance. I splash out on a taxi to take me back to the hotel because it'll take less than half an hour versus the hour-long train, and my eyes are drooping and my feet hurt.

The taxi ride, quiet and gentle, dark and warm, brings me back down to earth. We pass sign after sign glowing in the dark with characters I can't identify and the odd one I can, which I whisper out loud, 'Japan', '*su*', '*kyu*', 'forest'.'

By the time we reach the Park Hyatt and I've travelled the two elevators to my room, I feel wiped.

I head inside and plonk down my things, then sit for a moment gazing out of my window and let all those thoughts that keep drifting in and out and get pushed aside, come back to me for a while. What a perfect day. Matt would have loved it.

I think about how he would have laughed and laughed at me when I got a bit too into it on 'It's A Small World', singing my little heart out only to find it was the Japanese version of the theme song playing and everyone wanted me to stop ruining their magic.

And Disney Sea ... I know Matt hadn't been bothered about fitting Disneyland into our trip, but he whoops as much as the next person on a theme-park ride, and that was one of the most stunning theme parks I've ever been to – and I've been to quite a few in my time, thanks to my four siblings, Matt, and theme-park crazy Brienne. We'd have hung out, sunning ourselves on DisneySea's beautiful glittering harbour, drinking delicious frozen pineapple beer, with nautically themed 'ports' housing different rides and attractions. There was definitely a more adult vibe there. Not adult in a nudey girls and excessing swearing way, but the rides are a little more for the thrill-seekers.

We could have screamed together on my favourite ride – the Tower of Terror. We could have listened to the marching band as they wove through the park. We could have eavesdropped, together, on the excited chatter in quickly spoken Japanese and quizzed each other about what was being said, showing off what we remembered from our Japanese lessons on the app. He could have helped me eat the popcorn so I didn't make myself feel quite so sick.

It hits me like a come-down from a sugar high, melancholy washing over me, and I feel sad again, which makes me annoyed at myself for being such a spoiled brat. But from my darkened hotel room as I gaze out of my window at the city where over 9 million people are doing their thing, I feel alone. Matt should be here, we should be drinking a glass of wine and wearing our hotel robes, wondering what our friends and family were doing back home, chatting about how we should spend tomorrow, laughing over funny wedding stories that would keep us chuckling for months.

Matt would probably be itching to try out the hotel pool, even if he'd just had a bath. He'd be making up stories about all the people in the building across the road, and what they were doing and talking about. He'd have cracked open three of the mystery cans in the minibar for us to do a taste test on. He was a fun travel partner, entertaining to be around with his silly playful ways.

Now is he being silly with Katie?

Or is he standing next to a window somewhere in England, looking up at the overcast late-morning sky, and wondering what I'm doing across the world in Tokyo?

Chapter 5

Restless dreams, it seems,
Can bring ideas to me.
Call me Scorsese.

It's been a long day, it's now really late, I should fall straight to sleep … right? But my midnight mind seems to want to keep my thoughts whirling like the tea cups in Disneyland.

I lie with them for a long while before getting up and out of my luxurious bed and peeping through the curtains at the city, which is very much still awake down below.

Standing on my feet again reminds me how sore and overused they feel from today, and in a lightbulb moment I think of my big, deep soaking tub in the bathroom. A good remedy for tired feet and tired brains? Worth a try.

With the curtains pulled open so I can see Tokyo's moon above the city from my bathtub (don't worry, I'm so high up I'm pretty confident nobody can see my own

Tokyo moon) I let the hot water tingle around my pinked and sore feet. I'd read that in Japan the act of having a bath is taken seriously as a purely relaxing experience, and that you should wash your hair and body in the shower first and use the tub for luxuriating. I suppose that's what it's supposed to be everywhere, but I can't remember the last time I just lay in the water like this, easing my muscles. Enjoying the sensations. If I have a bath at home I usually spend no more than about three and a half minutes relaxing, letting a couple of pages of my latest book get soggy, and then get out the hedge trimmer on my leg stubble and the disinfectant for my hair. It turns into one furious scrub-fest and I come out glowing and squeaky but hardly wandering through the house with a dreamlike serenity. Not tonight, I think, trying to clear my mind and focus only on the ripples of warmth on my skin. Tonight I am in Japan, and we'll do this properly.

By the time I leave the bath, my mood has lifted a little. But I'm still not sleepy. I check my phone and my stomach drops to see an email from Amanda, the editor at *Adventure Awaits* that I'm due to report to.

Hi Charlotte,

We're looking forward to having you join us at Adventure Awaits *next month. I saw that you posted a photo to Instagram that you're off to Japan! I remember now – you're on your honeymoon, right? Congratulations. Let us know if you come across any great angles for stories, of course.*

Just wanted to drop you a quick note to confirm arrangements for day one. Please arrive at the office for 10am the first day and ask the receptionist to call me. You'll need to bring your passport for me to scan for HR. You'll also be starting your internship alongside one other recruit, Thomas, who'll be commencing an internship on our sister magazine Eco Adventures *at the same time. You may have met him at the recruitment day back at the end of last year. We'll get the two of you oriented together, and we'll take you for a lunch on your first day, so leave your sandwiches at home!*

Congrats again on the wedding and we'll keep an eye on your trip on Instagram, and look forward to hearing all about it.

Best wishes,
Amanda
Amanda Sakerson
Editor, Adventure Awaits

I really need to reply and let her know my decision. I just can't do it now, my mind is too fuzzy, too full of dancing Disney characters. So I push the problem aside, turn my phone over, wrap both robes around myself and snuggle down into bed under a cloud of thick duvets, and let my hair naturally dry into a curly-wurly frizz. I flick through TV channels until I land on an intricately illustrated anime movie about two young people who I think have swapped lives. The images in the movie dance across my vision, cherry blossoms and sunlight and mountains. It's simple yet so perfect and beautiful. Everything about Japan is beautiful and begs to be documented visually, it seems, through paintings or art or film.

I pick up my phone again, avoiding looking at my emails, and check through some of the footage I've taken over the last few days.

My videos from Harajuku last night are quite good, actually (thanks to the subject matter, I'm sure; the narration is foggy and I sound like I've swallowed a pack of tissues). They're colourful and with a little tweaking I manage to create a couple of minutes' worth of montage of arriving in Tokyo and my first evening. I add a couple more minutes from the shrine and Disneyland, and finally a little of the inside of the Park Hyatt. After a while of tinkering around, I've made myself a little travel vlog!

And I'm starting to yawn.

I'm proud of it, though, and I think I want to share it with my friends and family. It's a few minutes' long, so I can't just upload it as a regular Instagram video. I open the app anyway and after a little navigating and a smidge of procrastination watching a video from Reese Witherspoon, I think I've got IGTV, Instagram's functionality for longer videos, figured out. I sit up a little straighter in my bed, trying to beat the tiredness now it's finally here.

This could be fun. A side-project to work on if I'm feeling a bit lost, but without losing my sense of taking a proper break from everything. Because the thought of having to write articles and put everything into words right now feels draining. Should I add some commentary? Maybe next time. This time I find a nice song to put over the top.

There's just one extra scene, one finishing touch to add on to the end.

Propping my phone up on the other side of the room, I angle it to get a good shot of the window, and the Tokyo night beyond it. I press record and then skitter over the windowsill to sit, looking out, a la *Lost in Translation*. I heft a butt-cheek up on the thin shelf, grip the window frame and hope the double-glazing is fixed into place. Shakily, I let go, and – no – I'm going!

I tumble to the ground with all the elegance of a hippo. I laugh out loud, and on watching the video, I laugh again and decide to keep it in.

As my finger hovers about over the publish button I consider getting in touch with Benny or Mara or maybe

Brienne. *Adventure Awaits* follows me. What if they see it and it makes them cringe? Would a second opinion help? Should I send it to them to check? I should ask them what they think—

No. This is what's best for me. It doesn't matter what anyone else's opinion is, I like this video, I like this idea. I shake off my anxiety and publish my video, and then pack myself into bed, surrounded by a cocoon of pillows.

On TV, the anime movie is coming to an end and I let the images and the colours soothe me into a light but welcome sleep. Overall, it's been a good day. And although my whole world feels like it's in pieces, all I can do is put it back together one day at a time.

Chapter 6

I don't want to talk
about me tonight, so please
pass the wasabi

In contrast to the warm bath water, the silky waters of
the hotel pool at the Park Hyatt are cold. They wake up
my body and soothe the headache that developed
following my late night, some bad dreams and the odd
sporadic tear. It's too late for me to turn back time, to beg
Matt to take back his words and not feel the doubts he
held. It's too late to give up on this trip and go home to
England and put my broken wedding and heart back
together.

So here I am, the first one at the pool on the forty-
seventh floor at 6am. The glass atrium above streams
daylight onto the water, though it's overcast today, and
droplets of rain speckle above me.

I swim lengths, slowly and methodically, enjoying
the unstiffening of my limbs until they start to feel tired

and I rest my arms up on the side and look out the window. Only the very tops of the neighbouring towers are in my vision from up here.

I submerge my face back in the water, all but my eyes peeping out crocodile-style, and blow bubbles for no other reason than there's nobody else around and it's nice to do weird things and make noises when no one can hear you. Flopping onto my back, I float about for a while, staring upwards. My honeymoon tour starts today. Not until this evening, but when I get out of the water I'll be heading to the breakfast buffet and it's odd knowing that some of the other people there might be my tour mates. I'll have to see who looks like an irritating smug-married and that'll be them.

Is this tour going to be the most awkward thing I've ever done? Will the others think I'm insane for not staying at home?

Why am I so obsessed with what other people think?

I float into the side of the swimming pool and bump my head so I take that as a sign to get out and head back to my room.

Down at breakfast I'm on red alert, picking one of everything from the extensive buffet, filling my plate with glazed-strawberry topped pastries, chunks of dragon fruit, cheese, minced salmon – so much for a svelte, traveller's diet – all the while keeping an eye on other guests, checking out who might be there on their honeymoon and is likely to have booked onto a romance-filled honeymoon tour like muggins here. I feel a sudden flash of anger towards Matt for leaving me, for forcing me to face all these newlyweds alone.

I suppose that isn't entirely fair. No one forced me to do this. In fact, I adamantly decided this all on my own. Freshly single and on a group honeymoon tour. Why oh why have I done this to myself?

I shuffle back to my seat with my hoard and eat facing the rest of the dining room. I don't mind eating alone. I thought I would – I thought this would be one more kicker that I'm a million miles away from everything I know – but actually it's okay. It's just like eating in front of the TV, actually, with good grub and some quality people-watching.

Oh, now look at them, they definitely could be candidates. An attractive tall couple in their early thirties have entered the dining room with a definite air of jet lag about them. Her blond hair is swept up in a messy bun that I reckon she slept in, and he hasn't shaved since the plane left his home turf, I'm guessing. They still look good, but in a 'celebrities, they're just like us' kind of way. She curls her lip at the buffet and selects only a banana, which shoots her down in my estimation, until she uses it to poke her husband (?) and crack a joke, which I think must have been along the lines of 'this is all you're allowed', and then they both laugh and reach for big plates and start piling.

I look down at my food and wonder if Matt has watched my IGTV video. I'm not doing it for him. But a part of me wants to say to him, 'Look what I'm doing. Look what I can do without you.' Unfortunately, IGTV will only tell you the number of viewers, not who has watched, and when I checked the app after rinsing the pool out of my hair, my first vlog had had thirty-two views, which I decide isn't bad, although I'm not really sure how many is good, and I always have to remember to subtract a large proportion of that to accommodate each member of my family watching from their various devices. I don't know what I'm doing with this minced salmon. I don't think it should go on this matcha cake, so I spread it on a bit of brie and tuck in. Pretty good, but I do feel like I missed an essential instruction up at the counter so will have to be a bit more careful at tomorrow's breakfast.

The rain is coming down harder now, so I decide to do what Matt and I had planned for this day anyway. In fact, screw Matt, *I* planned this whole trip, I found all the fun activities and things to do. Sure, he was invested, but I was the one who spent hours trawling the internet, researching the holiday brochures, watching YouTube videos, preparing everything behind the scenes ready for him to take my hand and enter at stage left once the curtain had come up. And today's activity was something I wanted to do since I watched *James May, Our Man in Japan*, and the man himself visited there. So I'm not going to think of this as me doing a 'we' activity on my own. I am doing a 'me' activity.

Saying that, I do need to do a 'wee' activity first.

I navigate the route from Tochomae to Aomi train stations now like a pro, and exit an hour later at the teamLab Borderless digital art museum.

How do I explain the space at Borderless ... imagine some huge empty rooms absolutely covered in digital screens that project brilliant colours and images that interact with each other and respond to how you move past or through them. The only light comes from the artwork itself and it's disorienting but completely immersive and incredible. It's like being in a Missy Elliot music video perhaps.

I didn't realise that the gentle music, the swirling colours and patterns that glide around me like candy floss, the sense of calm, would hit me so hard and here I feel tiny and insignificant and alone and totally free and lost. It's weird, and I'm glad it's dark because I spend most of the time walking through these darkened spaces with my eyes flowing.

The 'crystal world' gets me first, where it seems to be raining a never-ending universe of stars around me. Then I go into another space and a big bear made of digital flowers walks protectively alongside me through the room and for some stupid reason I feel like it's Gray here with me. Then I move to the 'forest of resonating lamps', where thousands and thousands of lights (or at least the mirrored walls and floor and ceiling make it seem that way) warm from calming blue to comforting sunset pink as I walk through, lighting my way.

By the time I reach the 'floating nest' and lie down on what is essentially a huge hammock suspended above, under, and in between more screens, I'm more than ready to let these millions of butterflies flutter around me until I die.

I spend hours at Borderless, way more time than I intended to or ever thought I would, and I wonder if this is what it's like to meditate. I leave feeling a little detoxed, my headspace a little clearer, and I'd quite happily take the journey back to the hotel and climb in my bathtub and stay there for the next month pondering what I just experienced.

But I can't do that. Because in a short while, I'll be joining my fellow honeymooners.

I look back towards Borderless as I board my train and wonder if I can run back inside. Maybe nobody would ever find me.

I'm feeling very Bill Murray. I didn't do a runner from the UK just to live in Borderless for eternity, instead I put on a big brave face and some half-decent clothes and now I'm in the New York Bar of the Park Hyatt drinking a whisky on the rocks because it feels right, even if my taste buds tell me it's wrong. Beyond the floor-to-ceiling windows, the sun has broken through the blanket of clouds long enough to be waving us goodbye as it dips towards the horizon. It's late afternoon and I'm soon to meet my tour guide and fellow travellers.

I'm not nervous, you are.

Jazz is lilting from the speakers. If we were staying here into the evening, the jazz would become live. But since the brochure advertised, 'your first night you will be taken into the heart of Tokyo for romantic Japanese cuisine and entertainment', I'm guessing we're outta here.

The tall couple from breakfast have just walked in. This cannot be a coincidence. But instead of going up and questioning them, lest they think I'm a prozzie trying to lure them into a threesome, I side-eye them while sipping my whisky and trying not to squince my mouth up at the taste.

They take a seat and look around, their eyes drifting past me without hesitation, searching for other couples. It's only when a slight but strong woman – high heels, glossy hair, a wide smile and an air of authority – strides in and straight up to them, bowing and introducing herself, and they visibly relax, that I think this is my cue.

'Hello,' I say, shyness creeping in, and they all look up at me. '*Konbanwa*,' I say good evening to the woman I really hope is our tour guide because otherwise I've just been unforgivably presumptive. 'Is this the Honeymoon Highlights tour?'

'Yes, it is,' the guide enthuses in English. Her voice has the lightest of accents, calming and delicate. 'My name is Kaori and you must be Charlotte?'

'Yes,' I confirm, and take a seat. The travel agency clearly passed on the change in party number, which is a good thing.

The tall man leans forward, a huge grin on his tanned face, and gives me a stocky, animated handshake. He speaks with an Australian twang and he's instantly likeable. 'Hey Charlotte, m'name's Lucas, this is my new wife, Flo.'

Flo grins a megawatt smile worthy of Margot Robbie and leans in towards me too. She's also beyond friendly and greets me with a handshake that involves her clasping both her hands over mine, which is oddly comforting. '*Love* the name Charlotte – that's our first choice if we ever have a little girl. Great to meet ya.'

'Where's your husband?' Lucas asks, looking around and getting a pinch from Flo. 'Or wife?' he corrects himself.

'Well—' I start but then we're interrupted by a silver fox approaching the table.

'Excuse me,' he drawls in a soothing, growly American accent. 'Are you guys here for the Japan Honeymoon Highlights tour?'

'Yes we are!' Kaori answers. 'You must be Cliff and Jack?' She pronounces their names carefully and the man nods and steps aside for another tall, slightly-less-silver and just-as-handsome chap to step ahead of him and take a seat.

Lucas, Flo, Cliff, Jack, Kaori and I exchange hellos and names and I think I'd better get this out of the way before it becomes the elephant in the very posh room.

'Um, Lucas, you were just asking me where my husband is, this being a honeymoon tour and all, so just to say that we, well I, well we, um, called off the wedding a bit last minute but I didn't want the trip to go to waste.'

Jack reaches out immediately and puts a hand over mine, his face shocked and confused as to what to say, and that small gesture breaks my heart just that little bit more.

'Ah, I'm sorry,' Lucas says, sounding genuinely gutted for me.

'Ace of you to come here on your own though, it costs a dime or two so good not to let it go to waste,' adds Flo.

'What did he do?' Cliff, the first silver fox, asks.

'If you don't mind us asking,' Jack jumps in to say, putting a hand on his husband's knee. Cliff meets his eye and they both smile, their eyes crinkling.

'He didn't really do anything wrong, apart from have horrible timing, as usual, but I can't be mad at him for not feeling the same way I do any more. *Did*.'

'Sure you can!' says Lucas. 'I'd be mad as hell at Flo if she changed her mind about me.'

I laugh and admit, 'Sometimes I am a little mad.'

'Let's change the subject for now,' Jack says, and I feel close to him already. 'What are we doing this evening, Kaori?'

'Right,' Kaori starts, perched on the edge of the sofa, all eyes on her. 'Tonight we go for a delicious dinner, traditional Japanese, you will like it a lot but wear comfortable pants or long skirt because we sit on floor.'

Her eyes dart to my skinny jeans and I feel acutely aware of the builder's bum I'm currently flashing at the back-rest of the sofa and decide to run back to my room before we leave. 'Then we go to a kabuki show! Does anyone know what a kabuki show is?'

'I think it's a traditional Japanese play?' says Jack.

'Yes,' Flo clicks her fingers, she looks genuinely delighted. 'There's dancing and there's loads of drama, and aren't they long?' She checks her watch.

Kaori nods. 'They are four hours long sometimes, but in Tokyo we can buy tickets for single acts, so you can experience kabuki without having, you know, too much.' We laugh, and then she continues, 'We need to be at the kabuki theatre for eight o'clock for our act. So shall we leave for dinner soon and then we can all get to know each other a little bit more?'

As I head back to my room to change, I stifle a yawn. I'm fatigued, but that's partly because it's done now, introductions are over, the elephant is out of the room ... or whatever. Now I can settle back, relax into having some company and let other people make decisions for me. It's comforting, like a blanket.

I may not have a husband, but I do have *thirteen* courses of food about to be served to me. Granted, Matt was supposed to be here with me, but I'm very happy to comfort eat my way through this *kaiseki* meal. Kaori has brought us to a traditional Japanese restaurant where the chefs are busy preparing small but perfectly formed dishes for us to wrap our chops around. I'm practically salivating in anticipation.

Flo, next to me, shifts her bum about on the cushion on top of the tatami mat in front of our table. I've just been having a sneaky side-eye at her long, toned limbs and estimating that she must put in at least three hours of yoga a day when she says, 'I wish I hadn't just talked about starting yoga for the last year and had got on and done it. I feel like I'm letting the side down among all you floor-sitting pros.'

Cliff smiles. 'Honey, we're just too old to move once we're in this position.'

I wonder if anyone's clocked that I'm actually wearing my pyjama trousers. They're black and have little stars on, and they don't look a million miles away from those loose linen trousers people wear during the summer. Especially since I've tucked the tassels inside. They're so comfy and my builder's bum is nicely hidden, because most importantly they were the only trousers I had in my case that I could wear and be sure that I was not offending the Japanese family enjoying a birthday celebration on the table next to us.

We've already nibbled the starters, and as the mains begin to arrive, Kaori takes us through what's in front of us.

'So this is a tofu soup; this one is grilled wagyu beef – very tasty; this one is a nimono, which is sweet, boiled fish and bamboo; this is sashimi – my favourite—'

'That's my favourite too!' I interject. I love the delicacy of raw sliced fish and the deep pink of the salmon on the dish looks yum. I remember the first time I tried sushi. Marissa had made it during food tech at school, and had been given a high grade for her work (of course), so when she brought it home for the rest of us to try, I knew it would be good. Mum, who looked close to gagging at the idea, forced herself to eat a bite and had to admit the raw fish and seaweed combo was a lot more delish than she gave it credit for beforehand.

'Is that wasabi?' I point to a green blob but it isn't the bright green we tend to get in England, it's more of an olive colour.

'Yes, but it's quite a hot wasabi so try just a little at first. I have eaten here before and it can …' She mimes her head exploding.

Kaori talks us through a few more dishes, including a tempura and some pickles, tells us how to serve ourselves from the bowl of rice and then we tuck in.

I go straight in for a slice of sashimi with wasabi on top, not realising the whole table is watching me until I've stuffed it whole into my gob.

JESUS

I think my nose is dissolving!

I think my head is going to fall off and roll down the stairs and out into the streets and then I can only hope someone kicks it into a water-filled gutter!

My eyes water and squint and my nostrils are running and I grimace at everyone and pound the table and then after a few seconds it subsides and I'm panting and exhausted but I've made it. 'Yum,' I croak, and go in for a second bit.

'What do you do back home, Charlotte?' Lucas asks, after I've stopped sweating.

'Well, I'm not sure,' I reply, this question always feeling awkward to answer even when you're not going through a quarter-life crisis. 'I trained in journalism at university, but for the past couple of years I've worked at a local newspaper, copy-editing, but I just left that because my fiancé and I were going to be moving to London together after the wedding and honeymoon. I'm supposed to start an internship at a travel magazine.'

'That sounds exciting,' says Flo.

'It is … I'm still deciding what to do at the moment.'

And by deciding, I mean procrastinating, avoiding, burying my head in the sand, and doing everything in my power to *not* make a decision on it yet. My future was neatly boxed and now it's spilled wide open. I know I need to clean it up but right now, I'm just going to focus on the sushi. Focus on the sushi!

I change the subject, moving it back over to them. If I can avoid it, no more talking about myself from now on.

With full bellies and a little *osake* – alcohol – in our system, our group takes a slow walk between the restaurant and the kabuki theatre. We're walking alongside a wide road lined with office blocks, shops and restaurants, the city still bustling at seven thirty at night.

Flo and Lucas are just ahead of us, holding hands and she's walking with a lean on him, keeping warm against his bulk. They turn their heads from time to time to check they're still going in the right direction and we haven't veered off. Cliff and Jack are behind us, strolling at a slower pace than they look like they're used to. And I'm walking in the middle next to Kaori who is chatting away and pointing things out to me.

'Ooo, that looks nice,' I say, pointing at a large picture in the window of a Subway sandwich shop. I'm not sure what I'm pointing at, exactly, but it fills the silence from my side.

'Ah yes,' she replies. 'I like those. They're the subways with sweet red beans.'

I nod like I know what that is. 'Do you live in Tokyo, Kaori?'

'I do now, yes, but I was born on Ishigaki, which is an island way down in southern Japan – have you heard of it?'

'No, I don't think so, I'm afraid I didn't end up doing a lot of research on the southern islands as it didn't feel possible to add it on.'

'Oh, it's very easy to get to Ishigaki now; we have a low-cost airline that takes people there in about three hours from Osaka. It's very beautiful and tropical, you can do snorkelling and go on a kayak, it's very very different from Tokyo, and probably London.'

'Do you go back there often?'

'Yes, my parents live there so I go back and say hello to them and to nature a lot. Something for you to do next time you come to Japan?' She smiles and touches my arm, before waving at the others that we've arrived.

We're outside a vast and ornate building that resembles the structure of a temple with the grandiosity of a theatre. Billowing purple curtains hang above the entranceway, while lines of crimson paper lanterns light up the façade.

I kinda like that it's standing proudly in front of a whopping glass skyscraper with the stubbornness of somebody who isn't going to change or move for anyone.

Inside, the theatre is just as awe-inspiring. We shuffle our way into our seats, just six among nearly 2,000. Drums signal the start of the act and the audience shushes, and what follows for the next hour is spellbinding. Actors, singers and musicians, faces and bodies painted in whites, reds and blacks, take to the stage in delicately embroidered kimonos and other traditional dress. I don't really know what's going on, but it's very dramatic and I can't take my eyes off it. My favourite bit is when a geisha dressed in swathes of pink and purple dances slowly across the stage in front of a line of musicians playing Japanese 'shamisen' guitars. It's hypnotic, and I forget about all the people around me, including the couples to my right and left.

When the show is over, Kaori returns us to the Park Hyatt and bids us goodnight.

'Well, I think we'll go back to that nice bar we met in earlier and catch the jazz singer,' Cliff says, and Jack nods. 'You guys want to join us?'

Flo snuggles in towards Lucas, looking sleepy. 'Sure, we'll go for one, then let's go back to our room.'

'You want to show me a kabuki dance of your own, I bet,' Lucas jokes.

'Didn't you see? All the actors were male, even the female parts were played by men. So you have to do a show for *me*.'

'I never noticed! But if that's what you want, my love. Charlotte, you coming?'

I bow out, content to leave them to it and go back to my room. I have a lot to process from today. I set up my phone and sit in front of it to do my first 'this is me' for my IGTV, but I need to do a few takes to get the words out.

Because the undefined edges of Borderless, the cloud-touching hotel and the immersive music this evening have me feeling like I'm on a ledge, on a tipping point, ready to fall or fly. How can I say 'this is me' when I'm beginning to wonder who I am?

Chapter 7

On top of the world
I'm searching, searching, searching
But I can't see you?

I've been awake for an hour or so, but I'm still surprised when my mobile rings at 5.45am Tokyo time.

'Hi, Benny!'

'Hey, sis, did I wake you up?'

'No, I'm a bit all over the place so I was going to go and make use of the hotel pool again soon. I went yesterday morning and was the only one there so early in the morning.'

'Is the pool amazing?' he asks. 'I've watched both your Instagram videos at least twice.'

'You did?' I smile, sitting up in the beige chair from where I'm sitting wrapped in my PJs and my robe, watching the sun rising over the city, a cup of tea in hand.

'Yes, they're great! I showed all my uni friends. We love the falling off the windowsill bit, and Borderless looked so cool. I watched *Lost in Translation* this evening and had to call you to see what you were doing.'

'Are you missing me, little brother?' I ask, realising I'm missing him.

''Course not,' he replies, but his voice gives him away, I know him too well. 'It looks like Japan suits you. Travelling on your own suits you ...'

'Well, I'm not on my own any more; I'm with the tour group now.'

'What are they like?'

'All really nice. I feel like an absolute spare wheel but that's on me, not them. But how are you? How's the revision going?'

My little brother pauses. 'It's okay ...'

'What's up?'

'I don't know. I just don't feel like I have any motivation at the moment.'

'Did something happen?' Benny is always so sure of himself; he's not the most confident or outgoing but he knows what he wants. Something seems different in him today.

'No, I'm just ... maybe I do just miss you! So what are you doing out there today?'

I know a change of subject when I see it, so I let it settle for now but I'm going to keep a close eye on him, even from the other side of the world.

'I'll go for a swim in a minute – I'll take some footage of the pool just for you – then after breakfast we're all going on a bit of a Tokyo tour, I believe, visiting the Olympic stadium, going to a museum, or is it a gallery ...? And then later on visiting the Tokyo Skytree, one of the tallest buildings in the world!' I chatter on for a few more minutes, sensing he needs to sit back and listen to something distracting. If it helps, I'm quite happy to be his 'reality TV' for a while.

'Do you ever imagine what your home would look like if you were stinking rich but also needed to do a lot of thinking?' I whisper into the camera on my phone. I'm up at the pool and there isn't a soul around, but I still don't want anyone catching me talking to myself. I expect I'm also not supposed to be taking photos in this area if there's anyone else using the facilities.

'Wouldn't this be a good setting to rule over your kingdom or write a Jackie Collins-esque thriller?' I pan the camera off me and onto the huge glass windows beyond the pool that overlook the city.

Benny is on my mind ... it's weird not having him or my other brother and sisters around, but it's not the worst thing in the world getting a bit of space.

I wrap up my video then wrap up myself, and head to breakfast via my room.

I pay a lot more attention at breakfast today, making sure that I'm not only grabbing the traditional Japanese goodies, but that I note what is supposed to go with what, and you know ... it works better.

I'm on the lookout for the others and when Flo and Lucas walk in, I wave at them to join me.

'Morning!' I say, standing and hugging Flo before wondering if she would have found that weird, given that I'm still a virtual stranger who last night didn't want to hang out but is now desperate for company and a safety net. But she hugs me back, or at least pulls me into her boobs, since I'm considerably shorter than her.

Lucas, keen not to be left out, comes in for a hug too. 'Charlotte, you missed a great evening at the bar last night. Cliff ended up singing a song with the band!'

'He did?' I push my plate of breakfast sushi towards them but Flo declines. 'What did he sing?'

'No idea,' Flo answers. 'If I had to guess I'd say it was country, but he's got a good voice, and Jack is such a smitten kitten around him.'

Lucas gives Flo the same look now, and then pulls back and looks at me. 'Sorry, Charlotte, tell us to shut our faces if we get too lovey-dovey.'

'I wouldn't dream of it!' I answer, and laugh a little too hard so stuff a massive chunk of mango into my gob. 'So we've got the city tour today.'

'Yes, in thirty minutes.' Flo checks her watch. 'We'd better get on and grab some brekkie. You want anything else while we're up there, Charlotte?'

I shake my head. 'I'm good. I'll leave you to it and see you in the lobby in a bit.'

'Our first stop today,' Kaori says into an unnecessary microphone at the front of the minibus she's arranged to take us around Tokyo today, 'will be the new Tokyo Olympic Stadium.'

She pauses so we can clap or cheer, I guess, so I start things off with a loud and enthusiastic whoop like I think I'm on the Dallas Cowboys cheer team.

Kaori continues. 'Now the stadium is getting a makeover but it was previously used the last time Tokyo hosted the Olympics which was in ...?'

Oh no, it's going to be a quiz day. I can feel it. I'm shit at quizzes – even if I think I know the answer the words refuse to saunter their way from my brain to my lips quickly enough.

'Was it the sixties?' queries Jack and I think, *you know damn well it was the sixties, don't you, you sly fox?*

Kaori claps at him. 'Yes, it was 1964. You get Olympic gold medal, Jack,' she laughs and you can see the rest of us sitting up because even though we know it's only an imaginary medal, Kaori just raised the stakes. 'Who can tell me what the first sports event played in this new stadium was?'

' ... Was it football?' Jack asks.

'Yes it was, extra gold medals for you! Do you know the name of Japan's annual football competition?'

This time I stare over my seat at Jack and watch him pretend to think about the answer. Then when he starts to speak ...

'Is it—' he starts.

'Is it—' I read his lips and lay my words over his.

'The Em—'

'Emmm'

'—per—' Jack shoots me a surprised look.

'—prrr—' That's right, I'm doing this, even if I do sound slurry and undignified. Well that's just who I am, Captain Jack.

'—or's Cup?'

'—coop. Emperor's Cup!' Nailed it.

'That's right, congratulations, um, both of you,' Kaori smiles at us and sits down, unsure where to go from here.

I bow my head to Jack. 'Good game, but I think you got in there first on that one.'

In no time we pull up to the front of the stadium and I decide to stop being so awkward for the rest of the trip.

We climb out of the bus and look at the outside of the stadium, vast and dominant, while Kaori explains how this is where the opening and closing ceremonies will be, as well as many of the events. If I think Tokyo's busy now, I can only imagine what it'll be like when it's overflowing with the excitement of the Olympic games ...

28 July 2012
Saturday evening, 10.55pm

I had been thinking, maybe I should take up volleyball. Maybe I should take up any sport. But those girls looked so cool out there, and I wondered if I could ever be as athletic as them. I guess I couldn't have ever been as athletic, because they were Olympians, but ...

I pulled the waist of my jeans up and over my teenage belly as much as I could, hoping Matt didn't notice. He'd seen my belly, of course, but still, looking at those tanned and toned athletes from the US and Australia about to take to the court had me feeling like I needed to do a little more.

It was late and Marissa was yawning, though none of us wanted to leave. Mara had managed to book all of us – me, Matt, Mum, and all my brothers and sisters – tickets for the beach volleyball at the London Olympics and it was perfection. When we had arrived, the sun was just dipping over Horse Guards Parade and we took our seats in the big purple stadium, facing the sandy court. The atmosphere was electric, people were cheering and drinking beer and everyone was happy no matter which team won. It was the most exciting thing most of us had ever been to, and to think we nearly didn't make it.

We had been completely divided with what we wanted to try and get tickets for. Mum wanted to see synchronised swimming, Gray wanted to see athletics in the main stadium, Marissa was gunning for diving because she was in love with Tom Daley, Matt and I were praying for basketball and Mara said she didn't care but I know she wanted Benny to see the wrestling, since that had been her sport for a short while. We couldn't possibly see separate things, as you can imagine, so we went backwards and forwards until Mara, sensible Mara, bought a batch of tickets for beach volleyball so none of us could have been disappointed. And we sure weren't.

This is why I've always watched the Olympics, every time it's been on. Not because I was a big fan of any one sport, though there were certain ones I always enjoyed watching, *but because I imagined how exciting it would be to be an Olympian. To travel to a new country and be part of something as a team. But also on your own, responsible for your own training and destiny and results. To have a purpose that's all yours. And to remind me to take a trip to the gym once in a while.*

I take a last look at the Olympic stadium and imagine it spilling over with visitors and locals, happy crowds coming together to celebrate the hard work of others, while millions more watch from their television screens around the world. I take some video, and know I will look back on it when I'm back in the UK, joining the millions watching the Olympics on TV, soaking in the atmosphere as it spreads like lava around the world. I wonder if by then I'll have figured out what my purpose is.

The next stop on our group tour of Tokyo is the Sumida Hokusai Museum, dedicated to one of Japan's most famous artists, Katsushika Hokusai. He did a series of woodblock prints titled Thirty-Six Views of Mount Fuji and the most recognised one is called *The Great Wave off Kanagawa*.

Now, maybe you already know all about this image, but it isn't until Flo and I are staring at the piece inside the museum, with matching tilted heads and 'where have I seen that before …' expressions that it comes to me and I pull out my iPhone.

'It's the flippin' wave emoji!' I show Flo and she peers at my screen.

'You're right, it is, it's got the same claw-like little frothy tips, and the same formation of the water.'

'Fancy that. I've been a fan of Hokusai longer than I realised; I use that emoji all the time.'

'Same.'

We mosey through the rest of the museum as a group before Kaori has us all back on the bus for a short journey to the Asakusa neighbourhood, where we spend a couple of hours strolling about, nibbling on street food and shopping. We split up here, with Flo and Lucas taking a rickshaw ride, Cliff and Jack stopping in at a sit-down eatery to rest their legs, and I end up trailing about after Kaori, who is so sweet and doesn't seem to mind and, in fact, without her I wouldn't have tried *kibidango*.

After we purchase these sweet treats, which are warm little dumplings on a skewer, times five, covered in sweet powdered soy beans, Kaori walks us towards the river and Sumida Park to eat them.

'It's lovely weather today,' I say to Kaori once we reach the park and I've scoffed two of my five yummy skewers. 'Good weather to go up one of the world's tallest buildings.'

'Yes, *hare* – sunny.'

'*Ha-re*,' I repeat.

'Correct. At this time of the year there is often a lot more rain, like yesterday, but we're lucky.'

'It must be very *ha-re* on the island you grew up on. Do you have any brothers or sisters?'

'No, I am a single child.'

'Wow, I have four brothers and sisters, it's like a commune in our house.' I can't imagine being an only child. Who would tell me what to do?

We walk through the park, pretty with pale pink cherry blossoms on the trees, and down some steps so we're beside the river for a while.

'Do you like Japan so far?' Kaori asks.

'It's amazing, it's so different from anywhere I've been before and it's only, what, my fourth day here and I've done so much. Eaten sugary crêpes in Harajuku, visited a shrine, spent the day at Disneyland, had my mind blown at Borderless, dined on traditional Japanese cuisine, been to the kabuki theatre, stayed at the *Lost in Translation* hotel, looked at the Olympic Stadium, seen the wave emoji in real life … I'm actually a little exhausted!' I can't believe how much I've done already. Anyone would think I was trying to stay busy and distracted …

'Tomorrow will be more relaxing for you, just a lovely soothing train ride to Kyoto then free time until dinner. Maybe have some ...' She mimics falling asleep on her hands and then becomes serious. 'I am sorry about your marriage, Charlotte. I hope this tour is good for you and not too hard. Because of the nature of the tour I am obligated to make it, in some places, quite, you know, romantic.'

I'm just taking a bite into my last *kibidango*, and in my attempt to breezily shoo away her worries I snarf a plume of soy-bean dust towards her, which I then brush off her coat using equally dusty fingers. 'Gosh, sorry. Um, no, please don't worry about that, I don't want you to change a thing for me, the others all deserve a really lovely trip with all the romantic honeymoon frills they want. Just promise you'll pair up with me if we do any couple's massages,' I joke and then quickly eat the last few bites to hide my cringe at my inappropriateness.

But Kaori laughs and agrees; she's so lovely. I notice she has some *kibidango* left and get an idea.

'Kaori, I'm doing a bit of a vlog while I'm out here, which I'm putting on Instagram using IGTV. Could I feature you in one of the videos? If you wouldn't mind?'

'Feature me?' She looks quite chuffed! 'Yes please, would you be able to tag the tour company? My manager really likes it when our customers tag us on social media. What shall I do?'

I think on the spot, glancing around at the river, at the Skytree in the background, at the sunshine above and have a brainwave like I'm a Hollywood director or something. 'How about "Kaori's 5 Favourite Foods to Try in Tokyo"? Perhaps starting with *kibidango*, since you're holding one. If that's not putting you on the spot too much?'

She's great and bubbly on screen, waving to the viewers, and listing off five foods with confidence and certainty, peppering each with yummy noises, and luckily most things she says are morsels I've tasted over the past few days, so will be able to slot in a photo or video frame or two. Afterwards, she insists on taking the camera and filming me, walking by the river, looking up at the newly sprouting cherry blossoms, pointing at the Skytree, trying to speak Japanese to a shop seller.

'When we are up there and the sun is setting, let me take some more video with you in, it will be so beautiful and your ex-boyfriend will feel so stupid.' She then demurs a little as if worried she's crossed a line, but I laugh. I'm sure it will be beautiful at the top of the Skytree, but I'm also sure it'll have nothing to do with me.

*

That said, leaning my forehead against the warm glass, looking down over the city, I do feel like I might be quite beautiful now I'm up here, in a free spirit, face-to-the-sunshine way. We're 450 metres up in the sky, which is roughly level with the spike at the top of the Empire State Building in New York. In front of me is a rose-gold tinted soft grey Tokyo winding down for the day as the sun dips. I take a moment to just be here and to soak it in.

After a while and a walk around, where Kaori points out to us the sites of Tokyo, including the stadium, Tokyo Tower, Disneyland, the park we'd just been in and even Mount Fuji in the very distance, we come to a stop and watch the city light up the dark night. We climb onto bar stools at the cafe, in a row so we're all looking out at the view, and are presented with a glass of champagne to sip.

Cliff and Jack lean into each other, Flo and Lucas do the same, and I lean back in to my friend the window.

Another glass of champagne each, an extra hour into the evening, and the lights of Tokyo fully illuminated below our dangling feet, and the conversation has moved on to weddings. It was inevitable. And it's fine, sort of. Well, it's more fine than I thought it would be. It's quite soothing hearing Cliff describe in detail the simple ceremony he and Jack had in Carmel, California. The look of the ranch, the sound of the sea. And then in contrast Flo and Lucas were married in a big marquee in a vineyard in southern Australia in a ceremony that lasted days thanks to visitors from all over the country travelling far and staying a while. I can tell that at one point Flo feels a little awkward around me when she was passing round her phone to show the photos of her and Lucas walking arm and arm back down the aisle as husband and wife, as though she were somehow rubbing her happiness in my face.

'So Charlotte, what lies in store for you back in England?' asks Jack, drawing me into the conversation. 'You mentioned you're moving to London? Who are you at home when you're not adventuring around the world solo?'

I take a sip of champagne, letting the glass mask part of my face for a moment while I search for an answer. Going home meant starting a new life, one that had felt so mapped out and is now so unplanned.

'Yep, I'm supposed to be moving to London,' I say, and I grin through the fear. 'I'm starting an internship at a travel magazine that I've been a big fan of for years and it's really exciting.'

'That is exciting,' says Lucas. 'Working for a magazine sounds great fun, and London is a great city. I lived in

Fulham for a little while in my early twenties. Where are you going to be living?'

'Um, well, that's where the plan falters. I have two sisters in London who would probably let me stay for a bit but if I go I'd need to start house-hunting for a place of my own or, more likely, a house share with some strangers.' Did they hear my voice wobble at the end or did it get caught by the breeze and whisked away? 'The plan had been for me and Matt, my fiancé, to move into a flat together,' I explained. 'But, you know ...'

'Well, that's bloody bad luck,' says Flo. 'Though I'm sure you'll find somewhere fantastic to live, and I hope Matt's place has cockroaches.'

I spot Kaori shuffling about nervously, keen to get the conversation back on a happier track. Shit. She must be worried her Honeymoon Highlights tour is going to be one big downer thanks to yours truly.

I slap on a big fake smile and push the hair out of my face. I'm the odd one out here, these nice people deserve a happy, romantic trip. I will go with the flow, follow the crowd and mask my feelings. Maybe I can fake it until I make it out the other side of this heartache? 'Right, we've heard about the weddings, now please renew my faith in love. Tell me about how you all first met. Cliff and Jack, you go first.'

Kaori relaxes and pulls her sweater around her, and Flo pulls Lucas around *her*. I pull myself together.

Cliff smiles at his husband. 'Well we met a very long time ago, and we waited a long ol' time to be able to get married ...'

It's not actually that late, but we're all sleepy and silent on the minibus drive back to the hotel, ready to call it a night. I stare out of the window at the signs and the lights and imagine I'm an actress in a film noir wondering where her life got so derailed. I let out a dramatic little sigh.

Oh dammit, I forgot to get any video at the top of the Skytree! I reach for my phone and flick through my photos, hoping I can montage something together for my IGTV without it looking like a slideshow presentation from 1998.

A pop-up window fills my phone screen – *AirDrop, Kaori would like to share a video*. I glance towards Kaori, sitting up the front next to the driver and she turns around and gives me a thumbs-up, so I press 'Accept'. And there's exactly what Kaori promised – a beautiful video thirty seconds long, the rose gold sunset over Tokyo and me, my forehead against the window, taking it in, unaware of the camera, feeling free, and being completely myself.

Chapter 8

Fast as a bullet
I dive down into this hole
I'm burrowing deep

Have you ever been on one of those theme-park rollercoasters where you're strapped in and you're jiggling a bit with excitement and you're like *yesss bitch, let's do this* but also *I wish I'd tied my hair back* but it's too late now because any second the ride is going to *shoot* forward at a million miles an hour? This is how I'm expecting the bullet train from Tokyo to Kyoto to be.

I'm next to Kaori, she's given me the window seat, and I'm clutching my coffee and my Japanese snacks, which I'm looking forward to finding out whether they're sweet or savoury. Whatever they are, they're decorated with little smiling mascot cartoons, so that's nice. I'm holding everything really tightly for when we zoom out of the station, which – if rumours of rail service punctuality are to be believed – will be in three, two, one …

'What are you doing?' Kaori asks with a smile as the bullet train glides away from the platform with a gentle confidence. Am I supposed to scream if I want to go faster?

I look around, at the people in the seat behind me, at Cliff and Jack in the seat in front. 'Isn't this the bullet train?'

'Yes, it will speed up in a moment, but you won't really feel it, you will just see the scenery go by very quickly. I have seated us all on the right-hand side so you will see Mount Fuji if the weather stays nice.'

'Cool,' I reply. 'It feels like a normal train, then ... No, I don't mean normal, I just mean, you know, like the ones I'm used to. Very comfy,' I add, in case I've offended her. It is lovely inside this train – soft seats, good leg room, very peaceful, nobody on their phones.

I get out my phone. Not to make a call, though! Just to capture some video. I try whispering a little commentary but I expect that it'll come out sounding like I'm some pervert heavy-breathing behind the lens. It takes about two and a half hours to travel from Tokyo to Kyoto and I settle back in my seat, allowing the gentle rhythm to massage away the busy last few days. Mount Fuji greets us, sloped and snow-capped and looking every bit the picture-perfect holiday brochure snap. There is an audible 'ooo' from inside the quiet cabin, followed by *click-click-click* from cameras and phones. Mine included.

I watch it all the way until it disappears behind us. The last two nights of the tour will bring us back to Mount Fuji, where we'll be staying in a traditional Japanese *ryokan*. That'll be a little over three weeks away, and I take a deep breath and hold it for a moment. In three weeks' time I have to have my life figured out.

After Fuji, the rest of the landscape becomes less urban, greener, and we travel alongside glittery lakes and faraway mountain ranges. It's beautiful, but it's the unknown and even though I've only 'known' Tokyo for a few days it felt reliable, comfortable, a whirlwind I had tamed, and the further we stretch away from the city the stranger I feel, the unknown settling upon me and reminding me how derailed I am.

The unknown is good, change is good, I tell myself. And Kyoto is supposed to be amazing, the cultural centre of Japan. I know I'll love it. At least I think I will.

I turn in my seat and crane my neck to look back towards the long-disappeared Tokyo, at my past, and although I'm surrounded by people, I feel very alone.

I crouch down and peer into the tunnel I'll be sleeping in. So this is what a capsule hotel looks like. My pod is long and sparkling with what looks like enough room to sit up in. There's no window, but there is a personal lamp, a shelf, bedding, and a curtain to pull across once you're in.

'Is this okay?' whispers Kaori, putting her own handbag a few pods further down, and both Flo and I nod.

Men and women sleep on separate floors in this hotel – not ideal for a Honeymoon Highlights tour, which is why Kaori's guests have the option to switch to a regular hotel for their next three nights in Kyoto if they feel one night of this experience is enough.

The hotel is clean and simple and has all the sleek design and sharp technology you'd expect. We've been asked to leave our larger bags and our shoes in lockers, we've been shown where the shared lounges are, we have a little bag with slippers, a towel and *free pyjamas!!!* and now I've got my head inside pod 283. It's dark in the corridor between the pods, and no matter the time of day we've been asked to keep the noise to a minimum once you enter the space to let people sleep. It's so harmonious I'm forgetting it's still the middle of the afternoon outside and am stifling a yawn.

Kaori beckons us out from the women's dorm and we follow her to one of the lounges, where there is free tea on tap, which I help myself to, and then start browsing a shared bookshelf.

Once the boys have arrived, Kaori tells us, 'The rest of the day is yours to rest or explore or do whatever you like. I will be staying here in the lounge and doing some work, so if you need any hints or tips for things to do, just ask me, I have lots of ideas. Tonight we can eat together or alone; your choice. Kyoto is a very pretty and historic place and you will find lots of nice and romantic things waiting for you.'

'Sounds great,' says Flo. 'I could do with stretching my legs so shall we go for a walk?'

'Yeah, brill,' answers Lucas.

'Find a nice garden or temple or something to take a little walkabout in?' She turns to me. 'Fancy it, Charlotte?'

'Thanks, but I think I'm going to take it easy for the rest of the day. You go ahead.'

They wave goodbye, as do Jack and Cliff. I'm completely alone. I freshen up in the bathroom and look at myself in the mirror. I make a face and roll my shoulders.

'What shall we do with you this afternoon?' I whisper to my reflection. She answers me by rattling off a list of things I need to do: *you could reply to the email from* Adventure Awaits; *you could tell them you aren't going to be taking the internship any more; you could write some article ideas, like you promised yourself you would; you could have a good think about your future.*

Or I could just climb into bed. That feels like it could set me on a dangerous path, but succumbing to the loneliness feels like the only thing my mind and body are capable of right now.

I leave the bathroom then hesitate. If I take the elevator down, I'll be out in the bright, fresh air, in a new place with new things to take my mind off old things. If I take the elevator up, I'll be heading down a dark rabbit hole. I pull out my phone and consider WhatsApping my family, asking their advice, which would really be asking them to talk me into going outside. But even that feels like too much energy.

I take the elevator up, find my pod, let my slippers drop to the floor, climb in, put in my headphones, and close the curtain.

An unknown number of hours later, a feeling intensified by the lack of natural light, I wake to hear a small whisper outside my capsule. I pull out my headphones, which are uncomfortable inside my ears, the music long-since stopped, and sit up.

'Charlotte, are you awake?' the quiet, Australian voice says again.

I stay completely still for a moment, tempted to ignore her, but then feeling bad I open my curtain.

'Ahoy,' I whisper.

'Did I wake you?'

'No,' I lie. 'What time is it?'

'Eight. Lucas and I are going to head out to dinner together, do you want to join us?'

They are so sweet. But this is their honeymoon, they shouldn't feel they have to invite me, and I'm not going to be the person their friends and relatives see in every photo when they get home and ask, 'Who's that random girl?'

'Thanks so much but I have a bit of a headache, I'm going to stay in tonight and catch up on rest. That way I'll be bright and ready for the geishas tomorrow.'

'Are you sure?' she asks, already grabbing her purse.

I nod, and when she's gone, I crawl out of my tunnel and slide on my slippers. I shuffle out of the dorm and make my way towards the bright landing by the elevators where I spotted some vending machines earlier.

At the vending machine I'm faced with an array of instant ramen noodle bowls choices and I don't really know what I'm doing so I just feed in some money and press a button, hoping for the best.

I wait a few seconds. Then a few more. I wonder where I can find a kettle because if this is your average Pot Noodle I'm going to need some boiling water.

Ting!

I open a door near the bottom of the vending machine and, well, shit me, it's a proper, large bowl of hot soupy noodles topped with vegetables and slices of pork. This is nothing like the ramen bowls Matt and I would devour throughout university, let me tell you. Who knew?

I'm guessing my fellow bunkmates won't appreciate me eating this inside my capsule, so I shuffle towards the lounge and sit like the lonely little self-induced Billy-No-Mates that I am and slurp away.

It's delicious. I'm not being sarcastic, it's proper yum, and I feel hugged from the inside. Is the 'chicken soup for the soul' movement actually kicking in for me? I polish it off in record speed and then head back to the vending machine to find a dessert and end up taking a can of coffee and a matcha-tea-flavoured KitKat back to my pod with me. And once that's devoured I change into my PJs, put my headphones back in, and capsule myself back away from the world. Tiny me in my tiny hotel room, in a country with a population of over 120 million, 6,000 miles from home, completely out of reach of Matt, and he of me.

Guess what I did last night? You're going to kill me, I text to my siblings.

Turns out a can of vending machine coffee isn't the best nightcap and I had to slither out of my pod twice in the night for a wee. By the second time, I was very awake, and my head was beginning to ache for real as the room was getting stuffy with the curtain closed. So I padded to the lounge where a couple of other late-nighters were on their devices, and sat sipping on a water and cooling off.

Within seconds Marissa and Gray both reply with, *What did you do?*

I was wallowing, okay, hear me out. Wallowing, and intent on continuing my self-destruction, it turned out.

I looked at Matt's Instagram.

At this point, Mara jumps in. *Are you actually an idiot?*

WHAT it was right there like a big red button and I had a headache and shut up.

Believe me, every bit of me shouted at myself while I typed his name into the search bar but I did it anyway. His profile opened out in front of me, a tapestry of patchwork pictures of his face and our life and I scrolled like a twat, tormenting myself about what was no longer. There should have been some snaps from our wedding on here by now. In fact, there should be a photo of Matt in his own capsule on another level of this very hotel, and I could have done a cute matching one, and everyone would think we were annoying but we wouldn't care because we were happy. We were happy.

What did you see? asks Marissa. *I unfollowed him when you split up.*

Same, Benny jumps into the conversation. Lovely loyal lot.

Nothing at first, he hasn't updated it for five weeks, not since that photo of the sky with his thumb in.

Twat, Gray types.

Marissa, who evidently thinks the same way I do, adds, *Did you check for ones he'd been tagged in?*

Let me guess: of course you did, Mara states.

Yes, Miss Marple, I did – I just wanted to see if he was in any photos with Katie. But there was nothing.

So you called that a win and went to bed? replies Mara, and I know that she knows that I so did not do that.

What I did was, as I discovered five seconds later, something completely idiotic. I went to the list of people he's following. I typed 'K-A-T-' and she appeared. I recognised pretty preppy Katie from her gym-bunny icon alone and I clicked into her profile.

And there it was. A photo from five days ago. A group of friends in a pub, Katie in the middle, Matt next to her, their arms touching.

But she didn't tag him? Marissa asks. *That's a shady move.*

He wasn't tagged, but nobody else was either. I don't get the feeling they're trying to hide anything, she's just not a tagger.

Gray, instead of his usual 'wit and charm', simply types, *Sorry, Charlie.*

Do you want me to have a word with him about any of this? Benny adds.

No, thank you though. Just venting, I say, because if I can't share my feelings with these people any more, who else is there? *He looked happy, without me.*

For a while, after I'd closed Instagram, I sat with my sadness, staring at the dark sky outside the window of the lounge, the Kyoto street not quiet, but quieter, and let the dusty shatters of my heart settle inside my chest. Before I did any more damage to my self-esteem, I turned my phone off completely and went back to my capsule, but I don't think I slept any more.

But we're in a new day in a new city I have yet to explore. Today is all about spring and beauty and serenity here in Kyoto, because we're heading to the annual geisha festival that celebrates the cherry blossoms through dance and music. We're going kimono shopping, or viewing, I'm not sure which, and we're going for a long look around an exquisite temple.

Before we leave, I stand under the shower for a while, trying to wash off any lingering melancholy that sticks to my skin.

I hum 'I'm Gonna Wash That Man Right Outta My Hair' as I lather in a blob of shampoo, trying to trick my mind into no longer fixating on The Photo.

Because, whatever, right? Scrub lather. So he's at a pub with his 'wild oat'. I'm in *Japan*. Scrub scrub lather lather. I'm on the trip of a lifetime, seeing the most amazing things. I'm on my *honeymoon – alone*. Wait, that last one was supposed to be cool and empowering too.

Scrub scrub lather lather.

I know where I'd rather be. That's right, I would rather be here, scrub lather, than with him, pressed against him in a pub, I would rather be in Japan. SCRUB LATHER.

'Then BE in Japan!' I shout at myself, pulling my hands from my poor scalp. I breathe for a moment and step back under the water. *Be in Japan. Be present.*

I wish I could truly be here without him. I wish everything didn't circle back to him but I just don't know how to pull the threads of the two of us apart. I can't figure out who I am without straying into who *we* were.

The last of the suds wash down the drain. Time to get dressed.

Chapter 9

Folds of kimono
And layers of history
But still I undo

'Is that Kaori?' Flo squints into the sunshine outside our capsule hotel.

I look up from my itinerary and follow her gaze, but all I see is a woman wrapped in sun-catching floral silk, a kimono scattered with peach, pink and yellow petals embroidered into the folds. She wears a sky-blue flower in her hair with a matching sash around her waist and a proud yet slightly shy smile.

I remove my sunglasses. 'Jesus Christ, it is! She looks stunning.'

At that point, the three men leave the hotel and do a double take, and we all bustle around Kaori, taking in the details and marvelling at the exquisite fabric and intricate tailoring.

'You didn't have this in that suitcase of yours, did you?' I ask.

'No, I went early to a kimono shop I know very well. I will be taking you there this morning and you can try on kimono if you would like. I always rent the same one, I love this pattern, and today I plan to wear it all day because of the special festival.'

As Kaori walks us the short distance to the kimono rental store, I begin to notice something, a lot of very colourful somethings. 'Kaori, there are way more people wearing kimono here than in Tokyo, is that because of the geisha festival?'

'Yes, in part.' Kaori walks slowly and carefully. It's a nice pace after the hecticness of the city we left yesterday. I don't feel like I could move my legs fast and drag my heavy heart along today if I tried. '*Miyako Odori* – the festival – is a big cultural event here in Kyoto which is all about the geishas performing the spring cherry-blossom dances. Kimonos are not always, but typically, worn in more formal occasions or during cultural times like this, so you will probably see a few more women, and men, dressed in kimono. But also, Kyoto is more traditional than Tokyo, so you will see a few more people wearing them, even when it's not festival time. Many of them tourists. So don't be afraid to wear one.'

We arrive at the shop and while everyone is picking kimono to try on, I branch off to the side and study some fabric.

I hate feeling like this. Have you ever gone to a party and you love the host and the people are great and the atmosphere is awesome but you feel like an alien in your own skin? Like you can't – you wish you could but you can't – shake loose and just go with it? Everything you do feels stiff and forced and your insides are all tight and worried? I used to get that occasionally, unexpected bursts of anxiety that would make me feel like I was wearing someone else's mask. Matt could tell, sometimes (not all the time), and would hold my hand, making me feel less alone.

My fingers trace a waterfall design painted on a vast piece of silk hanging on the wall, the water spiralling down until I can't reach any further.

'Charlotte, which one do you like?' Flo asks, coming towards me with a hot-pink kimono in her arms, which is going to look just gorgeous on her.

'I'm not sure ... I'll look around a little more first.' Flo and Lucas go off to get dressed, with some help, of course, and I walk around the shop. Cliff and Jack are looking at the men's kimonos and chatting with Kaori, and the sales assistant walks over to me.

He bows and I do the same. 'May I suggest a kimono for you?' his voice is quiet and he speaks English carefully.

'*Hai, domo arigato*,' I reply and bow again for good measure. *Yes, thank you so much*.

He selects a turquoise and green kimono, decorated with a peacock feather design, and while I go through the motions trying it on, wishing I could turn off the thoughts in my head, I do acknowledge that it does look beautiful. Not because of how it looks on me, specifically, but because it is just stunning.

This reminds me of trying on wedding dresses. In particular, that time with Mum, when I had my mini meltdown. I felt like I was all dress and no inner peace there, too.

There is a shaded courtyard behind the shop with tatami mat flooring and simple calligraphy art on the walls, and Kaori has us pose for photos.

'Excuse me,' I ask the sales assistant. 'Would you please take a video of us all on my phone?'

He agrees and we pose for the camera a final time.

'So who would like to rent their kimono and wear it for today?' asks Kaori.

'Absolutely,' Lucas says, proud and tall in his petrol-blue ensemble, next to his pretty-in-pink wife.

Cliff and Jack, in their matching navy blue, decline. 'I think we old-timers have enough trouble getting around,

I can see one of us tripping and breaking a hip,' says Jack, though none of us think of them as old-timers.

I decline too. It was nice to dress up but I'm not in the headspace for any more attention on me. I'd like to be an invisible, miserable old bitch, please.

After I'm back in my own clothes and we're waiting for Cliff and Jack, the sales assistant comes over to me again. I'm running my fingers over the sea-greens and electric cyans of the peacock feathers printed on my kimono, the silk cool and heavy to the touch, and trying to imprint it on my memory.

He hands me something wrapped in tissue. When I open it, I see it's a palm-sized flat, rectangular bag made of the peacock-feather silk. 'For you,' he says. 'This is *omamori*, a good-luck charm.'

'For me?' Oh bloody hell, the tears are coming again.

'It is good luck to carry on the outside of your bag and you will know you're making good decisions.'

I love it and thank him a million times, and as we're walking away from the shop, I show Kaori.

'Oh, that's very nice, you will have a lot of luck with that,' she says. 'Normally, *omamori* are bought at temples and shrines, and they have different ones for the different things you want success with in your life. Inside is a prayer blessed by a priest, but you shouldn't ever open it and read the prayer because then it doesn't work. The kimono seller has a brother who is a priest at one of the temples in Kyoto and he makes them for him. This is a general "good luck" charm and doesn't have a prayer in it yet, but I think it has heart because it was given to you in kindness.'

Kyoto was once the capital of Japan, and it has such a different vibe from Tokyo. Centuries of history and tradition seem to tuck themselves into every nook, every passageway, and behind every doorway here.

We walk to the Gion district, also known as the geisha (or *geiko*) district, which is where the Miyako Odori festival will be held. Along the way we catch glimpses of sloping-roofed pagodas rising into the sky from different parts of the city. We walk along a quiet canal lined with willow trees and through narrow alleys between wooden buildings that house *ochaya*, teahouses.

'Have you read *Memoirs of a Geisha*?' Kaori asks us as we go past a particularly grand-looking teahouse with high red and dark wood-stained walls. A small crowd of people wait outside the closed gate. Some of us nod. 'This is Ichiriki Chaya, it is a very exclusive, members-only teahouse and this is where the author set a lot of that book. It is over three hundred years old and anybody who wishes to be entertained by geisha here has to develop a very good relationship with the *ochaya* first, as well as be able to afford it. It's *very* exclusive.'

It looks it. It looks like the kind of place where I'd be laughed all the way out of Japan if I set foot in there to ask to use the loo.

'Why are people waiting out the front?' I ask. 'Is there a celebrity in there?'

'The geisha are the celebrities around here,' Kaori answers. 'They are hoping to catch a glimpse of real *geiko* who work at the teahouse.'

We move on, fascinated, until Kaori stops us again in front of a low building with a curved lip of a roof over the entranceway and a taller, temple-like building behind. A cherry blossom tree drips pink on either side of the entrance and red paper lanterns swing in the soft breeze above a raised curtain of purple and white.

'This is the theatre for the Miyako Odori dance,' she says to us and we all say 'Ooo' and step inside.

The Miyako Odori geisha dance is both the same and opposite from the Kubuki show back in Tokyo. Where that was all men, and about the dramatics and stylisation, this is all women, and about beauty and detail. But both have an air of grace and great cultural importance.

Plus, the cherry blossoms here are incredible. Damn right they get a whole festival dedicated to them.

I settle in and watch the show, which unfurls in front of my eyes like a dream of times gone by. My mind drifts along with the music from time to time, but like the *maiko*, the apprentice *geiko*, who also dance on the stage, I keep practising bringing my mind back to the present, and to all these people around me, the beauty of the dance, the detail of the imagery, the ringing melodic music and the awestruck silence of the audience, and not to the parts of my heart that sit in my chest like the dropped petals of the cherry blossoms.

'What's hill walking like in that kimono?' I call to Flo, up ahead of me.

'It's fine,' Flo calls back. 'As long as I don't take massive strides.'

We're walking up to Kiyomizu-dera Temple, one of over 1,600 temples in this city, which sits on a hill to the side of Kyoto. On the way here, Kaori told us that it's a UNESCO World Heritage Site. Its name means 'Pure Water Temple' and it was built in the year 780 on the site of the Otowa Waterfall. So there you have it.

'You can taste the water near the bottom of the temple,' Kaori explains. 'It has been channelled into three streams and you can pick one and fill up a cup and you will get luck that relates to that stream, such as love or success.'

'Can you chuck back all three?' asks Lucas and I pretend to laugh along with the others but actually that's a bloody good question.

But Kaori shakes her head. 'No, the gods think that is greedy and it invalidates your wishes.'

And then there it is – in bright, vermillion red stands one of the many buildings that make up this temple. I'm learning that most temple gateways – *torii* – are painted in this reddish orange colour to ward off evil and symbolise vitality. One day, when I have my own home, maybe I'll paint my front door this colour.

Kaori has arranged a private tour led by an English-speaking priest, so we head to the main building to meet him. He greets us each by name and with a bow, his long black robes soft-looking, like his face, and his voice is as calm and as soothing as an ASMR video.

As he walks with us to the Otowa Waterfall streams, he explains a little about the temple.

'Here we worship the deity Kannon, who is known for her compassion for all people. We believe she can appear in many forms to help those that suffer. You will visit her a little later, but first ...' He claps his hands together and we're here, standing below three crystal clear streams of water that run over the top of a thick, stone archway. He hands us each a tin cup on the end of a long ladle. 'You can choose which healing water you would like to drink from. School, good health and longevity, or romantic relationships. The water will purify your senses and help your wishes come true.'

He smiles and steps back. Lucas and Flo cutely both go for the romantic stream, and then have a snuggly, coupley moment. Cliff and Jack both opt for the longevity stream, and Jack rests his head on Cliff's shoulder in contentment. Kaori chooses 'school' because, she tells us, she's studying languages on the side and hopes to travel and work abroad one day if she is successful.

'Which will you choose?' the monk asks me while the others are chatting among themselves.

'I'm not sure. I just had my heart broken so I suppose I should drink from the romantic relationships stream ...'

'Why do you suppose that? Would you like to find a new love?'

'No,' I declare.

'Would you like to be in love with the person that broke your heart again?'

This time I answer with less speed. "No ... I don't know if I'm out of love with him yet. But I think I want to be.'

'What would your wish be for yourself, right now?'

'To get to know who I am.' It sounds a little corny out loud, but I also know it to be true. 'He and I were together for a long time and it's so hard to unpick the fabric of the two of us and figure out, of what's left, what threads are mine.' I look at the view beyond the streams. I probably shouldn't be boring this monk with my tales of woe, but he stands quietly beside me for as long as I need. 'I don't suppose Kannan can help with creativity, can she?' I ask.

'She can, but the goddess Benzaiten might also be able to help with that, as she is goddess of the arts.'

'Hmm. Thank you. There's a part of my life that I need to go well, creatively, and it all feels a bit out of reach at the moment.'

Eventually, I hold out my pole and dangle the cup under one of the streams. I drink it with my eyes closed, focusing on the cool of the water, the sounds of the birds, the feel of the cold metal against my lower lip, and I make a wish.

From there we move to the lookout points and to inner sanctuaries, and he teaches us about the temple and about Buddhism. We visit Kannon's sculpture in the main hall, with her many arms to envelop anybody going through difficulty, and we're encouraged to offer her a prayer if we want to. The hall is dark and candle-lit, with incense lightly scenting the air and a warmth and stillness like a hug when you really need one.

Finally, our monk leads us to a private veranda overlooking the 'moon garden' for some meditation or prayer, and I sit quietly and close my eyes.

At first all I hear is the plinky-plunky trickle of the water feature, a never-ending background soundscape that is both relaxing and slightly makes me want to pee. But the longer we sit in silence, my eyes remaining shut, the more my ears seem to open out to other sounds.

A nearby bird chirps loudly and monotonously, moments of silence between each one as if waiting for the other. The song of another bird further away starts to filter in, a rhythmic *brrrr*. The wind whispers between the leaves of the trees and branches creak in the quiet. A small splash causes me to open one eyelid, and I see the orange and white flash of a koi fish dive back under water in the pond in front of the veranda.

Beside me I hear Cliff breathing, slow and steady. On my other side, Kaori rolls her shoulders and the fabric of her kimono rustles.

Would you like to find a new love? the monk had asked me earlier, and I'd said no. But I do, one day. I can't picture myself ever finding the closeness that Matt and I had with anyone else. But just because I can't envisage it now, doesn't mean it won't happen, I suppose, one day.

I'm exhausted, I realise. Ever since calling off the wedding I've been on the go, cancelling plans, rearranging other plans, explaining things, trying to forget things. I'm not sure I have the strength to keep sightseeing. I wonder if I could stay here for the next three weeks; just do this.

But that's not on the itinerary, so the temple tour must come to an end, something we all look a little blue about, having had such a special time.

We bid goodbye to the priest, and thank him, and walk back towards the crowds.

We round the corner, finding ourselves in a small yet busy courtyard behind the main hall, where people seem to be taking it in turns to walk with their eyes closed while their friends cheer and take photos.

Kaori laughs in delight. 'Now this is a very special place to see on a tour dedicated to finding your true partner – this is the shrine to the god of matchmaking and love!'

'Where?' Jack asks, looking at the various little wooden huts decorated in calligraphy and wondering what we should be looking at.

'There, I think,' I say, pointing down. On the ground is a rock, maybe knee-height, decorated with rope and gold ribbon, and a plaque. About twenty metres away is an identical one. 'Are people walking between the two stones?'

'Yes,' nods Kaori. 'The legend says that if you can walk from one love stone to the other with your eyes closed you will be lucky and find true love, very soon.'

Cliff pondered this. 'It'd be kind of awkward on our other halves if one of us walked that and made the trip successfully.'

Kaori laughs. 'Maybe those of you already in love stick to praying for successful and long marriages using the luck charms,' she smiles, then adds, 'which you can buy at the end.'

'Charlotte, you should try it,' pipes up Lucas and, to be honest, I was dreading that someone was bound to suggest this.

'No, thank you,' I brush him away.

'Yessss, go on girl,' Flo joins in, quickly followed by Jack.

'No, really, I don't need to find a new love any time soon.' I can't even imagine kissing anyone else at the moment. The photo of Matt with Katie rolls into my consciousness.

'We'll all help ya!' Lucas cries.

Kaori waves her hands. 'Actually, you *can* help her but if you do it will mean that Charlotte will need a matchmaker to help her. She will only find love on her own if she can do it by herself.'

'Can we at least jump in if she's about to fall off the side of the hill?' asks Jack.

'Well, yes, because if she is dead she will not find love on her own anyway,' Kaori answers completely seriously.

And then they're all back at it again, egging me on, thinking this will fix me and I feel like a big single show-pony. When Cliff says, in his deep voice, 'You never know, kid, this could be good for you,' I give in. I'll play along to get this spotlight off me because it's too much.

'Okay, okay, okay,' I say, and take my position.

'Do you want help or do you want to be left alone?' Kaori asks.

I close my eyes. 'I want to be alone.'

I do want to be alone. I don't want to be praying to the gods for a new great love. I don't want everyone and everything reminding me of my heartache.

The closing of my eyelids gives me the sensation of a black cloud rolling in, and I'm unable to keep it at bay any longer. My feet walk forwards, and I keep my eyes squeezed shut, not because I'm desperate to complete the challenge successfully but because I'm afraid of them spilling over if they're open. I hear the others walking beside me, whispering to each other and trying to stay silent. They mean well. If I can't figure out what I need or don't need, I can't expect them to know.

I wobble on the spot and stop, feeling like I could crumble. I can't do it. I can't do this, I'm not ready.

Just get through it, get to the end, put on a brave face and then go for a walk. I step forward again, carefully, trying to keep in a straight line and I hear Flo whisper, 'yay!'

On I shuffle, this never-ending walk that seems to fill everyone else here with hope and laughter, and my hands are outstretched, praying not for a new man but for the end of all this.

And suddenly, *bump*. My shin hits the second love stone and I open my eyes, and everyone cheers and hugs me and it does make me laugh a little, which helps me disguise that I'm mopping away a couple of tears.

'How much longer do we have here?' I turn to Kaori.

'We have about another hour so you can look around on your own, go back and take photos, and then we'll meet back near the entrance.'

'Great, thanks everyone, I'll see you in a bit!' I flash them a smile that drops the minute I walk away.

I walk fast, my heart pumping, away from the crowds and following a path up into the gardens of the temple. I walk past water features and ponds, past squat, mossy bushes, over a bridge that reflects in the still stream and I find a spot with a stone to sit on, cherry blossoms above me, and a view of Kyoto poking through the pink petals and green leaves. It's deathly quiet, and I sit down and breathe, and pull out my phone. *Is anyone free for a chat?* I type to my sisters and brothers. *Need some help.*

Mara answers almost immediately. *Group call?*

Marissa replies, *I have Benny with me, we can dial in.*

Yep, says Gray.

No matter how busy they all are, they'll drop everything for me, and I don't think I can do this without them any more.

Mara starts a video call, dialling us all in, and their wonderful, familiar faces fill my screen. I don't even realise how obvious my tears are until Gray gets close to the camera on his phone and says, on full alert, 'What's happened, Charlie?'

'I think I need to come home.'

'Why?' Marissa and Benny ask in perfect unison.

'I can't be here any more, on this trip, I can't do it. What the hell was I thinking, coming to the place we planned our honeymoon on my own? I'm coming home.'

'Charlie, it's okay, tell us what happened,' says Mara.

'How did I ever imagine I'd breeze around Japan like everything was fine?' I plough on. 'I'm in these beautiful places with these lovely people, but my heart is just a big pile of shit and who wants to be around a big pile of shit?'

'Where are you right now?' asks Marissa.

'I'm at a temple in Kyoto, in the gardens.' I turn the camera around so she and the rest of them can see.

'Wow,' Marissa continues. 'It looks gorgeous.'

'It is, and I want to enjoy it, but there's always this black cloud over me and—' I sniff in a lungful of snot.

'They made me do a love stone walk because I'm the only unmarried.'

Gray looks very confused but says nothing.

'Well, they didn't *make me* but I felt embarrassed and on the spot so I did it and I only went and bloody completed it and now if it comes true I'll be lucky in love.' This causes me to choke a sob out and I see Gray's confusion triple. 'I don't want to fall in love with someone else, I want to be left alone. I want to come home. I can't do this.'

Mara adjusts her glasses on her nose. Uh-oh. 'Sorry, why can't you do it?'

'Because it's too hard?' I ask, hoping that's the correct answer.

'And the only possible solution is packing it in and coming home? To do what? Are you planning to just mope around Mum's?'

'Mara, you're such a hardarse sometimes,' Marissa scolds. 'I think she should come home if she isn't having a nice time. Come and stay with me, Charlie, you can sleep in my room and I'll accidentally make loads of extra petit fours to bring home for you every day.'

'What about if I came out there?' pipes up Benny.

'You what?' I sniff.

He leans closer to the camera. 'I could come there and join you for the rest of the tour. I could be on the next flight out. Don't tell any of my mates I'm on a honeymoon tour with my sister though.'

'Excuse me,' says Marissa. 'You're supposed to be staying with me for a couple of days, we have plans, I've booked time off work.'

Gray snorts. 'Japan versus Marissa's flatshare, tricky one.'

'Benny, you're in the middle of revising for your exams, you can't fuck off to Japan,' says Mara.

'No, I can, it'll be fine, I really want to. What do you reckon, Charlie?'

'That's really sweet but I don't want more company; I want to come home and lie face down on a carpet for a while.' He looks a little deflated, and I feel bad. 'Gray, what do you think I should do?'

'Wouldn't you be wasting a load of money if you quit now? Isn't that why you went in the first place?'

Marissa jumps in. 'Yes, but she'd also be saving money because they said some of the hotels might refund her, plus she'd save on all the food and drink and activities.'

I would miss the food if I went home. Have I mentioned how much I'm enjoying the food?

'I think she should do whatever she wants to do,' says Benny. 'If she wants to come home, she should do that, and if she stays I should go out and keep her company.'

'What do you want to do, Charlie, or what would you like us to advise you to do?' Mara asks.

'I want to come home.' I say it quieter this time, feeling a little less sure of myself, my heart a little less poundy.

'Do you?'

'Yes.'

Mara raises her eyebrows. 'Interesting ...'

'What?' I ask, taking her bait.

'Nothing, I just never realised that all this time you were with Matt was partly because you can't handle being in the world without a man.'

Marissa and Benny erupt into a loyalty-filled tirade and Gray laughs his head off.

'Don't bloody reverse-psychology me,' I scoff to Mara. 'You know that's not true at all! It's not that I *can't* do this on my own, it's that I don't want to.'

Mara tilts her head and I know she's deliberately being extra-patronising to push my buttons. 'I think you were the one who said you "can't".'

'Well, I *can*.' God damn my big sister; she's winning and it's a train I can't stop. Checkmate.

I see an elderly couple strolling across the bridge, enjoying the peace, and I know I need to hang up. 'I have to go, thank you for all your help,' then I whisper to Mara, '*Except you.*'

'You're welcome!' she sings. 'Call us when you're at the airport in case you need me to find a man to come and pick you up.'

I hang up, fuming. But as I look at the view with the tiniest trickle of the stream my only soundscape, and breathe in Japan, I realise I have a little more thinking to do before hauling my arse to the airport.

I know it's an awful thing to think when you're on the site of a holy ground, but deep down I say this with love, I promise: God damn my big sister.

I'm still all scrunched up and tangle-headed when I get back to the pod hotel later. Thoughts are whizzing through me like all the bullet trains in Japan are going at once, only I don't know where any of them are going. I need to take back some control. I need to jump off these trains.

I've got to do it now and then it's one less thing to think about. I need to write to Amanda and tell her I can't possibly take up the internship. It's just too overwhelming. And if I'm not going to rush back and try and impress *Adventure Awaits* then I might as well call it a day with Japan as well. I've seen some of it, more than many people who visit here, probably. And I consider myself lucky for that. But it's time to jump.

I tap through to the *Adventure Awaits* website, buying time before I rip the plaster off, telling myself I'll find a recent article by Amanda herself to compliment her on within my sucky email.

An advert to the side of the homepage catches my eye. *'Looking for your next adventure? Click here for latest job opportunities with the* Adventure Awaits *group'*. I do as I'm told and click here, and see three words that make my mind suddenly become very sharp and focused indeed. I sit up.

'Junior Travel Writer'.

I pore over the job specifications, racing through the words, feeling my heart quickening. Full-time, paid, permanent, working in the digital department creating content for the magazine's website, deadline in six weeks. Must have a proven passion for travel, a great eye for detail, be familiar with the brand and writing styles, and have some journalism experience on a national publication. Well, I don't quite have that, but I do have a degree in journalism and have been at the paper, albeit copy-editing, for a solid couple of years. What is it they say? That often women hold themselves back because they won't apply for a job if they don't tick all the boxes, but men will apply if they tick at least some of them? I don't need this to stop me, not at all.

But wait a minute, this isn't part of the plan. *What plan?*

But they won't consider me for a job so soon after chucking away the internship. *So don't cancel the internship.*

But ... wouldn't it be wrong to go ahead with the internship if I apply for this? *Who knows ... ask them? Maybe they'll be impressed by your ambition?*

I can think of a lot of reasons not to think any more about this role, not to add an extra thing to think about into my already bursting braincells, but I can also think of just as many reasons why I should put the brakes on and consider applying. This is the job I want. This is something I could do, and that I love, and that I could get paid for. This is a dangling carrot to put my life back on a track. This is something I can control. This is the adventure I, maybe, should catch.

But how can I go chasing adventures, when I'm still struggling to pick myself off the ground? I'm so conflicted on what to do, on who I am, and what the best decisions to make are. If I go to London and all that happens is that I sit and pine for the way life should have been there with Matt, then maybe London isn't for me, after all. Maybe neither is working on a big, giant magazine in a big, giant city. I can't uproot myself and move away from everything I know on a 'maybe'.

Can I?

Chapter 10

Slow down, girl, slow down
We are on island time now
Sayonara, *Matt*

By the following morning I've made a decision. All the opinions in the world couldn't tell me if it's the *right* decision, but it's *my* decision, and I owe it to myself to trust it.

I'm completely surrounded by bright, dewy green right now. Kaori had us up at the crack of dawn to head to Arashiyama Bamboo Grove before the crowds rolled in, and although I can't stop yawning my head off, it's worth it to have the tunnel-like, reed-lined pathways to ourselves.

The path weaves its way through the long, thin bamboo that stretches so high into the sky that you can barely see any blue up above. The trees creak with quiet satisfaction as the breeze tickles their leaves, and the air is tinted with a fresh, forest scent. It's serene. The perfect ending to my time on the tour.

'Kaori, could I have a word?' I ask, touching her arm. She falls back into step with me, leaving the other four to continue on ahead, tilting their necks back and taking a million photos.

'How are you today, Charlotte?' she asks.

I hesitate, unsure how to put this in words when the last thing I want is for Kaori to think this is because of her or the tour she's organised.

'I don't know if you've noticed, but I'm struggling a little bit.' She nods, and I think she has noticed. I continue, 'Ever since calling off my wedding everything has been such a whirlwind and I think it's just starting to sink in now. I thought coming on this trip would be a good distraction, but also a good way to get a bit of alone time. I don't really know who I am and when I try and work on that at the same time as try to be present and included in all of the amazing activities you've planned for us, I'm getting a bit overwhelmed. I'm worried that if I continue with the tour, everybody else isn't going to get the best out of it, and I don't want to be the cause of that.'

'I understand,' Kaori says in her soft voice. 'It's very hard to be yourself and follow your heart when you are with strangers and being told where to go and what to do.'

'Please know, though, that I think the tour is incredible. I've already done so much and learnt so much, thanks to you. I think I need to step back, figure out who I am without any noise, and travel on my own for the rest of my time here.'

So that is my decision. I'm not going to leave Japan, but I am going to leave the tour. If I need – and *want* – to be just me, myself and I for a while, then Mara was right: the solution isn't giving in and going home. I have a twenty-one-day rail pass, I have a little spending money still, I have my Duolingo app, and I have to do this.

'I will be very sad to see you go, but I think this is a good thing for you. It's a very Japanese thing, actually. Have you heard of the term *ikigai*?'

I shake my head.

'*Ikigai* is a concept in Japan which is about finding your purpose and living happily. I think you should look it up, it might help guide you a little.'

'Thank you, I will.' I'm not sure I'm ready to find my life's purpose, though; I'd be happy to just find my own voice at this point.

'You know, *ikigai* has foundations in the Okinawa Islands, of which Ishigaki – my home island – is one.

Okinawa is one of the world's five blue zones where people live long and happy lives.'

'Funny you should mention that, because Ishigaki has been on my mind since you mentioned it the other day ...'

Back in the heady days of honeymoon planning, there had been one doubt that hovered in my mind about Japan being the perfect post-wedding destination. Everybody kept telling me, *you'll be absolutely shattered, just pick a beach break and relax*. Were we going to be crawling about on our hands and knees dying of lethargy if we attempted an action-packed month-long expedition in a brand-new country with a brand-new language barrier?

But as much as the idea of zonking out on a sun lounger and being brought a kaleidoscope of cocktails sounded pretty ace, we just kept coming back to Japan. We would be between jobs and renting anyway, so when else would we get a string of weeks to jet off and see the other side of the world? If I tried to take a month off in my new career it would wipe out my whole year's holiday leave quicker than you could say bullet train.

However, now I have the opportunity to have the best of both worlds. Kaori mentioned the low-cost airline that goes to Ishigaki from Osaka, a city not far from

Kyoto that I could get to using my rail pass. I'm going to treat myself to a few days on a sun lounger.

'That's so fantastic!' Kaori cries. 'You can get in touch with me at any point while you're there if you need any tips or anything. Try the snorkelling! Ooo I'm jealous.'

At that point, Flo turns around, looking very *Survivor* hottie framed by all that bamboo, to see what Kaori is cheering about.

'Can I speak to you all for a minute?' I ask, and when they've gathered around I tell them my plan. They're understanding, of course, but they say what they can to convince me to stay.

I shake my head, touched by their kindness. 'I'm sorry. I hate to be all "it's not you, it's me", but that's honestly true. You're all lovely and have made me feel so welcome and taught me a lot,' I say the last part to Kaori. 'But you all deserve to have the best honeymoon possible, and I need to do a bit of soul-searching. A big part of why I came on this trip was to prove to myself that I could be by myself for a while and stand on my own two feet, and I haven't done that yet. And I don't think I will by being on this tour. If I keep hanging around and using you all as my comfort blankets, I'm never going to take that leap of faith that I need to do to figure out how to think for myself. So if I stay, none of us are going to get what we need out of this trip.'

'You're a brave girl,' says Cliff in his magnificent drawl, and leans in to give me a stubbly hug and a fatherly pat on the hair, which I haven't had for, oh, a very long time.

'I hope you understand. And I hope to see you again at another point in the tour. I know I can't get all my hotel monies back so if the stars collide perhaps I could join you for dinner or something, somewhere.'

'I'd bloody love that,' answers Flo, throwing her arms around me and squeezing me, as warm as she was the first evening we met. 'Keep in touch with us all as you go around, okay?'

I agree, and we all swap details and say our goodbyes. 'Oh—' I say, almost forgetting. 'If you're on Instagram connect with me, because as you know I'm vlogging my way around Japan. The video Kaori was in the other day has been watched over two hundred times!'

Kaori cheers and I double check if they'd all be happy to give their permission for me to use footage I'd taken with them over the past few days on my channel as well. They are, and as they all crowd around Kaori's phone to watch her starring moment, I quietly back away down the bamboo-lined path and say a final, silent farewell.

Kaori catches my eye when I look back and she bows her head at me and smiles. I do the same back to her.

'Now,' I murmur to myself as I stroll back towards the train station. 'Where the chuff is my *ikigai* ...?'

By early afternoon I'm in Osaka airport, clutching my ticket for Peach Aviation to take me to the island of Ishigaki for five whole days. It's not the airport I thought I'd be in, or the destination I thought I'd be flying to, when I spoke to my siblings yesterday afternoon, but I made a change to my situation and I think that means I am super grown-up and mature now.

I've also spent the last forty-five minutes finding out everything I can about *ikigai*, ready for this epiphany I was due to have.

Here's some cool things about the concept of Ikigai:

1. *Ikigai* is all about figuring out what makes you happy, what makes you want to get up in the morning, and how you can live your everyday life by it.
2. When *ikigai* refers to 'life's purpose', it doesn't need to be this massive, all-consuming, on-your-deathbed revelation for being in the world like we in the West would usually think of the term 'life's purpose'. It's about finding happiness and purpose in everyday life. What makes you happy and gives you purpose *today*.

3. Because of the above, your *ikigai* can also evolve and change over time, and we don't need to be worried that it's set in stone.

4. In Okinawa people get super-old and some studies attribute this to their everyday sense of *ikigai*.

I can find my purpose, figure out what *I* want to do, without Matt, without anybody else's opinions, then I think I can move on and plan this future that's just opened out in front of me.

I look back at the job advert, which I've checked at least fourteen times today. One of the requirements for submission is to create a dynamic and interesting vlog of five minutes that I think would be interesting for visitors to the website. I don't know what kind of thing makes a vlog stand out, so I guess I'd better do some YouTubing once I get to Ishigaki, but I'm sure some of the footage I've already shot and shared could be used to create something exciting at the end of the trip. I hope.

Another thing I've been perusing while loitering in the airport is accommodation for when I get to Ishigaki Island. I've chosen an inexpensive little guesthouse right near a quiet-looking beach, where the interiors are painted a sea-turquoise and soothing cream, and the room looks small – not capsule hotel small – but with a big window that faces the ocean.

At the airport I've treated myself to a can of coffee, a big hibiscus flower hairclip and a pink 'Isigaki' tank top to get me in the mood (and because I wasn't expecting to go anywhere tropical on this trip and could do with an extra top where my armpits can go wild and free).

I'm nervous, sure, but I'm ready to branch out on my own again. Picking my own hotel, sitting here with my toes tickling to get out of my shoes and on to sand, choosing my own 'how' and 'how long' … it's all pretty nice.

As the announcement calls me and I board and peer out of the window at mainland Japan, and then the plane sweeps me up into the clouds, I have a little word with Matt inside my mind:

Once upon a time, when you proposed to me, you said you'd never leave me. Well now I'm going to try and leave you.

I drive my rental car with the windows down, the warm wind kissing my face, the flower in my hair and freedom giving me another shot. The sea, in marbled blues and greens, basks on my left, flat and slow, and low palms mix with the greenery to the right of the road.

I'm on island time now, and I'm in no rush at all.

My guesthouse is just as pretty as the website showed, and the owner – a woman with dewy skin and a deep tan – pointed out to me in easy-to-follow Japanese and hand gestures where the shared bathroom could be found, the fridge of goodies that I should help myself to, a bell to ring if I need anything. She presses a map of the island and a can of soda into my hand and bows as she leaves me in my room. The first thing I do is fling open my window, rest my feet up on the sill, let the breeze investigate my soles, and take a big drink.

The job advert is playing on my mind, but it makes a nice break from wishing my time here away all because I can't check out of heartbreak hotel. If I apply, I have to admit to having zero experience with vlogging, outside of the handful of IGTV episodes I've put up so far. But they're just footage, mainly, nothing particularly dynamic or interesting. Apart from that episode with Kaori in Kyoto, that seemed popular.

I take my phone from my pocket, connect to the Wi-Fi, and watch a few travel vlogs on YouTube. Hmm. Each sweeping drone shot and stylised title sequence makes me realise how amateur my attempts have been so far. I need to seriously step up my game. But *Adventure Awaits* are recruiting for a junior member of staff, right? They wouldn't expect videos of this quality ... right? Well, maybe they would.

What can I bring to the table?

I remember then something that was said to me once: *Tell* your *story of how the adventure feels to you. Make it authentic, and tell your story.*

That's it. Ariel was right. I'm not just a girl travelling around Japan, I have an angle. I'm on my honeymoon, alone. I've broken off from my group tour. I'm getting over heartbreak and I'm learning who I am. That's my story, and without a drone, or a laptop full of editing software, that's going to have to do. I can start with my IGTV vlogs, and hopefully I can piece together something great to show the magazine at the end. If I apply, of course.

Before I can change my mind, I set up my phone and face the camera, the breeze from the open window ruffling my hair, and I feel like I'm looking directly at my followers without a mask for the first time.

'Hi, everyone,' I start. I'm going to wing it. I can always edit it later, and I know myself: if I try and script something I will sound unbelievably robotic. The very opposite of authentic. 'I've gone a little off-course here in Japan, but before I tell you about it, I should explain my situation for anyone who doesn't know. For the past week, and for the next three weeks, I'm travelling through Japan … on my honeymoon. Only, the plot twist here is that I'm taking my honeymoon alone.'

I know the difference between being authentic and oversharing, so I keep some of the more personal details surrounding Matt and my fallout to a minimum – no need to slam him all over the internet, that's never going to make me look good – and focus on explaining the journey I'm trying to take, and how it's taken a swerve. 'A happy swerve though,' I laugh, glancing out of the window towards the beach. 'I mean, look where I am – on the island of Ishigaki, and it's a million miles away from the big city lights of Tokyo. In fact, the only light here at the moment is from the sunshine dropping down towards the ocean. I'm going to head down to the beach in a minute, but thanks for listening, and keep your fingers crossed for me to find my *ikigai*, okay?'

I switch the video off. That felt good, really good. I guess it was like journaling, in a way. I watch it back, just once, and decide I like it just the way it is, even with that strand of hair blowing sideways throughout, and my eye make-up sweated off.

Bugger it. I share the video to IGTV.

All right. And now I shall succumb to the wishes of my toes and take them down to the sand.

Breathe in, two, three, four, hold, two, three, and out, two, three, four. I'm hanging on the beach, this beautiful little tropical beach that's pretty close to Taiwan, and the sun is setting off to the side. With that comes a sky the colour of a motivational quote on Pinterest. Do you know what I mean? The kind that says 'dare to dream big'. A pastel watercolour of soft blue and millennial pink, and the sea reflects it effortlessly.

My thoughts return to the topic of *ikigai*. It feels waaaaay too big to decide what my whole life's purpose is, but I've done some reading and *ikigai* can change and evolve and you only really need to focus on the present. What do I want out of this trip, now that I've buggered off on my own?

That's a hard question. I watch a couple further down the beach as they play-fight in the waves, laughing their heads off. A tiny part of me wants to go and join them but I think they'd find it mega-weird.

I want to see Japan, as much as I can, including all those places I would have liked to have included but that the tour didn't incorporate. I want to try some new things. Oh ...

As the girl down the beach does a perfect mermaid dive into the water and rises to the surface a few metres away, her curls glinting in the low sun, I realise something I need to do. I get my phone out, check there's nobody in earshot, and start a piece to the camera with the sea behind me. Two in one day! You can't shut me up now, it seems!

'Hi adventurers,' I start. Filming isn't the thing I need to do, but you know how sometimes it takes telling people you're going to do something to force you to do it? 'I'm on the beach here in Ishigaki and I just realised something about myself, and it's freaked me out a little bit but I think I have time to do something about it. If any of you have ever said to me, what do I like to do in my spare time, I've always probably said travelling, holidays, adventures. That's been my "thing". One of my sisters has always been the chef. My other sister has always been the CEO, like, her whole life. I was the explorer. I've always thought of myself as a big adventurer, happy to go anywhere and do anything. I read novels about people who go on adventures around the globe, I've subscribed to travel magazines since I was a little girl, I'm due to go and work at a travel magazine when I get home from Japan. In fact, it was a travel writer called Ariel Cortez at that very magazine who, maybe ten years ago, wrote an article about Japan and I've wanted to come here ever since. I saw her give a talk once and she said I should catch every adventure, which I thought I'd been doing. But ... I think I might be a massive phoney ...'

I look away from the camera for a moment, my thoughts drifting out to sea.

'Maybe phoney is a harsh word, but I think I'm only a *wannabe* adventurer. And that would be fine, except, have I been kidding myself? Thinking that reading the magazines and books while never taking any real risks or following through on my ambitions is enough to call myself an adventurer? I've never swam in the sea. I've paddled and I've been in boats but I've never actually lifted my feet off the sand within the ocean. I've never stayed in anywhere that wasn't a hotel or a holiday home. I've never camped outside the UK.

'You might be thinking, *who feels sorry for you? You're in Japan!* I'm not saying this to make you feel sorry for me, or even to belittle the trips and the things I have done that were adventures, but my point is that I talk a big talk and have a big bucket list for someone who rarely strays off the beaten track.

'It's hard when you're in a relationship because you compromise on the type of vacation you take. Plus you're tired from work and life and would just like a break rather than turn it into a life-changing moment in time. But I'm on my own now, and I have nearly three more weeks in Japan with no real timetable, so I think it's about time I prove to myself that I'm who I claim to be.'

The sand becomes cool under my legs so I stand and stretch, propping my phone up on my bag, and remove my shorts and T-shirt. 'Shall we tick one thing off the list now?'

I have swimmies on! Panic not, Ishigaki.

I head into the ocean in case my *ikigai* is in there having a swim, and I sit down in the shallows, letting the chill water lick around my neck and arms. I glance over at my beach neighbours again and they are both floating on their backs, holding hands, like two serene otters.

I shuffle further into the water. This will definitely need editing down because nobody wants to see me spending ten minutes creeping further away from the shore in slow motion. Although if I'm suddenly swept away by an undercurrent it will make a great final viral video.

Why would I think that right now?

It's not that I'm scared of the water, it's more that it's now become ~a thing~ so it feels like a big deal, although it probably isn't.

Come on. I know how to swim. I'm already in the water. And look how cute otter-couple look. So I lift my feet behind me, push my arms forward, keep my face out of the water and hold my breath as I kick off, and take my first swim in the ocean.

I stop, and put my feet back down, and stand tall, my torso out of the water and my arms held high. 'Woooooo!'

I whoop. One small swim for woman, one large swim for adventurerkind.

Even if I don't do anything other than sleep, eat, roll about on the beach and take tiny swims for the next five days, I know I've made the right choice.

I do decide to do a little more than that while I'm here though, and the next day I spend a while compiling ideas for how to spend my island time wisely, but also in a shoot-the-breeze, easy-going way. I settle on a mix of gazing at the views, trying the local chilli oil, checking out a palm grove, walking along Kabira Bay, relaxing on 'my beach', and trying something I've never made a high priority before, due to the whole swimming-in-the-sea wall I'd built up: snorkelling.

My guesthouse serves up a breakfast of breads, rice, salad and fresh pineapple smoothies and I have a touch of each, filling my belly with these heart-healthy morsels ready for my day ahead of doing very little.

'*Domo arigato,*' I say to my host after I've helped wash the dishes and shown her photos on my phone of me in a kimono, which she probably had no interest in seeing but, oh well.

I'm slowing everything down today. No rush, no timetable, no worrying about connecting with the wider world. I start by sitting by my open window again, practising a little meditation as taught to me by the priest at Kiyomizu-dera temple, and then I wander back down to the beach for a mid-morning mini-swim.

My days uncurl along with my body, getting used to the sunshine, getting used to the pace of life. I let my thoughts drift about and I come up with a little trick. Any time I think of Matt, or I worry about something hypothetical, or I let doubt or sadness pay me a visit, I turn from whatever direction I'm facing and I look at the sea. And I imagine those thoughts to be waves, coming to check in on me and then drifting back into the ocean. If they want to stay I let them, I have the time to stew now if that's what I want to do, but aside from the sadness, which sometimes lingers a little longer to enjoy the pity party, the others tend to slide away again pretty quickly.

On my third day on Ishigaki Island, after I've had a cursory check on Instagram to see that, to my surprise, views of my last two IGTV posts have more than doubled (I guess I must be doing something right?) I decide to take the plunge, as it were, and take a stab at this snorkelling lark. It turns out, snorkelling trips take you to a beach and then to a manta ray point off the coast.

Before I leave my guesthouse, I show my host what I'm up to and she scurries off only to return with armfuls of things for me to take, which she keeps piling up on the table. She's loaning me flippers, which she squeezes my feet into, a mask and a snorkel, a small cool bag that she stuffs with snacks, and a clear plastic box on a lanyard, which I have no idea what it's for until she nicks my phone, throws it in there and then lobs the whole thing in a bowl of water.

'Oh, it's waterproof casing!' I say. 'I hope ...'

Lastly, she gives me a big tub of waterproof sunscreen to take with me. She's so great. And off I waddle.

I meet my guide at Kabira Bay, a picturesque beach dotted with tour boats along the turquoise shore. I remember having a poster on my wall at uni – the same poster most people had – which was of a tropical beach with boats on. I expect it was of Thailand, but this vista reminds me of that poster. Hmm. I wonder if uni-me would have ever imagined I'd be somewhere like this in real life. I expect so. I always thought, *'one day'* ... Well, today is 'one day', lady!

'Ohayo gozaimasu,' I greet the blue-shorted, white T-shirted guide who stands with a clipboard beside a sign that reads 'Manta Tours Ishigaki'. A few others are loitering around as well, some with all the clobber, like me, and some brandishing nothing but bright red sunburn.

I picked a tour with an English-speaking guide because although it isn't the most out-there option, let's face it: this isn't the time to practise my basic Japanese while submerged in water off the coast surrounded by massive manta rays.

Yuya is a man with a big smile and bare feet. He can't wait to get us all into the sea and from the moment he's loading the ten of us onto the minibus to the moment he's offloading us at Yonehara Beach he's telling us all about the fish we'll see, the coral reefs, the island.

'But this is so important, snorkel team,' he enthuses. 'Don't take anything home with you except smiles and photos. The coral takes thousands of years to grow and it's their home out there. You wouldn't like it if a manta ray came to your home and stole your front door? Would you?'

We all shake our heads.

'And no taking Nemo home, okay? You saw the movie, right? They don't like it. You will cause a lot of stress for Nemo's dad.'

We all nod.

'Let's go in the water!' He legs it off down the beach.

Dumbo here had already put one flipper on so I struggle to keep up, lolloping my way across the sand like an idiot, but at least it gave me a little extra time to admire the scenery. Aside from the white sand and sparkling sea (*ohayo*, ocean!), there are more of Ishigaki's distinctive hills on all sides, densely packed with green palms and other flora. There are parts of the beach where the palms have snuck right down to overhang the water, hoping to catch a glimpse of the fishies themselves.

All along the shore, people are walking in and out of the water, those coming out have their snorkels pushed up on their heads and they smile as they push the sea water and snot from their noses, and laugh with their friends, excited about what they've seen.

Well, I don't have any friends here to point things out to, so I'm going to be content with pointing things out to myself. But I choose to make use of the waterproof case the guesthouse host loaned me, so before I jump in I switch the camera on and clip it all back shut. 'Fingers crossed,' I whisper.

I don't realise at the time but the first fifteen minutes of my video is of my own stomach in extreme close-up, thanks to the lanyard having flipped the case around and so I filmed myself instead of the fish.

While we're all standing on shore, Yuya asks us if any of us have never been snorkelling before.

I, and two young boys, raise our hands.

'And you are making your first-ever snorkel on Ishigaki Island? This is fantastic!' says Yuya. 'Okay, let's all go in the water, just a little way, and get used to how the equipment works, yes?'

We wade in to nearly waist-deep water and Yuya asks us to sit down. The sea bed here is soft sand and we're now sitting with our shoulders above the water, swaying gently with the current.

'I know some of you are thinking, *Yuya, I need to go and see the fish! Let me go!* But I am the boss and we will go through the basics altogether. And then you are free to explore but I will help our three new snorkellers a little more. Step one: spit on your mask please.'

I laugh out loud, assuming it's a joke, but everyone else is dutifully gobbing onto the glass on the inside of their mask and giving it a rub around, like over-enthusiastic aunties cleaning chocolate off the faces of unsuspecting children. Even the two boys, who have as little idea as me as to why we're doing this, are only too happy to be given permission to spit on their belongings so are copying their parents with glee.

Yuya glances at me but addresses everyone so as not to single me out. 'The spit helps to stop your mask from fogging up when you are under the water. It's weird but it works.'

I'm hocking up my third spitball when Yuya adds, 'That's probably enough now, so go ahead and rinse your mask a little in the water, also splash a little water on your face to cool it down because the hotter the face the more danger of fogging.' At this point he darts his eyes to the chap with the lobster sunburn like he has no hope. 'Now put the mask on your face, like this, and tighten the straps ... like this.'

The straps snag at my hair and the rubber mask suctions at my face and squashes my nose. I stare through the glass at Yuya and back up at the beach and feel a fizzle of excitement. I am here. I'm about to snorkel in the sea.

'Now this is your snorkel,' Yuya says, holding up the tube. 'This goes in your mouth, in case anyone is not sure. You put the end with the rubber mouthpiece in your mouth, not the end with the orange stripe because that end is what I use to check where you are when you are floating about.'

I suspect there's more to it than he's letting on, but nevertheless I make a note: do not stick snorkel into your mouth the wrong way round. Do not stick your snorkel into mouth the wrong way around.

'With these snorkels you will breathe underwater but I would not suggest submerging them completely unless you take a pause of breath. If you get a splash of water in this type of snorkel you can let out a sharp breath, like if you are doing a breathalyser, and the water will shoot out, but you don't want to breathe in with the *whole* thing underwater otherwise you will be having a second breakfast of seawater and fish.'

With that, Yuya gives a little direction about where to swim for those who are confident to get the ball rolling. I stay behind, willing some courage to find its way out of me to dunk my head and try breathing through this weird plastic tube.

I kneel in the water, the sun warming my shoulders with encouragement, the water still swaying me from side to side. I stare downwards through my glass box, and grip the mouthpiece with my teeth, my lips stretched over the outside. I take a breath, hold it, and plunge my face into the sea.

Seconds later, I pull my head back out and only then open my eyes, which rather defeats the point, I guess. I pull the snorkel out of my mouth, my lips tingling with salt, and I realise I didn't try breathing either. Yuya raises his eyebrows at me but says, 'There is no rush, the fish do not have meetings to go to.'

As a trickle of water creeps down from my hairline and tries to get into my mask, a thought concurrently trickles past, that same old song of *I wish Matt were here to try this with me*. I can picture exactly what would have happened. He would have sensed my fear and found my hand under the surface of the sea and held it as we dunked our heads together. I look up at the horizon and feel the current wash through me, and I tell myself, *Totally fine to feel like that, Charlotte, but he isn't here so get your flippin' face in that water. And open your eyes. For crying out loud.*

I've got a point. I take another deep breath, stuff the snorkel back in my mouth, squeeze my eyes shut and plunge my face back in. This time I open my eyes under the surface and – wow.

I'm only looking at my own legs and some sand, granted, but this is incredible. I can see Under The Water. Way better than I could if I just opened my eyes under there; this feels like a porthole into a whole other world. I've been staring down for a while so the time has come to try this breathing lark, I guess.

Whoa, here it comes. I very very slowly exhale the breath I was holding. That went well, now time to breathe in. My lips are cold and stingy in the waves, my teeth chomped around the rubber, and I try and keep everything super still as I breathe in ... and it works!

I mean, of course it did, there are literally fifty other people on the beach right now doing this exact thing, but it still feels weird to have your mouth underwater but still be able to breathe. I feel like Ariel, or one of those escaped convicts from an old movie who hides in a lake with just a straw poking up so they can get air.

A few more goes at this and I'm ready to see more than just my own legs, so with a thumbs up from Yuya,

I very carefully swim towards the others, my face under water, the snorkel sticking out.

Let's say 'swim' in this instance in the loosest possible term, because I'm more gliding with the tiniest movement possible, paranoid about kicking up any water that might jump into my snorkel and drown me. As my view changes from pale sand to the beginnings of craggy beige coral, my first fish whizzes by: a tiny blue fella who takes one look at me and darts in the opposite direction.

'MMMMM!' I sound into my snorkel, pointing at where the fish was and turning my head from side to side to see if any other snorkellers are around for me to show them what I saw. This action, unsurprisingly, causes my snorkel to scoop out a lungful of sea water, a little of which trickles into my mouth, and next thing I know I'm doggy-paddling back to the shallower part of the beach, coughing and spluttering, my mask fogged up like I'm on stage at an old *Top of the Pops* taping. I sit down in the sand and catch my breath. That was BRILLIANT.

Wiping off a trail of snot and gobbing into my mask again (maybe it's not such a bad thing this isn't happening on my honeymoon, after all) I head back in.

This time, I don't bother trying to alert anyone else to the fish I see, instead I just 'MMMMM!' and point for my own benefit. I could spend every hour of the rest of this whole trip doing this. I could travel to every ocean and never do any other activity ever and just float about being part of their world. I wonder if *Adventure Awaits* would like a snorkelling correspondent on their books.

But after a while someone taps me on the leg and I look up to see that Yuya is waving for us all to come in.

'Did you see the fish the colour of rainbows?' I ask one of the little boys who I've fallen into step next to as we reach the shallower water and push our legs to reach the shore.

'Those are called parrot fish,' he tells me in a loud, happy voice. 'They poop sand and they save coral because they eat the algae off it. They spend *all day* eating.'

'That's a nice life,' I reply.

'They're my favourite.'

I agree. 'Mine too.'

Up on the beach, Yuya is handing out chocolate bars, and I realise I'm famished. So is everyone else by the looks of it, because we all sit facing the sea, sand in our bottoms, and chomp down on our choccie.

'How did you like it?' Yuya asks, taking a seat next to me and handing me a bottle of acai berry juice.

'I liked that ...' How do I put this into words? 'I liked that so much that for every minute I was out there it felt like I was cancelling out an hour of anything bad. Can we go back in?'

'Yes,' he says, but reaches out to stop me as I stand. 'But not here.'

A short drive back on the bus, at which point I remember to stop filming on my phone (oops, that would take some editing this evening before I run completely out of storage), and Yuya files us all onto a little boat for a trip out to Manta City!

I know this sounds like a shopping mall, but it's actually an area with a really high concentration of manta rays off the northern coast of Ishigaki Island. Yuya warns us that it's not quite prime manta-viewing season yet, but the warm weather has brought a few in early, so we might get lucky and, if not, it's another place to see fish.

The boat ride is short and sweet, just enough time to slap on some more sun lotion and let the ocean breeze whip my hair into a candy floss of tangles, but I don't give two hoots about that. I close my eyes and let the salty spray hit my face, ready to dive back in the minute I'm given the okay to do so.

When the boat pulls to a stop, bobbing on the surface, we're expected to slide out of the back. Yuya holds onto my arm to help me down, my breathing shallower, not just from the cooler sea this little bit further away from the coast, but because of exactly that: that we're that little bit further away from the coast. I can't touch the bottom here even if I wanted to – I'm in open water.

Before I let my thoughts get the better of me I dip my face under the surface, and this time the hidden world is bathed in a shining sapphire blue. A school of yellowy-black fish take a group tour over the coral, several metres below me. A parrot fish swims by and gives me a high five.

Okay, maybe it doesn't give me a high five, but it feels like it, and anemones wave about as if they're doing the hula.

I'm counting the number of different coloured fish I can see when I sense something bigger and darker creeping along into my eyeline, like seeing a plane on a summer's day, but from below. And there she is, Ms Manta Ray, drifting along like a boss, huge and shadowy, with rippling fins and a long spear for a tail. She's stunning. In fact, I have no idea if she's a she or not, but I want to move like her in the world.

I stay completely still and watch her disappear into the blue as quickly, or should I say slowly, as she appeared.

I surface and tread water for a moment, letting it all sink in. Pulling my mask up onto my head and spitting out my snorkel, I bring the waterproof casing up so my phone is level with my face.

'I don't know if the audio will get through this case, or whether you would have seen any of that, but we just met a manta ray. I can't ... I can't believe I nearly didn't do this.' I look off to the side, back towards Ishigaki, and it's all a little overwhelming. So I turn back and smile to the camera. 'I'm very lucky.'

Later on, back at my guesthouse when editing my videos together, I see that not only did the camera catch the manta ray, but because of how it dangled in the water, my phone saw her before I did. You can see my shaky finger point in her direction at the exact point I notice her looming behind me. I hadn't realised what a big smile she had!

Also, the audio didn't pick up, but what did was the big mask ring around my face, and the trail of snot hanging from my nose.

I take a little drive on my last morning in Ishigaki en route to dropping my car off at the airport. I've been meaning to come to Tamatorizaki Observation Point since arriving on the island, but alas I was too busy burying myself in the sand and scurrying in and out of the sea on the beach by the guesthouse with the borrowed snorkel and mask.

And then this morning, I did a whoopsie again. I was packing up my things when I couldn't stop my fingers doing the devil's work, and just like that I was back on Katie's Instagram page, scouring her latest pictures for clues of just how together she was with my man. Was he with her in any pictures since the pub one? No, just a couple of quite pretty photos of herself in a flower meadow. Had Matt liked them? One of them, yes. Had he posted anything of the same meadow, a sure sign that it would have been him taking the portraits? No. Still nothing new on his feed.

I was this close to going down a rabbit hole, my happiness drifting towards the open window on the breeze, when I managed to shut down the app and stand back, pulling my happiness back inside and shaking off the anxiety. And that's when I made the decision to leave for the airport early and come here.

I pull up at the small car park below my destination and put on my sunglasses. The air is sticky-warm today, a little nudge and wink towards the summer weather that will follow soon.

I follow the curve of the path as it winds around the cliffs, past the palms and the ferns that spread out from their places and tickle my ankles, until the view on my right opens out and I can see the sea in all her shiny glory again.

The closer I get on the short walk to the Observation Point, the more pristine the pathway gets, with greenery trimmed back, a short wooden fence alongside a manicured hillside. And when I reach the stone-walled gazebo at the summit, the island opens out in a panorama in front of me. I have lush mountains and hills behind me, a peninsula stretching away surrounded by slivers of sand and white frothing waves, flat green fields with orange rooftops dotted among them, the ocean – the wide, sparkling ocean – showing off its marbled turquoises of the coral reefs and more muted blues of the deeper seas further out.

I take a big lungful of warm, tropical air, pleased as punch to have made it down here. When Kaori first talked about the island, I never expected to have found more than simply a place to relax for a few days. What I found was a renewed sense of adventure, more wonderful people and, I think, a step towards finding some *ikigai*?

Today, I'd be heading back to the mainland, to cities and trains and many more experiences I'm sure I can't even imagine yet. Will I find anything I love as much as snorkelling?

I take a last, long, drink of the island. Come on, Charlotte, let's go and find out.

Chapter 11

There's nothing like a
Little bit of perspective
To live a little

My mini summer holiday within a holiday has been amazing, exactly what I needed. After the rollercoaster of emotions whizzing around me, from feeling free and alive in Tokyo to crashing down to loneliness in Kyoto like a dip after a sugar high, I am happy to say that I'm now feeling a little more reset.

My train chuffs its way along the Japanese countryside from Osaka airport to the city of Hiroshima. Had I remained on the Honeymoon Highlights tour I would have done this destination by now and would already be heading north. I wonder what Flo and Lucas, Cliff and Jack, and Kaori are doing right now ...

I spent the flight back from Ishigaki editing together some of my extra footage from the island, and when I uploaded it to Instagram using the airport Wi-Fi as I waited for my train, I spotted something that made me feel a little proud, actually!

My videos were being watched by a lot of people, more than the usual amount that visit my page. It helped that I was starting to add hashtags, and I guess a lot of people will be visiting the country when the Olympics take place, so I'm not saying it's because of me, but still … chufty badge.

I've planned three nights in Hiroshima, two full days, and then on the third day I'll be taking a long day of travelling to get the trains right back up to Nagano, an area sort of central within the main Honshu island of Japan, which is really mountainous and beautiful, by the looks of it. And there are monkeys who sit in hot springs; that's my main reason for wanting to go.

Back to the present, since I'll be rolling into Hiroshima station in the next ten minutes or so. Outside the window the view has become more urban, but enveloped with the protective embrace of green-covered hills around the city. One of the things I can't wait to see while I'm here is the Miyajima Shrine, one of the most iconic views of Japan, but that will have to wait until my last day because with no set plans to follow I'm leaving that until the day with the sunniest forecast, so I can see the colours in all their glory.

Ding. My phone alerts me to a new private message on Instagram. Thomas Day. That name sounds familiar. I hope it isn't because I've seen him on the news as a serial sex pest and I'm about to open a dick pic.

Hello Charlotte!

Hope you don't mind me getting in touch, and if you don't remember me, hope you don't mind me sliding into your DMs – I promise I'm not a creep! We met just before Christmas at the Adventure Awaits recruitment day? We swapped Instagram handles after pairing up during the awkward journalist–reader role play, though if we're both being honest I think you were just humouring me when you said you were interested in seeing my travel photos, ha ha.

Right, I do remember him! Of course I do. Thomas, with the dark-stubbled face and big smile. Thomas, with the kind eyes that sparkled with excitement when we talked about his next big trip to the US and the sights he wanted to see and photograph, and mine to Japan, and how he wanted to stay in touch so I could tell him all about it.

Anyway, I'm pretty sure you're the Charlotte who got the internship over at the main magazine, and if so, congratulations!

If not, this is even more awkward that the role play. When Amanda sent me an email about our (?) first day she just mentioned 'Charlotte'. I wondered if it was you, and then I watched your video the other day and you said something about starting at a magazine when you're back from your holiday, so ... here I am!

Anyway, just wanted to say hey, and looking forward to catching up on day one.
Thomas (Day)

That was so nice of him to get in touch. I'd all but forgotten our encounter at the recruitment day, but I genuinely wouldn't have landed the internship without his help.

7 December, last year
Saturday morning, 10.40am

My palms were sweating and I couldn't stop touching my hair. I knew I couldn't, every time I went in for another fiddle I scolded myself, but then went in again. Mara would have smacked my hand out of the way for me, but she wasn't here, it was just me.

Me, and about thirty other hopefuls. I looked around the room, where we were all peacocking like IRL-influencers, trying to have the most winning smiles, the biggest laughs, the most serious, studious faces when listening to the recruiters. I tugged at the sleeve of my grey blazer, looking stuffy among the others in their peach blouses and flamingo-print skirts. They looked a lot more like they'd fit in at a schmancy London travel magazine headquarters than dowdy old me.

This was so not the place for me. I mean, I wanted it to be, but I'd never been to a recruiting event before and I hadn't mentally prepared for how cut-throat it would feel.

I texted Matt: I don't know what to do, everyone is just standing around at the moment networking but I don't know who to talk to.

He replied instantly. Talk to anyone. Literally anyone. But get off your phone!

Shit, he was right, I hoped nobody saw and jammed my phone back into my suit trouser pocket immediately and looked around for someone to chat to.

'Do you want to see something embarrassing?'

And there was my someone. He was tall, with dark hair pushed to the side and a stubbly beard, but in a smart yet relaxed way; he didn't look scruffy. Far from it. He was, like me, buttoned into a sharp grey suit, he even had a tie. The other guys striving to land a job at the end of the Adventure Awaits *group's recruitment day were in a rainbow of sky-blue linen, forest-green moleskin, cool khaki slacks.*

He smiled down at me, his hands in his pockets, his eyes kind. 'Do you? Do you want to see something really embarrassing for both of us?'

'What?' I asked.

He looked around like he was checking who was watching and then peeped open his blazer, shifting his tie to the side, and flashed me his shirt underneath. White, with lemons printed on it. A 'colour pop', Brienne would have called it. A quirky little detail in your outfit to stand out but stay professional.

I know ... because I had the same shirt on.

I laughed and covered my mouth. 'So did I accidentally shop in the men's section of H&M, or did you shop in the women's section?'

'I don't know, but I think we're both rocking it.' With that, he unbuttoned his suit jacket and loosened his tie, and stood proudly, his shirt on display. I did the same next to him, and noticed one of the recruiters look over at us, mid-conversation, and smile.

'Thank you, I needed that,' I said, turning back to the man. 'I'm Charlotte.'

'Thomas. You ever been to one of these before?'

'Nope, I'm terrified, you?'

'Same.'

We chatted easily, him telling me that he was into travel photography, me telling him I was more on the travel-writing side. He paid attention when I talked, and his gentle charisma meant that I did the same for him without even trying. Around us, other conversations seemed peppered with darting glances of 'is there someone more important I should be talking to'. But we had all day to impress, and in that moment I was grateful to Thomas for saving me from running away before I'd even tried.

Oh, that's so nice to know that if I do go ahead with the internship, or apply for and get the job, he'll be there too. I shoot off a quick reply, asking how he is, telling him where I am at the moment and then sit back, ready to roll on into a new city.

I've booked into a hostel in Hiroshima, and that's where I head now, a few minutes' walk from the station.

'*Konnichiwa*,' I bow to the receptionist when I walk in, and she doesn't respond for a second, watching the screen of a TV off to the left. I turn to look and see a baseball game being played, and somebody just about to take a massive thwack (you may have guessed I don't know a lot about baseball).

'Oh noooooo,' she says when he missed and then turns to me. '*Konnichiwa*, checking in?'

'Yes, please, I booked a bed in the dorm, *watashi wa* Charlotte *desu*.'

'*Konnichiwa*, Charlotte, welcome to Hiroshima, have you been here before?'

I shake my head. 'First time here, first time in Japan.'

'Do you like baseball?' she asks.

'Sure,' I lie.

'The Zoom-Zoom Stadium is only about ten minutes' walk from here if you want to see a home game by the Hiroshima Toyo Carps.'

I'm not sure what she's talking about, but in the spirit of adventure, maybe I will check this out. Tomorrow. For today I think I just want to get my bearings, and some dinner.

She takes my passport to photocopy and I fill in a few forms, then she gives me a quick tour. 'Big communal space, have a relax in here, this is the kitchen, help yourself to any of the sauces on that shelf, and to the tea. You can rent towels and bikes and a load of other things from us, just let me know if you need anything. Okay?'

'Okay.'

I'm a little sleepy from the travelling, but determined not to fall into the trap I did in Kyoto – crawling into bed on arrival – so I go for a quick shower, washing the last grains of Ishigaki sand down the drain, and head out into Hiroshima.

As I pass reception, I reach past a group of Japanese guys a couple of years younger than me who are checking in, and take one of the free maps on the counter.

Outside, I take a long walk beside the Enko River, one of several rivers that ribbon their way around the city. I pass sparkling office buildings, quiet parks, blue water and green trees, the grey tips of Hiroshima Castle in the distance. I have no destination in mind for my walkabout, I'm just letting my legs take me on an adventure.

The next day, I wake early and head into the city before breakfast, wishing to reach my destination for today before any crowds arrive.

In 1945, Hiroshima was mostly destroyed by the first atomic bomb during the Second World War. Today I'm going to visit the hypocentre.

The morning is sunny, the rivers gentle and the streets quiet. I cross the Kamiyanagi Bridge and make my way towards the Hiroshima Peace Memorial Park. This was once the city's commercial heart, but four years after the bombing it was decided to turn the area into a place for remembrance.

I see what they call the 'A-Bomb Dome' first, one of the only structures left standing due to being directly under the bomb; today, the metal and stone ruins are a UNESCO World Heritage Site.

I stand for a while on the edge of the Motoyasu river, looking up at the dome, shielding my eyes from where the sun glints off the metal frame. Things like this ... they have a way of putting things into perspective. I turn, and head for the bridge that will take me into the memorial park itself.

Thousands and thousands of birds, all colours of the rainbow, rest in glass cases beside the Children's Peace Monument. The origami cranes, intricate folds of paper delicately constructed and sent to Hiroshima from all over the world, are an ongoing tribute to a little girl named Sadako Sasaki who died from radiation poisoning-related leukaemia in 1955. Sadako believed a Japanese tradition that folding a thousand paper cranes would bring a wish, and her wish before she passed away was world peace.

I walk through the Peace Memorial Park, exploring the monuments and taking in the history, though it's hard to imagine how the city looked all those years ago compared to the metropolis here today.

My heart tells me it needs to process what I've seen this morning and reflect before moving on with thoughts of adventures. I stand on the edge of the park and wonder what to do with myself. What will take up the afternoon but requires little noise or action. I could visit a gallery or museum; I hear Hiroshima has some fantastic art. I could see if there's a baseball game but ... I'm not really in the mood. I mean, I can think of something I'd like to do, but whether I could arrange it on short notice ...

Spotting a sign for an information centre nearby I trudge over and stand in a queue. And after a near-miss where I almost booked myself onto a three-day tea-making expedition, I manage to secure an open spot on a traditional Japanese tea ceremony, which sounds exactly what I need.

Not least because I'm busting for a cuppa.

The directions the information assistant gives me lead me out of Hiroshima City itself and towards a port town called Tomonoura, a short train and bus ride away.

When I step off the bus, I could be back in Europe at a Mediterranean fishing village. The sunlight pools yellow, reflecting off the stones and pathways, and small boats bob on the water in the harbour. Islands pop out of the glittering sea and fishermen string lines of sea bream out to dry in the afternoon spring air. As I follow my directions through the neat, sleepy alleyways, I love how off the beaten track it all feels.

I reach the outside of what I think is the teahouse I'm heading to, and it's a low building bathed in sunlight, with sloping roofs and a stone pathway leading to the door. Beside the pathway is a small wooden sign with 茶 の湯 carved onto it. I remember that first character being associated with tea, because it makes up the second part of the word *ocha* (お茶 – tea). And the only reason I remember that is because I associate the little character with looking like it was a 'T' inside a house. And Japan has a lot of teahouses. Bear with me, okay.

So if tea is there on the sign, and this is where my directions lead me, I'm reasonably confident I'm not going to walk up to a random villager's door and demand a cuppa. I doubt it says, 'Move on, tourist, no tea here for you today'.

Later on, I'll realise this sign literally says 'Way of the Tea', while pointing me towards the teahouse, so it really couldn't have been clearer.

Following the pathway, I reach the door, where a stone basin and scoop invite me to wash my hands before entering. The gardens are so simple, all neutral tones of beige and green, no fancy flowers, no strongly perfumed shrubberies. And looking at the building itself, it follows the same colour palette, with clean lines and humble decoration.

Tea ceremonies in Japan are quite special and sacred, so thanks to me planning for Matt and I to partake in one during the Honeymoon Highlights tour – and knowing what a bumbling idiot he could be at times – I'm pretty clued up on the etiquette I need to follow. Probably not perfect, but I'll try.

The doorway is purposefully low, and when my host, dressed in a deep sea-blue kimono, meets me at the entrance and beckons me inside, I bow, as I'm supposed to in order to show humility, and remove my shoes.

For Brits, who drink 40,000 cups of tea per day, their home or office kitchens a steam-filled conveyer belt of PG Tips being dunked and squeezed, the 'way of tea' in Japan wouldn't really work. Here, it's a careful, intricate, drawn-out ritual to appreciate every moment and every drop. Here, it is perfect.

It turns out I'm the only one here for today's ceremony, a bonus for getting a little further away from the hubbub of the city. I take a seat inside the tearoom on the tatami mat floor. Natural colours of creams and browns add a calming serenity to the room, the only decoration being an alcove with a hanging lilac calligraphy scroll, and the delicate ceramic and bamboo equipment that my host is setting out in front of us.

Using a cloth plucked from her kimono, she cleans the equipment methodically in front of me while I watch. The process reminds me of those fireplace videos you can watch on Netflix, where there isn't a lot of action but it's just lovely to gaze at and experience.

Flavoured KitKat's aside, I think I'm about to try matcha for the first time. She reaches a teeny scoop into a pot and pulls out a spoonful of green powder, which she then stirs with a cool little bamboo whisk into some water. I've been fancying jumping aboard the trendy matcha train for a while so this is very exciting. And then she pulls out some little lilac blobby nibbly things and, well, you know I like food. I can't stop thinking about them.

'*Amai?*' I whisper, '*sweet?*' because I'm not sure if I'm allowed to say anything.

But my host meets my eyes and smiles, nodding.

I then point to the tea. '*Nigai?*' I ask, which I think is the word for bitter, though whether I'm using it correctly is anyone's guess. But she nods again, and then puts on the floor in front of me a little bowl filled with the green matcha tea.

She passes me one of the sweets first, a fruity jelly globe which is yum, and then gestures for me to drink the tea. Now, have I remembered the next bit correctly? I watch my host for signs of shock and horror in case I bugger it up, but I reach out for the bowl with my right hand, place it in my left hand, turn it so the front is facing away from me, and take a sip.

Oh, it is a little bitter! Nice, but, well, I'm glad for that sweetie.

After a few sips I return the bowl to the mat and bow low, thanking my host.

We sit in a companionable silence for a while, drinking more tea, and enjoying the tranquillity, and when I notice the light outside beginning to fade from yellow to mauve, I decide I'd better leave this little fishing village and make my way back into Hiroshima. I leave the way of the tea in Tomonoura, but keep the way of tranquillity with me.

One day, I'd like to live somewhere I can catch a ferry to and from work. Can I do that in London? I think that some people do. And if I don't go to London ... maybe it won't be so bad. As I sit here the following morning, leaving Hiroshima City and sailing the ten minutes to Miyajima Island, I feel worrisome thoughts drift away in the breeze, like broken spider webs. And it feels good.

My hair will be a haystack by the time we arrive, but I refuse to go inside, instead leaning my arms on the side of the ferry, face to the sun, waiting for us to be close enough for me to see one of Japan's official top three views.

I wonder who picks the top three views ... surely dream views mean something different for each person, and I wonder what would be my own so far in Japan.

The view under the surface of the water on Ishigaki, for sure. The view of the moon garden from the veranda of Kiyomizu-dera Temple in Kyoto. And what else …

When I see a glint of bright vermillion centred in the azure water, I stand up straighter, and get my phone out to take some footage. I think I just found my what else, and I might just agree with the mystical top three list creators.

The Itsukushima Shrine's *torii* gate appears to float during high tide, and if you'd ever casually flicked through a Japanese holiday brochure, as you do, you will absolutely have spotted this. And here it is, in real life! It's fifty foot of wooden gloriousness and I bow my head at it a little, just in case I'm supposed to from this distance.

Stepping off the ferry and onto the island, I join the other passengers in taking 10 million photos and fourteen hours of video footage before dragging my gaze away to go and explore the rest of the shrine, and the island. What would my top three views have been if I'd never come to Japan? That's a question I'm happy that I don't have to worry about.

I'm really loving this bright, orangey red on the shrines. It causes the bridges and the tunnels and the buildings to pop with colour in a way you rarely see elsewhere. I spend a happy few hours on Miyajima, making videos, taking pictures, exploring the shrine, which even has a whole room dedicated to barrels of sake! I wonder if I'll try any more sake on this trip. Probably shouldn't just start helping myself to this collection, though.

I follow a walking trail up to the Tahoto pagoda, passing deer on the way, and reach a viewpoint that lets me experience the beauty of Japan laid out in front of me, with the *torii*, the islands, a few cherry blossom and this beautiful sixteenth-century structure. Hiroshima City glitters in the distance, strong and proud.

I lift my head to the sun and take a deep breath. There's something about this city that makes me want to be the same. It makes me want to live a little.

Chapter 12

Lit from within, and
Actually I'm not thinking
About you at all

I'm back in the hostel early evening, squished deep inside an armchair in the communal lounge just off reception when I hear a lot of chatter in Japanese. I look up from the tattered Jackie Collins novel I found on a 'take one leave one' bookshelf that it looks like many people have loved before me and try and catch a word or two. I keep hearing the word for six, and one, and sorry, but that's about all I can distinguish.

'Excuse me,' the woman who checked me in at reception is leaning over her desk, calling to me.

'Me?'

'Yeah, hello English girl.'

'Hello.'

'Do you want to go sake tasting?'

What? 'When?'

Rather than the receptionist, it's a Japanese guy with playful eyes, a cute face and caramel-coloured let-me-run-my-hands-through-that hair who pokes his head around the corner, causing me to sit up in my chair and stop picking at my spot. He's dressed in jeans and a white, slim-fit shirt, rolled up at the sleeves, open at the collar, with a flash of olive skin peeping out at me and I hold his gaze for a fraction longer than is appropriate of me. He grins at me and my loins melt a little, if that's a thing and not something to be worried about, medically. 'Now,' he says. 'With us.'

I put my book down and clear my throat. 'What?'

The receptionist continues to holler at me. 'The guys have booked a sake tasting but the tour company won't go unless there is a minimum of six people and they are only five.'

Cute guy adds, 'If you don't come with us, everything will be ruined.'

'Everything?'

'*Everything.*'

I mean, I did have big plans to get a vending machine ramen and take it out to eat it next to the river, but I suppose I could go drinking with a bunch of strange men instead? Is that dangerous? Probably. I'm still weighing up the decision when a couple more of cute guy's friends emerge from around the corner. They all look to be about my age, or perhaps a bit younger, and they're all smiling at me encouragingly.

The receptionist comes out from behind the desk, holding a phone in her hand and covering the receiver. 'If it helps, the tour guide is a woman, and that one there,' she points at one of the other four guys who have now all edged into the common room to see who their mysterious chaperone might be. 'That one is my little brother. You will be safe. And he and his friends will divide the cost of your tasting.' She talks sharply to the one she pointed to, who looks a little put out at, presumably, being told they have to cover my costs if they want to drag me along so they can still go.

This is new territory for me in so many ways. I've spent my whole life with an entourage of siblings, my boyfriend, my close circle of friends. I've never gone to a party on my own. I've never walked into a room and had to make friends without at least one friendly face already by my side. I've always thought of that as a good thing, but maybe I was wrong. *Catch every adventure*, Ariel Cortez once told me. And I suppose sake tasting in Hiroshima is a little more adventurous than ramen eating by a river, so ... bugger it! I agree, and before I know it a bus is pulling up outside, I've barely had time to haul my arse back to my room to change into something more appropriate for nightlife (which is basically just the one going-out top that I brought with me, underneath a black sweater), and we're off.

Caramel-haired hot guy sits next to me on the bus, and introduces himself as Riku.

'Hi, Riku, I'm Charlotte.'

'*Hajimemashite*, Charlotte.'

'So why is this sake trip so important to you all?' I ask him.

'It's kind of my fault,' he admits. 'We are all at university, but this summer I'm moving to the US to do a year abroad – I study engineering with English language. This is a vacation week in Japan, and it's going to be the last time we can all be together for a while. We're all studying in Tokyo, but none of us had visited Hiroshima before now, and we get free accommodation through my friend's sister at the hostel.'

'So they want to send you to foreign lands with one last sake knees-up?'

'Why are my knees up?' he asks, looking down at his legs.

'No, it's just an expression.'

'Like this?' Riku brings his knees up towards his chin, tucking himself into a strange ball between the seats of the minibus.

I laugh with him. 'No, you don't need to actually put your knees up, it's an expression, I mean you are going to have one last night of sake-style fun together.'

He unfolds himself, looking shy but pleased at having made me laugh. 'Yes, you get it, I knew you would be a good companion. Where are you from?'

'England. Your English is very good, by the way.'

'My mother spent a long time in England before having me, so I've grown up trying to learn it really well. How come you're in Japan on your own?'

I pause. 'Well,' I start, quietly. He leans in towards me a little and, if I'm going to be completely honest with you, I want to push that lock of hair out of his face and go in for a kiss. What is wrong with me! My whole life I have never so much as looked at another man who wasn't Matt. No need to take that too literally; I do have a minor ogling obsession with the Hemsworths. But I have never found myself cosying up to a stranger that I met in a hotel reception, especially not a stranger with such soft, dark eyes ... I realise that Riku is staring back at me, waiting for my response, and in a snap decision, I choose to not to be a Debbie Downer and regale him with my sorrowful tale, so instead I say, 'Just having an adventure.'

Ammmm I flirting? I think I might be. I think those teen mags I used to read, when I wasn't nose deep in my travel mags, would probably say that yes, all this flittery eye contact and leany-leany-body language is indeed a dash of flirtation. I kind of like it, it makes my heart race. And what's more, he's flirting back.

It turns out, a sake tasting is quite the thing to do in Hiroshima; they even have sake districts, which people visit on day trips and where you can hop from brewery to brewery. We, instead, are going to a sake bar in downtown Hiroshima and our guide will talk us through different sakes from these same breweries. Riku says there'll be food as well, which is jolly good news.

'Have you tried sake before?' he asks me.

'Yeah,' I say, though I must have made a bit of a face because he laughs.

'It's not everybody's favourite. To be honest with you, we would usually drink beer, but this is a bit of fun. I'm sorry now for any silly behaviour. Sake tends to sneak up on you.'

'Don't be – nothing wrong with a bit of silly behaviour,' I say, without meaning that to sound quite so coquettish. You know what, actually, I fully meant it to.

The bus stops and I look out to see crowds of locals and visitors filling the street, dark skies above and those neon lights glowing all around me. It's certainly busy, and when we get off the bus, our guide, Moko, leads us straight into an adjacent bar where we all have to duck to get in and go straight down a flight of stairs. Riku reaches behind him and takes my hand, just to keep us all together, of course, but it sets my heart ping-ponging. I haven't had my hand held for ... well, it feels like for ever. It's only been a month or so, really, but when you get used to having someone hold it every day and then they're gone, I guess I'd been reaching out to feel that touch again without even realising it. There is a split-second where I don't know how I feel. It could go either way. I could either lean into it, or make my excuses and go home. I let him hold it as we move through the crowded bar, feeling comfortable but also electric, and at one point, just for a fleeting second, Riku glances behind him and holds my gaze. He half-smiles and turns back in the direction he's moving and it's everything I have not to let my fingers squeeze into his. If this were a teen movie, that bit would have been in slow motion, and to be honest I kind of feel like I am in a teen movie right now.

'We'll sit here,' Moko calls to the group politely for my benefit, and then repeats the same in Japanese. She points towards three empty seats at the bar and leans in to say into my ear so she can be heard, 'My English is not good, I'm sorry.'

'No, it's fine, you weren't expecting me to be on this tour. I'll figure it out, please don't worry.' God, everyone has been so nice to me since I got to Japan. I remember how nervous I was getting on the plane about not speaking enough Japanese, but it hasn't been an issue at all. Everyone has been so accommodating and kind, continuing to apologise that they don't speak enough English, when my grasp of their language is so clearly appalling. There are seven of us, including Moko, and three seats, so before I can even protest, Riku angles himself beside one of the barstools and gestures for me to sit.

'No, you sit down, it's your thing, I'll stand at the back.'

'Please, I insist,' he grins. 'I can stand behind you.'

Well ... okay. The room is too loud and jostley to have a ten-minute debate about it, so I climb up onto the stool facing the bar and Riku rests on the back of it.

Moko leans across the bar to the bartender, speaking to him and showing him a piece of paper, which I'd guess is a booking confirmation, and whoosh, all of a sudden seven little cups, almost like egg cups, are placed in front of us, and the barman is unscrewing a bottle, decanting the almost clear liquid into them. He explains the type of sake and Moko repeats it to the boys. I catch the word *amai*.

'Sweet?' I ask Riku.

'I'm sorry, what?' he says back and leans in closer, so my lips are near his ear.

'Sweet?' I repeat. *'Amai?'* Oh my.

'Yes!' he cries, and reaches past me to pick up a cup. *'Kanpai!'* He cheers first me and then the others.

I knock back the sake and only realise afterwards that that is clearly not how you're supposed to do it, because everybody else has taken a sip and I'm trying not to cough my guts up. 'It's very nice,' I wheeze, and the barman laughs and tops up my cup.

Riku holds my cup up for me again and I take it. He brings his towards his mouth and says, 'Like this. *Kanpai.'*

Gently he clonks his cup against mine and then sips, and I watch him like I'm being a very good student when all I'm really thinking is ...

Seriously, what is wrong with me tonight?

Or ... what is right with me? It's not that strange that I'd be feeling an attraction to a good-looking guy again when Matt and I haven't been together for over a month, is it? When Brienne broke up with her boyfriend last year, she watched *Magic Mike* every day for seven weeks, until we had to have an intervention because I found her looking at flights to Las Vegas and wearing a backwards cap.

I'm not saying I'm sitting here wanting Riku to be my new boyfriend, but I am a straight woman, and he is a man and he is just, well, delicious. And it's nice to feel a spark again in my cold, dead, crumbled heart.

'*Kanpai*,' I reply to him and we both take a sip. This time I can feel the sweet, but not too sweet, liquid dispersing in my mouth, exploring the flavour, like a wine. It's much more palatable this way, and I quite like it. Luckily. Because inadvertently I'm now one-up on all the other drinkers.

'Do you like it?' I ask Riku.

'I do like it,' he replies. 'Not my favourite-ever sake, but nice. Do you?'

'I like it more than the one I tried at home. So all the sakes we're trying tonight are local?'

'I think so.'

Somebody bumps into Riku from behind and he sways towards me a little, steadying himself by leaning more against me. 'I'm so sorry,' he says. 'Are you okay? It's busy in here.'

'That's fine,' I say, shuffling a little to make way for him by turning my body, and oh no, I guess I'll have to rest my arm on his arm.

The barman serves us another sake, this time from a different bottle, and Riku listens to the description before turning to me and repeating it for my benefit. 'So this sake is from a place called Kure, which is on an island an hour or so from Hiroshima. It should be really good, being from there.'

This one is cloudier and I take a sniff before sipping, breathing in an almost tropical scent. I sip and taste sweet coconut, but I could be imagining that because of the coconut milk look of it. 'I really like this one,' I say to nobody in particular.

The music, the noise, the closeness in the bar, and yes, the alcohol content in the drinks, is all adding to the fun, intimate atmosphere. At one point, warmed from the inside with the rich sake, I take a moment to soak in the surroundings.

I am here, in a city in Japan, living my life. Being in a downtown bar, drinking with some Japanese boys, one boy in particular, isn't how I imagined my honeymoon would be a few months back, but is it worse? I look at Riku, I drink my sake, I breathe in the thick air and I let the sound of Japanese chatter and music fill my ears. No, it isn't worse. It's new.

With every cup of sake, Riku and I move closer together, and I don't think either of us are doing it by accident. What started with his arm on the back of the barstool, and then my arm on his, has slowly, slowly moved to his arm being around my back and my hand on his shoulder, leaning into him.

We've moved onto some bolder sake now, apparently, from the Saijo region which is the main mecca for sake in Hiroshima. The sweet sake is a thing of the past, and now we're onto a butterscotch-hued version which punches like whisky. Cor blimey.

How many sakes have we tried now? Maybe six? We've sure been at this bar a while. Mmmmm.

'I think I need a sake break,' says Riku. 'May I buy you a beer?'

'Sure,' I agree. I could do with something cold and refreshing; it's hot in here. While he orders a round for the group, I listen to the music, which is kind of Japanese hip-hop. I've not heard it before, but I like it, it's got a good bass and the melody has me loosening up, dancing a little in my seat.

When Riku passes me a cold bottle of Asahi he adds a warning. 'Charlotte, I need to tell you before you drink this. Sake won't give you *too bad* a hangover but when we add beer, well, make sure you drink a lot of water before you go to bed tonight, okay?'

I laugh. 'Okay, will do.'

'Are you in one of the dorm rooms at the hostel?' he asks and I think, *damn boy, nice segue.*

'I am,' I reply boldly, and take a drink from the beer. 'Are you?'

I see him breathe in, trying not to blush, looking over my whole face with those deep eyes and considering his answer. But he plays a safe shot and says, 'I'm just saying, you don't want to feel ill in a room full of other people. Drink water.'

Okay, I nod. And we have a moment of eye contact. I love this part, the flirty looks, the loaded words, the back and forth. It's just a little bit of very intense fun, and I laugh out loud and give him a wink and command in reply, 'Drink.'

Riku and I both lift our beers to our mouths and after all that mouth-coating sake the frosty, bitter bubbles cleanse my palate.

Riku's friends are laughing their heads off as they order what I gather is a really strong shot of something for themselves but I wave a no. Think I'll just mix the two drinks tonight, as I have an epically long train journey tomorrow.

After Riku knocks back his shot he pulls me into him, pressing his face against my hair. 'Wooo,' he says. 'That was so strong. Don't let me drink any more of those, Charlotte.'

'I can't promise that,' I put my hand up to hold onto his left, which is dangling around my shoulders and he laces his fingers into mine. 'You're having fun with your friends, right?' I ask him. 'Don't feel you have to talk to me.'

'I'm having a great time,' he answers, and I pretend not to hear him so he has to get really close to me.

Riku, who I suspect may be on to my tricks, let's a small grin twinkle across his mouth before moving his mouth right up next to my ear. Letting go of my hand with his left, he replaces it with his right hand, so now we're face-to-face. With his left hand he tucks my hair behind my ear and lightly holds the back of my neck in place while he leans into me and talks to me. I'm tingling against his body and could really do with just lying in the middle of the floor and taking a minute. 'I'm having a great time,' he repeats, his breath sweet wine. 'Are you?'

'Yes.'

His fingers linger a moment longer at the back of my neck, and for an instant of time we're locked in a dance, the tango that is happening between people enjoying nightlife all over the world right now. But at the same time, in that moment, it's just him and me and we breathe together, not knowing what the rest of the night holds, but knowing we're too far into the dance to pretend it isn't happening.

One of his friends pulls at Riku, causing him to drop his hand, and they want to pose for a photo together.

'Charlotte, come in the photo,' Riku calls, his hand still stretched out and holding mine.

'No, no, I'll take one of all of you.' I take the phone that's being passed over and the boys crowd together, piled onto each other, a happy bunch of tipsy friends.

'Now one of you two,' Moko says, and puts her hand out for my phone.

I hand it over and Riku passes me my sake cup, which still has a small dribble of the strong stuff left in, and we pose with our heads together, and then he says '*Kanpai,* Charlotte,' to me again, and we clink our cups and drink the remainder of the alcohol, keeping contact with each other's eyes.

Afterwards, when Riku excuses himself to use the restroom, I realise Moko has captured the whole thing, not just the posed photo.

'Are they good?' Moko asks. I nod, pleased, and she follows with, 'Your boyfriend is very nice.'

'Oh, he's not— we just met.'

'You should—' Moko runs out of English words, so makes me nearly wet myself with surprised laughter when she uses her fingers to mime sex.

She laughs too and turns back to the bar to order a drink and I look back at my phone, smiling at the photos, and Riku reappears behind my barstool, his body leaning over me from behind while he looks at the photos of us on my screen. He says, over the volume of the bar, 'You should send me those.'

'I will.' I put my phone away and look up at him, studying his jawline, and he glances down at me.

'What?'

'What?'

Here's what I want to do. I want to lift my hands and pull him down to me by the neck. I want to feel his kiss and then maybe just jump him here in the bar. BUT. I'm enjoying the chase too much so rather than tearing into him like some kind of thirsty praying mantis, I'm going to see how it plays out. I'll know when it's the right time.

As we grow further into the embrace of night time in Hiroshima, Riku and I grow closer. I'm not talking about spiritually, I'm talking literally. We stick beside each other, he's my prop when the sake starts to be the reason for my giggles and I'm the one whose shoulders he continues to rest on when he wants to say something to the group but can't quite speak loud enough over the volume in the bar unless he leans right in.

'Let's go,' Riku shouts to the group, and then says it again in Japanese.

It's late and we've been there for hours, but when we step back on to the street, damp so it must have rained, the night feels young. The atmosphere in the street is just as neon as in the bar, and the cold breeze picks my hair up and gives me a thin excuse to bring Riku's arm back around me.

'Oh, it's cold out here,' I say, swaying a little, and Riku – all body warmth and satin skin – wraps his arms around me, pulling me into his chest while we wait for the others to all pile out of the bar too. Ha, oldest trick in the book and worked like a charm.

'Are you feeling okay?' he asks me quietly, like a gentleman. 'You tell me if the sake makes you feel ill or anything, okay?'

'I feel fine, happy,' I reply. 'But also hungry. I could do with soaking up a little of this alcohol.'

'In here,' says Moko at that moment, and we all tumble into a tiny restaurant where the lighting is bright and the seating is tight. At the counter, the chefs are making what looks like stacks of noodles with tortillas on top of a vast *teppan* hot plate.

'Is this *okonomiyaki*?' I ask, realisation dawning. *Okonomiyaki* is a Japanese dish that I've heard is big in Hiroshima, even having its own 'Hiroshima-style' version where all the ingredients of this savoury pancake are stacked up on top of each other, rather than mixed together before cooking.

Before us, the chefs use sharp, straight-ended spatulas to layer batter, noodles, cabbage, egg and meat on top of each other before drizzling with sticky, smoky sauce and sliding it over to the nearest customer.

'Have you had it?' Riku asks and I shake my head. 'It's Hiroshima soul food.'

After we've filled up on *okonomiyaki*, soaking up a little of the alcohol and then replacing it when I go and order another round of bottled beer for us all, Moko addresses the group in Japanese, and whatever she says causes them to all start protesting and shaking their heads, banging their beers on the table. She turns to me and says, 'The tour is finished now,' she laughs.

'Okay, okay,' says Riku calming the others down. 'The tour is over but we don't have to go home, right?' He faces his seat to me and pulls himself forward to be closer to the whole group, and it means I'm sitting with my legs together, between his knees, and his hands rest on the outside of my thighs, and he looks towards his friends and they have a quick discussion in Japanese.

I like his hands on my thighs, and I lean forward, mesmerised by his mouth as he speaks in his native tongue. Mid-sentence he glances over, catching me watching him and simply says, 'Oh my God, you,' and then continues talking, and I nearly pass out.

Among the plans being made, I hear the word *karaoke*, I'm sure of it, and sure enough, Riku then says to me, 'Have you been to a karaoke bar in Japan yet, Charlotte?'

'No, Riku, I have not, I am not very good at karaoke.'

'That's never stopped any of us. Would you like to go? No pressure.'

I look over at Moko. 'Will you come to karaoke?'

She nods an enthusiastic yes. 'I know the best karaoke in Hiroshima.'

'All right then,' I clunk my beer bottle with Riku. '*Kanpai.*'

'*Kanpai!*' Everyone cries, all joining in and clunking their bottles against mine.

'Come on.' He jumps up and holds his hand out for me. Riku tells me it's a bit of a walk, so we stroll the wet streets of Hiroshima's Nagarekawa 'party district', walking under neon signs that curve over the top of the streets and past nightclubs, bars and eateries. Familiar and unfamiliar music pours out into the road, merging together and filling my ears.

We walk hand in hand, this handsome stranger and me, and a part of my hazy mind tries to think of Matt, and walking hand in hand with him. But the tipsy parts of me, which is about 80 per cent of me, pushes that thought away. And I push it away quite easily when I hear Jason Derulo pumping out of one bar and I lead Riku into a twenty-second dance party as we go past.

We're behind the rest of the group now, dropping back, too focused on each other to keep up. On our left beside the bar is a small alley off the main street and

Riku pulls me into it by my hand and spins me so my back is against the wall, which is cold and wet but I don't care. I can feel the music still, the bass pulsating through the stones.

Riku stands in front of me with his hands against the wall, boxing me in, his hair dropping down over his forehead, the olive skin of his upper chest glistening and level with my face.

I meet his eyes and I think this is it, all the heat from the night is between us, and he moves one of his hands down so it's on my side, just above my hip.

We're an inch apart, our mouths closer than that, and though I could freeze this and stay in this position forever, the anticipation is also killing me.

'Riku?' we hear on the breeze. *'Riiiiikuuuuu?'*

'Sounds like we'd better get back to your friends,' I say.

'No, I don't know them, let's stay here.'

'RIKUUU?'

'Come on,' I press my body against him as I push past and take his hand, pulling his arm around my shoulder and we exit the alleyway and catch up with his friends.

We both know this is mainly a fun, physical attraction. I don't know a lot about him, beyond him being kind, inclusive, intelligent and ambitious. But I like all of those things. And maybe he thinks I'm brave, open minded, easy-going and adventurous. I like to think of him feeling that way about me. Mostly, right now, I'm just enjoying how we seem to be making each other glow.

A little further on and we hit the karaoke bar that Moko has been leading us to, and when we enter I see we aren't in your typical British pub with a SingStar hooked up in the corner. Instead we're led to a small private room for the seven of us with microphones, a screen and an electronic menu where one of Riku's friends is already ordering more beer for everyone. The room is intimate and warm, the lighting low and blue-toned, giving the feel of being in a private booth at a nightclub.

Moko starts us off singing, and she has the voice of an angel. I don't know the song but I'm guessing it's by a Japanese pop group, and she sings it like she's part of the band. One of Riku's friends, the one who ordered the drinks, is frozen with his bottle halfway to his mouth.

'Your friend is in love,' I whisper to Riku.

'I have an idea,' says Riku, and when Moko is done, he steps up to the microphone, pulling his friend with him and they launch into the Japanese version of 'Mic Drop' by BTS, and we're all screaming because they're so *hot*.

That might not be why their friends are screaming, I guess, that might be because they're good rather than hot, but I am all about the way Riku is fanning himself with his shirt and spitting verses into the microphone without even needing to look at the prompter.

After that Riku returns to his seat, next to yours truly, and the clocks tip past midnight and into the early hours, music and laughter rolling the time away with us.

We're huddled together on one of the long sofas, our legs tangled together, ignoring the rest of the world.

'You know,' I say into his ear. 'I don't usually follow strange men to karaoke bars.'

'And I don't usually ask strange women to come with me. I guess there's something about you.'

I'm dying to touch his hair. His hand is burning a hole through my jeans by resting just above my bottom, so it's only fair.

I shuffle closer and steady myself with one hand on his chest, my skin touching that triangle of his skin that's been teasing me all night. With my other hand I reach up and take a caramel lock between my fingers. It's soft and a little damp from sweat and using just my fingertips I brush it back into the rest of his hair until my nails graze the back of his head and he shivers a little, making us both laugh.

Riku moves his hand up my back, tilting me towards him and now we're as close as we were in the alleyway, closer even. I hook my hand into his shirt, pulling it a little lower and we both know what we want.

And that's when I feel a microphone being prodded into my back.

'Ariana!' says one of Riku's friends, and holds the microphone to my face.

'He told me earlier he thinks you look like Ariana Grande, and now he wants you to sing,' Riku explains.

That is 100 per cent not true, and he is clearly plastered, as the only thing Ariana and I have in common is that we're both brunettes, and I don't even have my hair in a ponytail but hell, if he's dishing out this compliment, I will eat it up.

Just like that, Riku and I are back to the dance, but you know what, I don't mind at all, I will play along. I take the microphone and flip through the touch screen until the opening bars of 'No Tears Left to Cry' come on and I begin singing in my very not-Ariana voice.

As the melody and beat pump through the room and I sing my little broken heart out, I'm having the time of my life. Who knew karaoke could be so fun? I always thought I hated karaoke, but being here with this crowd of excited, non-judgemental, near-strangers in a little room in a Japanese backstreet has changed my mind.

The sake has given me confidence. We're all up and dancing, and I'm strutting my stuff like I really am the princess of pop. I sing to Riku without embarrassment, and I have his full attention. Near the end of the song in a rush of, I assume, booze-endorphins, and much to the whooping of the others, I slide super-close up against him, our bodies pressed together to sing the closing lines. Since I can't keep away I reach back in and sweep a fistful of that sexy caramel hair to the side. He leaves it there, looking exhausted, while I step away and bow.

'Yessss, more Ariana!' someone screams, so they must be drunk too. But within seconds one of the other boys has grabbed the microphone again and has launched into a very skilled version of Nicki Minaj, which has us all up and dancing.

While Riku and his other pals are being a great posse to their Minaj-loving friend, Moko and I have a shimmy together. I think it's safe to say we're all feeling the sake in our systems. Moko is great fun. They're all great fun.

But there's my boy; I feel hands on my hips and turn to see Riku and we dance close in more ways than one, until we find ourselves in a corner, where it's just a little darker.

Riku sits down on the sofa, taking my hands and pulling me with him, so I'm sat on top of him.

His forehead is moist, his hair still pushed to the side, his lips parted and his shirt open an extra button.

'Here we are again,' I say, enjoying watching him watch my lips.

He lets go of my hands and moves both of his to behind my back. I lean forward, propping my forearms on his chest and trace his jawline.

'You make me dizzy,' he says. 'I can't keep away from you.'

'You can't?'

'Can't you tell?'

I move my head closer so that my lips are side-on to his, and say to him, 'I don't know, maybe you're all talk.'

Next to mine his mouth curls into a grin, which I return. 'I'm not all talk.'

'Show me.'

Those hands sweep up my back, up my neck, and into my hair. I take a breath as his lips, still grinning, close in on mine.

He kisses me, strong and soft, squeezing into me and I feel like the both of us can't stop smiling throughout. He tastes of sweet sake and smoky air. He's everything I anticipated, and I like it.

I grab his hair and run my hands over the ripples of his chest and shoulders. He brings his hands down and wraps his arms tightly around my back, brushing my behind, just lightly. And in case you're wondering ... I don't think about how for the first time since I was fourteen years old I'm kissing the lips of someone who isn't Matt. I don't think about how Riku feels different to Matt. All of that comes much later, but for the next two and a half minutes I don't think of Matt even a little bit. I'm not even trying not to, but all I'm thinking about is this moment in time, and this person in front of me.

Yes, I feel weird, but no, I don't feel guilty. Matt and I broke up over a month ago, and I'm not ready to move on – I can't even begin to tell you how much I *don't* want a new boyfriend – but I'm free now. I'm so free. And that means if I want to get a little drunk and do a little kissing with a cute boy, then I have just as much right to do that than any of the things I'm trying on this vacation.

I'm not necessarily trying to claim this in the name of *ikigai*, but imma give Charlotte what she wants.

Uh-oh, we've gone into third person.

He's so cute though and he's only a couple (*cough*, *four*) years younger than me.

We don't leave the karaoke bar for some time, and by the time we do, we all have scratchy voices (and some of us have chapped lips). The yawn-to-not-yawning ratio has gone up so it might just be time to call time.

Riku pauses at a vending machine on the street to get us some water while we wait for taxis to take us all back to the hostel.

I don't want the evening to end. Tonight the neon lights have been on inside me and I've buzzed and glowed and I wouldn't change a second of it. Although ask me that tomorrow because I'm pretty sure I'm going to have a hangover.

In the cab, Riku and I lean our heads together, watching the city rush by, flashes of streetlamps and shop signs illuminating his face in the dark.

'You leave Hiroshima in the morning?' he asks, quietly.

I nod, eyes locked.

'How early?' A wicked twitch in the corner of his lips.

I think I mentioned that I didn't want the evening to end. So I say, 'Not *that* early.'

Chapter 13

Cherry blossom breeze
Bring memories back to me
Monkey stole my shades

I did have to leave early and it's a long journey back on the train from Hiroshima to the city of Nagano, right back up level (ish) with Tokyo. Famed for its snow monkeys and hot springs, I'll be spending at least two or three nights there, and hopefully by the time I leave again this sake hangover will have gone.

Oish, this hangover might even beat the one after my twenty-first, when both Matt and I had to lie face down in our bed for a good twenty-four hours afterwards. Matt had been lovely after we finally got up, doing a run to the shops for bacon and potato waffles, and he must have cleaned up more than his fair share of puke from a couple of party guests who hadn't managed it themselves. He didn't even crash about in a grump like he usually did if I had a hangover, bothered by the fact that

I was trudging through the house like an extra from *The Walking Dead* instead of snapping back to normaldom like he could.

Actually, no, the hangover after my twenty-first was worse, but both were worth it.

I use the journey to think things over, and in doing so, I find a lot of my thinking revolves around my just-been-kissed lips, which curve into a smile.

Ah, Riku. What a yummy interruption you were. We exchanged details but I doubt our paths will cross again, and that's okay, he can stay a happy memory, one of my happiest, and one of the many fireflies that this trip has presented me with that I'll keep in a box in my heart for ever.

I'm rather proud of myself, if I'm honest with you!

Oh that reminds me, I had a text from Brienne last night. I go back and read it again.

Hey Charlie, just checking in at the midway point. We all miss you! I know you need space away and to think but just say the word if you need to chat at all. Saw Matt today moping about – he's grown a bit of a beard and it looks awful on him, just thought you'd want to know. What are you up to tonight?

Smiling to myself at the image of Matt trying to grow a beard I tap back, *Good morning, sunshine! Sorry for not getting back to you last night. I was somewhat occupied ...*

Minutes later, Brienne flashes up again with another message. *DOING WHAT???*

I check the time. *Isn't it the middle of the night in England?*

I don't care, I am wide awake now, girl, tell me what happened.

… I might have done a little kissing …

Brienne stays texting me for the next twenty minutes, asking question after question, but imagine my surprise when I finally get her to go back to sleep and open my Instagram, only to find Mr Weirdy-Beardy himself has made an appearance in my notifications.

Among the handful of new 'likes' for my photos from the past few days, there is Matt's name. So he *is* looking at my Instagram. And the photo he's liked is of me grinning from within a snorkel from a few days ago, which is interesting.

I wait for the heartache to wobble over me but … it doesn't come. I'm not saying I feel good, although I am a little smug that he's seeing what a good time I'm having, but I don't have the craving I did back in Kyoto to start cyber-stalking him. Is this indifference?

Settling back against the train seat and letting my eyes close, I forget my ex-fiancé for now, wallowing in the apathy that comes hand-in-hand with my little sake hangover, and I let the train rumble me forwards.

*

I've made it to Nagano, and these snow monkeys are a *vibe*. I'm transfixed by one gal (or guy) sitting in the steely-grey water of the hot spring, steam rising around her, submerged up to her shoulders and with her eyes closing like she's having a bath and a glass of vino following a bastardly long week at work. She looks serene and deserving, with her khaki fur in chilly, wet spikes around her pink face.

She rubs her eyes. *You've got the weekend to relax now, Karen. You chill, girl.*

And she's not alone, though maybe she wishes she was. Because around her are many of these wild monkeys who live here and wander to and from the natural hot springs of Jigokudani Monkey Park every day of the year. What a life! Three of the dudes are literally propping themselves up at the side of the pool, posing for a line of snapping cameras.

After that loooooong journey yesterday and a sleep interrupted by dreams about Matt and Riku turning out to be long-lost brothers, I boarded a bus early today to get over to the monkey park before too many visitors arrived.

There's a gasp and some whispering and pointing from one of the other visitors this morning, and I follow her line of vision.

I take out my phone and start a video, adding a little quiet commentary. 'Alert, alert, this is not a drill. We have a *baby monkey* going for a swim in the hot spring. He just showed up with his mum and dad and all of us in the crowd are beside ourselves, but in the most restrained way so we don't scare the animals.' I pan to the onlookers, who appear to be holding their breaths. 'Seriously, every one of us watching might pass out with cuteness overload.' I crouch down to get some shots of the baby, plus my favourite relaxing goddess who is now tipping her head back and letting the warmth envelop her.

It looks lush and I want to get in too … wait a minute … 'Hey!'

Someone just tried to slide my sunglasses off my face. I turn to the side to see another young monkey hanging from the fence, little hand stretched out as he tries to pilfer my Primark aviators. 'Excuse me,' I say, keeping my phone on video, holding it low in front of me and hoping I'm getting him in the shot.

He makes eye contact with me and reaches out again, stretching his tiny fingers with determination. 'These are not for you, the frames aren't right for your face,' Guffaw. 'You're not supposed to be over here, why don't you head back into the pool with your mum?'

We're supposed to keep a good distance from the monkeys, but we've also been advised that if they come to us, we should let them, rather than making an issue of it or running away. But I don't think I have to actually give them my sunnies.

When he sees I'm not playing ball, my little monkey pal whizzes back towards his friend, the other baby monkey, and splashes her with hot spring water before screeching and bumbling in the other direction.

I stay for a while, watching the monkeys, some of whom are watching me. The smell of sulphur from the hot spring is in the air, along with the soundscape of bubbling water, padding little feet, sudden happy screeches and the cli-click of long-lens cameras.

Eventually, I tear myself away, feeling inspired to go and have a bath myself. But I know when I get to Mount Fuji, where I plan to stay in a *ryokan* (a traditional Japanese inn) which has its own *onsen* (a Japanese hot spring, but usually for humans not monkeys) it's going to be even better. And like my gal pal in the water, I plan to submerge myself up to my shoulders and let the water help me feel serene and deserving.

Remember how I said Japan has a population of nearly 127 million? I think all of them must be here at my hotel in Nagano. After the serenity of monkey bath time over at the park, I find myself at the back of a long check-in queue that weaves from the reception desk, back and forth like a Disneyland ride, and I swear I can feel the breeze from the lobby door coming in. Looks like I was lucky to get a room yesterday, and I'm glad I booked this in a week ago when I was in Ishigaki. I think I'd be turned away if I'd thought I could just rock up today instead. Thankfully, I'm just queueing to pick up some info on the local area, which now that I've been in the queue for a while I'm wishing I'd just looked up on my phone, but I like to practise a little Japanese when I can.

I wonder why it's so busy? These don't look like business people, so it can't be a convention. And those already checked in seem to be walking briskly through the crowd to the door, clutching cameras and picnics.

And that's when I hear a word I remember learning, *sakura*. It's stirred into several conversations around me, and when the line moves forward a little I notice a big photo board to the right-hand side. Cherry blossoms. They must have opened up here, and *that's* why the crowds have come to town, to admire them.

I've seen a few cherry blossom trees at various stages of bloom while I've been here, but not managed to be in the exact right-place-right-time for the full open experience. This is a really special time for the Japanese and visitors from around the world check forecasts months in advance to try and catch *sakura* season in all its glory. I gather the thing to do is take a picnic and a blanket and sit under the trees, appreciating their fleeting beauty and taking some time out to be with nature. Well, sign me up, you had me at picnic.

Eventually the queue rolls on and I get a map and a guide about some local eateries, and take them up to my room. I send a photo of the monkeys to my siblings, and my mum, and then I pack my day bag with my camera, the little tripod I bought in Hiroshima, the snacks I have left (but I noticed a small essentials store in the lobby so I might pick up a few more), my sunglasses and, on a whim, a pink lipstick I'd been carrying with me since England but had yet to wear. It will coordinate well with the cherry blossoms!

I'm going to take a wild guess that I go left out of the hotel, judging by the quick-footed excitement of the other guests. I'm buoyed up by their keenness and I too have a spring in my step as I follow the path that takes us back on the road, down a hillside and towards where the blossoms must be.

We see the tops at first, a blanket that looks like the field has been swallowed by overflowing foam that's been dyed a pale blush. Then as we descend, the blanket rises, until we're under it looking up at this canopy of pinks and whites and a baby-blue sky that you can only just make out. It's absolutely breathtaking, and I stand there without taking a breath until somebody bumps into me from behind because they've also been staring up.

'*Sumimasen!*' We both laugh – *sorry!* – and I remember to take in a little oxygen rather than pass out and miss the whole thing.

I make my way through the crowd and find a tiny spot under a tree a fair distance from the opening of the park where I lay out my hotel towel (I didn't have a blanket) and crack open my can of coffee. I then slick on my lipstick, totally vibing with nature already, and lie back to look at the scenery.

From this viewpoint, the trees seem tall and proud, though compared to the bamboo trees in Kyoto they're much closer to the ground. But as I lie here I like how they stand, lifting their branches, showing off their finest garments, like teens the first time they dress up for prom and they feel special and for once don't automatically cringe at the compliments. Or like brides on a wedding day.

The folds and the layers of the petals, the sunlight bouncing off the whitest highlights, the elegant ruffle of the branches that is so similar to the sound of thick fabric being shaken out and positioned around you, it was all very much how I expected to feel getting into my wedding dress on the day that never happened.

I lie for a while, giving myself time to feel these feelings and wondering if I'll be able to let them go when it's time, like the branches of these trees will let go of their flowers. Maybe one day it'll happen for me again and perhaps, if the timing is right, I'd incorporate a little cherry blossom in somehow, because no matter what, it keeps finding itself again and coming back.

A thought enters my brain, courtesy of the part of me that is acting as my side-kick and my travel companion while we're away. She shoves in a little memory, designed to make me laugh, about another time in my life that a marriage of mine fell through, and the suddenness of this makes me snort out loud with laughter.

4 May 2003
Saturday, 10am

I appeared at the kitchen door, where my mum was making her fourth batch of marmalade this year. We had way too much marmalade and I didn't think we were ever going to get through it but Mum seemed to think it was very important to make a lot of marmalade now Daddy was gone.

This would cheer her up.

'Mummy?'

She looked up from the pan, her face beaded with sweat from the steam. Her eyebrows jumped up in surprise. 'Well, hello, where are you off to in that fine outfit?'

I twirled for her, showing off her own white cotton nightdress that billowed out from where I'd tucked its too-long length into my knickers. Around the waist was my purple woollen scarf and on my feet were some zebra-print kitten heels I pilfered from the back of Mara's wardrobe that Mum didn't know about yet. 'It's my wedding day.'

'Is it?' Mum said with interest and took off her apron. 'Is the wedding now?'

'Yes, and you're invited!'

'Jolly kind!' She turned off the hob. 'Should I put on a mother-of-the-bride outfit?'

I stared at her like she was mad and pointed at her jeans and jumper. 'You're wearing one.'

'Oh right. Who are you marrying?'

'Benny,' I told her and pointed at my little brother, four years old, sitting on our sofa in the other room where I told him he had to stay. He looked a bit grumpy, but I wouldn't let that ruin my wedding day.

'You're marrying your brother?' Mum clarified. 'Where did you get those shoes?'

I ignored the second question, I'm no snitch. 'Yes, me and Benny will be the mummy and daddy now so you don't have to any more.'

Mum pulled me into a big hug, which could have been because she was pleased she didn't have to make marmalade any more and she held me like that until I said, 'Mum, the vicar is only available for an hour so we should get on with it.'

'Of course, who is the vicar?'

'Mouse.' Mouse was our cat and she'd found a nice spot in the sunshine on the windowsill so I guess that was where we were getting married.

'And Benny, do you want to marry your sister?'

'No,' he replied, folding his chubby little arms across his chest.

'You said you would!' I shouted.

Foreshadowing, amirite?

'If Benny doesn't want to get married that's okay,' said Mum. 'I'm happy to carry on being the mummy.'

I squinted at her, not sure if she was telling me the truth.

Mum continued, 'It would be a shame for your lovely outfit to go to waste, why don't the two of you just have a wedding reception instead? I'll put a CD on and you can have a dance party, how does that sound?'

I sat on the sofa next to Benny. 'Well, Mara's shoes hurt a bit.' Oh look at that, I was a snitch, oops.

'Right-o, then how about half an hour of TV instead, a thank you from me for being so thoughtful.'

Mum didn't have to say TV twice and Benny and I kicked off our shoes and curled up beside each other, instantly glued to Dick and Dom in da Bungalow.

I looked at my brother and reached over to hold his hand, which had unclenched now, and he leant on me, and actually I was glad I didn't marry him today. I think it would have ruined our friendship.

This memory floats about in my head and brings a smile back to my face as I look up at the cherry blossom. I must give Benny a call this evening. He sounded so unlike himself the last time we spoke. After a while just gazing at the view and allowing myself to be present in the moment, my tummy growls, so I sit up.

The park is less crowded now, only just, but I've been lying here a while and the sun is lower in the sky, the cherry blossom beginning to lose that bright reflective light a tiny bit. I pull out my phone to take a bit of footage, which I'll edit together later, and then I turn the camera on myself, lying on my front so the pink flowers are behind my head and I tell my followers a little about what's been on my mind. When I first started these videos it was strange, talking to an unknown quantity of friends, and strangers – and maybe Matt? – about my wedding, or lack thereof. I didn't even like talking to the four people on the Honeymoon Highlights tour about it, it was excruciating for me. Now it feels less effort to be authentic, be myself, and share what's on my mind.

'… So if you've ever wanted to know what it feels like to be wrapped inside the most beautiful, delicate wedding dress, with a soft, floral scent filling your nose and your whole world, then this is the place to come, at this time of year. Because I didn't think it was my time to feel like that, as you know, but this is a pretty good substitute.' I let the camera slide away from my face and point up to the trees. 'No stress, no worrying about the perfect day or sticking to timetables, just enjoying the moment.'

I take a slow walk back to the hotel, feeling in no rush to skirt past the crowds and instead just be swept along back up the hill and into the lobby.

Inside, I round the corner to see a meeting room, it's double doors ajar, with people spilling into the corridor listening to the speaker. Creeping closer, one of the women standing in the doorway catches my eye, and she smiles, and bows her head a little before shifting to the side to let me stand next to her. I bow back and peer in, leaning against the doorframe.

At the front of the room is a couple, perhaps in their fifties, presenting a slideshow of deep green forestry, close-ups of ferns, vistas of mountains and brush strokes of rivers. The man and woman speak in quick yet companionable Japanese, easily handing the narration from one another using prompts the rest of us can't see.

The audience laughs at something the man says and his face lights up like he's excited to have found these kindred spirits.

The woman points at things on the screen – a branch, a leaf, and then turns back to the audience and closes her eyes, breathing in and exhaling with her face held high. She gestures for the audience to do the same and they do, and although I'm only picking up maybe one in every hundred words, I find myself swept along for the ride and I breathe in, and exhale with my face held high.

Nobody seems to mind me having joined them so I stay put, listening to the rhythmic language and watching the slideshow, until two English words are spoken and it snaps me to attention.

'Forest bathing,' the woman at the front says, looking directly at me and smiling. She repeats it. 'Forest bathing ... *shinrin-yoku.*' She points to a picture on the screen of her and the man (I presume her husband) standing within a big majestic forest, holding hands and looking up at the trees.

I nod with understanding, though I don't quite understand. I struggle for a suitable word and end up saying, *'Onsen?'* which is actually a hot spring or public bath but is the closest thing I can think of right now.

A few members of the audience chuckle but not impolitely, and the man picks up the top sheet of a stack of print-outs at the front and signals for it to be passed back to me. When it reaches me, he bows and I bow back and then read the top couple of lines, which is a print-out in both Japanese and English explaining what the bloomin' heck 'forest bathing' is.

Spoiler alert: it's nothing to do with getting into your swimmies in the middle of the woods.

Shinrin-yoku, aka forest bathing, appears to be a way for people with busy lives (that is, everybody in these modern times) to take some time out and let nature re-centre them. By spending some time outdoors and focusing on what's around you, rather than being plugged into an audiobook or talking on the phone, it's supposed to let your mind settle and let you enjoy life more. I guess it's mindfulness, with the help of the big wide world rather than just being left to the devices in your own mind.

I don't know about you, but my mind really struggles to shut the hell up, and although I've been beginning to do it more over the past couple of weeks it's tough to stay present when you're thinking about, what does that character mean? Where shall I spend the night after tomorrow? How cool was that thing I saw? Where's the nearest place I can buy mochi at 2.30am? Will my vlogs be enough to write some articles to show *Adventure Awaits*? Why didn't he want to marry me (Matt, not my brother)? How hot was Riku? And who the hell am I anyway?

So in short: forest bathing sounds ace, and probably what I need. I'm diving in.

When the talk is over and everybody has applauded and started filtering out, I go up to the couple at the front and say in clunky Japanese after bowing, *'Konbanwa, domo arigato, watashi wa* Charlotte *desu, hajimemashite.'* I get it out all at once for fear of losing confidence, but hopefully I said something along the lines of 'Good evening, thank you very much, my name is Charlotte, nice to meet you.' I follow with an extra thank you, gesturing to the paper I'm clutching and then point to the screen and say, 'Where?' because I don't know the word and hope my imitation of the shrug emoji combined with an interested face might indicate what I mean.

The lovely woman taps my arm kindly, and says, 'Japan Alps.' The man shuffles his papers and pulls out a print-out of a map of Japan and she runs her finger down a section of it on the main island. 'All Japan Alps.'

She then points out the window because Nagano is, in fact, in the Japanese Alps, so of course that's where the couple would be offering a free talk to the tourists.

I thank them again and wave and bow a goodbye, and then carry on up to my room where I splash out on room service, ordering some tempura, rice and miso soup, because I have some planning to do.

Chapter 14

Back to basics, and
Back to nature, but I think
I'm moving forward

It's decided – I'll be taking a detour! Well, it isn't really a detour because I hadn't planned in the next section of my journey, but I'd been thinking about hanging around Nagano for a couple more days before investigating staying in a Buddhist monastery (something Matt would never have agreed to, not in a rude way, but he just would have got itchy to Do More Things) and then on to my final stop of Mount Fuji.

You know, it annoyed me a little, Matt refusing to entertain the idea of the monastery stay. He knew it had been something I'd liked the sound of, ever since I'd read about it in my trusty Ariel C article, but he thought we'd be visiting enough temples as it was. 'The very fact we're going to Japan means you're already getting your way,' he would kind-of joke when I'd protest. 'Can I have my say on some of it?' And I would give in, because he was kind-of right. But looking back ... I didn't force him to come to Japan, he loved the idea, and went along with it willingly. And I involved him in every decision, even though he was more than happy to leave me to do all the research and detailing. I didn't force him to do anything. Anything!

Digression aside, instead of going straight from Nagano to my monastery, tomorrow I'm heading into the wilderness! I can get a train from Nagano to a place called Matsumoto, then jump on a bus which takes me to the village of Kamikochi, a hub within the Chubu Sangaku National Park, where visitors can go on hikes, follow trails, camp, relax or just enjoy nature, maybe dipping their toe into a little forest bathing.

I lick my fingers after I've eaten the last morsel of buttery-coated tempura prawn, brush the crumbs off my hand and pick up the phone to call my little brother.

'All right, Charlie!' he sounds muffled when he comes on the line and I hear him leave somewhere crowded and step outside, voices replaced with birds chirping.

'Benny! Is this a good time for a chat?'

'Sure, I was just sorting out a couple of things in the students' union.'

'Everything okay?'

He hesitates a millisecond too long and then says. 'Yeah, all fine. What have you been up to today?'

I'll circle back to him in a mo once I've got him chatting. 'Today I've been looking at monkeys chilling in a hot spring, and gazing up at cherry blossom trees, and tomorrow I'm heading into the Alps for some hiking!'

'Japan has Alps? I thought they were in France, or Italy or ... Wait, you, *hiking*?'

'I like hiking!' I protest. At least I think I do. I've only done a few hikes in the past during holidays, but the idea of doing one of those month-long, hauling about a tent and a tin mug kind of trips somewhere beautiful and dramatic like the Rocky Mountains or the Camino de Santiago trip in France and Spain, has always appealed to me. Not enough to have done anything about it, *yet*, but maybe that could be my next trip, if this goes well. A camping trip would certainly be better suited to what will be a severe lack of funds ...

'Anyway,' I say, 'tell me what's going on in your life.'

'Nothing interesting, just wish I was out there with you.'

'No you don't, once you've finished uni you'll find much more interesting people to go on holiday with than your sister.'

'That's probably true,' he jokes. 'But ...'

I wait a while to see if he's going to continue.

'... I don't know. I think I'm just not sure what to do when I finish uni, full stop.'

'Nobody does,' I try and reassure him.

'Some people do. You did.'

I pause. I know that this is one of those older sibling moments where I have to be careful with my words, because my brother is counting on me to say the right thing. Did I know what I wanted to do? I moved home after university so that I could save money and Matt and I could get married, but was that really what I wanted to do? After everything that happened, I'm starting to think that I just sort of got swept along with the wedding planning and the move to London and actually I didn't know what I was doing at all. I don't remember stopping to consider if the decisions I was making about my life were really what I wanted.

'I thought I did. I suppose I still do, I think, but if there's one thing I'm discovering while walloping about Japan on my tod it's that it doesn't matter how planned out you have things, stuff changes. Shit happens. So I might know what kind of job I want but I don't know a lot else about myself any more.'

'But you're discovering it out there.'

'And you'll figure it out. Don't beat yourself up, little bro, enjoy your last few months of uni and we'll work out the rest once it's done.'

He sighs, but says, 'All right,' and then changes the topic to, 'Did Gray tell you he's got a new girlfriend?'

'Shut the front door, tell me everything.' I cross my legs on the bed and rip open a cellophane-wrapped mochi ball I'd squirrelled away inside a shoe and had found earlier, by putting my foot in it. I munch on the soft, sweet squidge and listen to my brother tell me tales of home, while I sit in my hotel in Japan, smiling as he talks. He might not have wanted to marry me when he was four years old, but he's going to make someone (not related) very happy one day.

When I get off the phone to Benny I take a quick look at how my latest IGTV episode is doing and, scanning down the list of new followers, which seems to grow each day, I'm shocked to see a couple of blue ticks beside names.

'No way,' I whisper, noticing that a couple of travel influencers I've followed for a while have returned the favour.

But what's more shocking? The message that's come in. From Matt.

Just one line, in response to my latest video under the cherry blossoms. *You always looked pretty in pink.*

My heart stops. Did I read that right? I can't ... I don't know what to make of that.

And then, what did he have to do that for? Should I be pleased about receiving his greeting-card flattery?

Because at the moment I feel more annoyed at him invading my space. *Go and tell your new girlfriend she looks pretty*, I think. She won't be his girlfriend yet, though, will she?

I'm not going to let it bother me. I stand up and let the shower water run over me, drowning out the noise. I'm not even going to let it in.

I arrive into Kamikochi mid-afternoon of the following day. The further I travelled into Chubu Sangaku National Park the more excited I felt, and I was pressed against the bus window the whole time, my face upturned to see every mountain peak and craggy rock face we passed.

Stepping off the bus, finally, my trainers hit the ground and the smell of thick forest and pine trees fills my nose. The air is warm and that distinctive thud-thud of walking boots on a dusty road harmonises with the birds hanging out in the trees above me. It's the very start of the season here, the park having only been open a week or two, but already there are lots of visitors milling about, propping themselves on walking sticks, filling their water bottles at taps, and taking selfies with the mountains behind them.

I stop for a selfie with the mountain behind me and then navigate my way to the information centre.

'*Konnichiwa*,' I greet the information assistant behind the counter with a bow, which she returns. 'Um ...' Oh bugger, I have no idea how to say what I want to say here. I tried so hard to learn some Japanese phrases but I just clam up when it comes to using them. Plus I didn't think I'd need to know, *what overnight hike would you recommend for an inexperienced but enthusiastic Brit on her own?* Instead, I end up waving at the map stuck to the counter and saying '*Ichi yoru*, um, *aruku*, um, easy, *kudasai*?' This roughly translates, but not really, as 'One night, um, walk, um, easy, please.' I supplement my bad use of language by using my fingers to look like legs walking on the map.

Luckily, the woman is very kind and hands me a leaflet in English that explains some of the common walks and points out things like overnight accommodation.

'Tent?' she asks.

'No ... do I need one?'

'Yes.'

Oh, okay. I thank her and head back out into the sunshine, where I take a seat on a nearby rock and study the map until I find what sounds like a lovely trek, with rivers, forest, mountains and hopefully lots of adventure. I take a big inhale of the mountain air. This feels right.

*

By late afternoon, when the sun is dipping behind the Hida Mountains and weary travellers are returning to the campsite with their muddy boots and sweaty faces, I'm feeling very Reese Witherspoon in *Wild*. I'm also feeling quite Ariel Cortez when she did a big backpacking trip in Indonesia. I made Mum let me camp in the garden for a week after I read that piece. Now, I haven't gone anywhere yet, but I look the part, next to my rented tent, sitting on a tree stump ready to eat my instant ramen, my camping essentials lined up neatly.

I thought camping would be a cheap option, but after hiring one of the Kamikochi campsite's fixed tents and all of the gear I was lacking (camping mat, sleeping bag, pillow, a mug) I could see why an impromptu trip to the Northern Japan Alps is something most people plan a little more in advance.

I kick up a couple of leaves and poke my noodles, my heart bouncing in my chest. I knew it, I *knew* I would enjoy this kind of thing. It's taken five attempts for my camping gas to stay alight and I didn't bring enough sweaters but I feel ... I don't know. A bird catches my eye and swoops overhead, framed by the tips of the tall trees before shaking out its wings and heading off wherever it wants to head off.

Tomorrow I'm doing it, maybe only for one night but I am heading off for an adventure. But I'll have to tell you all about it in the morning, reader, because my noodles are done and it's nearly six o'clock so I need to go to bed now, ready for my big day tomorrow.

I lie in bed, using the term 'bed' pretty loosely, my rented sleeping bag pulled up to my neck and the sounds of the wildlife outside my tent. I had hoped to fall straight to sleep ready for my big day, but I was looking for inspiration on how to film some epic national park footage and have now worked myself up a bit to the tune of *Charlotte, you dum dum! You'll never get the job!*

Why? Because I searched for the tag #Adventure-AwaitsJob and found quite a collection of uploaded videos from people who were clearly pro travel vloggers ready to take the leap and apply for a coveted role at the magazine. The videos were stylish, beautiful, the guys and girls full of bounce and nose piercings and muddy knees but shaved legs and I thought about my silly little tries where I blabber to the camera about my big fat failed wedding while Japan happens behind me.

I'm being a little hard on myself, so I try and shake it off. It's okay, a little healthy competition is fine. What I have is passion and history with the magazine. It's got to count for something, right? And I try to remember that

I wouldn't have been picked for the internship if they didn't think I was good.

To distract myself, I look through Thomas Day's Instagram page, which is dedicated to his travel photography. He must have been to the US recently, to a snow-capped mountain, because he has all these icy-blue close-ups of vistas capped with setting and rising suns.

Just checked out your recent photos – they're gorgeous! I tap to him in a private message. *Eco Adventure will want to hire you as their photographer in a second!*

He responds quickly. *You just made my morning! Or evening. Where are you now?*

At a national park in the Japanese Alps, I'm off hiking tomorrow. What are you doing?

I am fixing my parents' garage door. So just as glamorous, thank you very much.

I smile at that. *Where were the snow photos taken?*

Colorado – have you been?

No, but I want to now.

As he was typing his reply, I imagined him for a second, standing in the spring sunshine outside his parents' house, maybe on a cul-de-sac, wearing jeans and a T-shirt with bare arms, a little sweaty from the manual labour. I wonder how accurate that was, and then his reply comes in.

It's so amazing there – so quiet. I love snowboarding but nobody I know does, so I sometimes just go on my own and I barely speak to anyone for a week, but it's great. I mean, you know how it is, you love travelling too.

I do. I hesitate. I've wondered whether to mention the next thing to him, in case it diluted my own chances, but he threw me a bone back at the recruitment event by talking to me when nobody else was, so I can't not tell him about the job. *Did you see that Adv. Aw. are recruiting for a junior travel writer?*

I saw that – you're going to apply, right? Your videos would be perfect for it.

That's nice of him to say. *I was thinking about it ... are you?*

No, he writes without pausing. *I love photography but am pants at videography, and besides, my goal is to become a photographer for Eco Adventure mag, so I don't want to lose that foot in the door, even if I'll be living off dried pasta for a year!*

Now that's out of the way, we talk a little more into the evening, until I remember he is supposed to be fixing his parents' garage door and let him go. Lying back I close my eyes with a smile on my face. It was nice chatting with someone who shares my love of exploring the world. I guess that's what my life could be like every day ...

*

I spread the contents of my day pack out on the grass, checking I've got everything I need one last time before handing over my suitcase to storage, giving it a night off from hanging out with me. Snacks, water, my first-aid kit, poncho, a lovely sensible fleece, spare snacks, a whistle I picked up at the camping store, my power bank to charge my phone, spare undies, cash, toothbrush and emergency extra snacks.

'I think I'm good to go,' I say to myself, and put it all back inside the bag. I look up at the sky, which is overcast but with brightly lit-from-behind clouds and only a faint mist dampening the air. Probably better that it's like this than sunshine beating down on me ...

Because ...

Today I'm doing six hours of hiking, from the village of Kamikochi to my overnight accommodation in Karasawa Hyutte, which sits in the basin of the Hida Mountains in the Northern Japanese Alps at a little over 2,300m above sea level. I'm staying the night in a mountain hut, which makes me feel very Cheryl Strayed and like a proper hiker, even if I am wearing gym leggings from H&M, thick ankle socks and slightly battered trainers. Then I come back down tomorrow. *Like a hero.*

It's early, but most of the tents near mine have their flaps open and an array of Gore-Tex-clad hikers of all shapes and ages popping in and out of them, getting themselves ready for the day. This village does seem to be quite the hub, be it for families looking for gentle riverside wanders to show their kids a little spring nature, or for the serious multi-dayers, already with a thin layer of mud and sweat covering their belongings, who are up stretching and ready to take on the next peak.

I say a goodbye to my rented tent, which I'll see again in a couple of days, roll my shoulders, take a gulp of water and then refill it, do a couple of squats because I see some other people doing them, and then head off down the road through the village to the start of my trail.

Plod, plod, plod. Feeling pretty amped up with vitality right now.

I wonder when I should have my first snack, just to keep myself going …

Soon, I leave the tarmac of the road and crunch off onto a gravel path that takes me beside a shallow river, a sliver of blue topaz that ripples under the watch of the green mountains. A lot of people are snapping photos at this early stage, so I join in, not wanting to be the idiot who didn't get the money shot during her time in the alps. I also take a little video.

'As you can see,' I narrate, holding the camera steady in front of me, the view on the river. 'It's pretty quiet here today, at this hour at least. Some tourists and trekkers are here on the beginning of the trail with me, but I read that when the autumn leaves are out, or during the summer holidays, it can be completely packed. So springtime feels like a good time to come, as long as the snow has melted enough.'

I switch the view to myself briefly. 'Hello, by the way, good morning, *ohayo*. Slept like a log in my tent last night, if the log was on a white-water rafting trip. But that's okay because I think the first four hours or so of today is fairly flat and then tonight I'm in my mountain hut where I get dinner cooked for me – yummyyyyy – and I'm sure I'll be shattered from a day of walking.'

My face is getting freckly! I thought I'd developed a tint of a tan after Ishigaki and seeing myself on camera just now I noticed for the first time a dusting of walnut-coloured sprinkles across my nose and cheeks. It's quite nice this being outdoors lark!

I settle into a pace for the first couple of hours, walking along flat, well-maintained pathways and over wooden bridges, past mossy, reflective ponds, and my mind wanders about as if on its own walk. I think over the past two and a half weeks of my time in Japan and how it hasn't quite gone according to plan, but what has in my life over the last two months? And I feel happy right now, so perhaps an imperfect plan isn't the worst thing in the world. If I hadn't looked in on that forest-bathing talk at my Nagano hotel I would never have been here right now. If I hadn't left the tour, I may never have found myself solo in a karaoke bar somewhere in late-night Hiroshima, kissing a boy I'll never see again. If I hadn't taken the plunge and come on my honeymoon without a honey, I wouldn't have seen and done everything that's lead me to hiking beside this river with the sound of birds above my head and the crunch of the gravel below my feet and the taste of the peanut butter granola bar I just ate in my mouth (oops).

I'm smiling to myself as I follow the pathway and then notice a group of female Japanese hikers stopped up ahead, pointing and laughing. Not at me, I hope. I stride closer until one of them waves her hands at me to stop and then points upwards into one of the trees.

'Monkey!' I almost shout in surprise, and said monkey flicks his head around to look at me, all pink-faced and hairy. And that's just me! Haaaa, ba-boom.

Anyway, the monkey, who is also the pink-faced and ash-blond hairy kind, looks very similar to my friends from the hot springs a couple of days back in Nagano. He stares at me for a second and I shrink my head into my neck and stay very still, mid-stride, so as not to be the stupid, peace-disturbing tourist any more.

Eventually, monkey looks away and carries on grooming his knees, and I watch him for a bit. I take my phone back out to take a sneaky bit of footage before sliding my way past him and the others and carrying on my way.

I'm nearing the four-hour mark and just about ready for a change of pace and some bathing in the forest when I see the pathway starts to take me on an ascent upwards. Although my legs are tiring, that's a good sign, because if I'm already heading up I'll probably get there soon; I must have been hiking at a good rate.

There are a lot less people around now. The families haven't come this far and the more serious hikers left a little earlier than me, but I still pass by someone maybe every twenty minutes or so.

Ooo, now this is what I'm talking about. I climb up a series of large grey rocks, moss spilling over the top like icing on a Christmas pudding. The trees are getting denser and the air cooler the higher I go and the further we get from the valley and the river. In fact, the direct sunlight and the breeze isn't making it through the leaves, so there's a stillness about the place which *could* be creepy but isn't.

I keep climbing upwards, and it's a big change from the path below. This isn't just a gentle incline, I'm needing to grip my fingers around the tree bark to pull me up, and my thigh muscles are beginning to ask me what the hell I think I'm doing.

When I reach a bit of a clearing, where the trees still huddle together and everything around me is green, but I'm no longer confined to a tunnel-like pathway between rocks, I take a moment to breathe.

I take out my piece of paper from my leggings pocket and unfold it. This seems like as good a spot as any to practise some forest bathing, and if it means stopping for a little while, then fine.

Now, it sounds like for proper forest bathing you should give yourself a couple of hours, but I've still got a way to go, I think, and I'm not sure it's going to be very relaxing to get stuck on a mountain in the dark. Instead I'll do the beginner's version and be mindful as I go, aside from little breaks.

I remind myself of the guidelines and then tuck the paper away.

My eyes close, I inhaaale, and then they open again for a quick check that nobody is around, and then they close again and exhaaaaale.

So. Charlotte. What can you hear? Apart from yourself, talking to yourself.

I clear my mind and try to focus. I hear my breath, I hear the stones under my feet because I keep shuffling,

I hear the trees, their leaves and branches swishing. I hear ... birds? And is that a waterfall? And far off in the distance maybe a helicopter or a plane? Wow, you really can notice more when you're paying attention.

After listening to the forest for a while longer what I start to hear are my own thoughts again, trying to picture what I might be having for dinner up at the mountain hut, so I open my eyes and carry on walking a little further. As I move, I'm paying a lot of attention to the nature around me, like the guidelines told me to. Rather than just watching my own feet I'm noticing the curves of leaves and the crags of the mountains that I can just make out beyond the trees. Talking of trees, I'm checking out their rough and wrinkled trunks and wondering if they're checking mine too as I pass.

At one point, a group of four friends pass me, hiking downwards, their legs propelling them speedily down the slopes and through the forest, and they look like they've been on a great big trek and can't wait to finally make it to the village. I stand out of their way acting like I'm being totally normal and not gawping at tree bark on my own, and they pass me with a smile and a wave.

When I'm alone again, I find a spot to stand still and close my eyes for a second time. This time I'm concentrating on what I can feel and taste, so I stick my tongue out. Mostly I taste the chocolate I keep gobbling, but I also taste a dampness in the air, on my tongue, which tastes like the type of water you get at a spa, infused with green stuff like herbs and cucumber. I'm quite enjoying this forest bathing. If you'd have told me before I came to Japan that I'd find more zen up a drizzly mountain than in the soaking tub of a luxury hotel, I would have bopped you on the nose. But back at the Park Hyatt in Tokyo I'd been jet-lagged and blue and I was desperately trying to force the zen, whereas now I am letting it come to me.

The mist settles over my outstretched bare arms and breathes on my forehead and my neck. And then it trickles down my nose – hang on.

It's raining, dammit. I put down my rucksack and pull out my poncho, and then begins a ninety-second furore of putting the poncho on with the rucksack over the top, then taking it all off again to put the rucksack on first and then poncho over everything. 'Oomph,' I say, going to whip the hood up only for it to cover my face because the poncho is on back to front.

By this point, the heavens have opened. Considering how tightly packed these trees are, it's impressive how penetrating the raindrops are, but it's pouring down on me like someone's released a whole bag of pinballs above me and they're clattering their way down past all the leaves as if the forest itself was a giant pinball machine.

Well, this is fun. I was enjoying forest bathing a lot, and I'll do it again, but I didn't want to *actually* forest bathe, thanks very much. I use my drenched poncho to wipe the rain from my eyes, and you can imagine how much good it did.

The path gets steep again up ahead; through the blinking I'm faced with another slope of rocks to scramble up, only now there's a layer of muddy water stroking the top of the stones as the rain has a go at creating an impromptu water feature.

'What do I do?' I say out loud to nobody. Going up seems like a bad decision, but going down could be just as treacherous, and at least here I'm only maybe an hour or so from the hut, as opposed to five hours from the village.

What noise am I hearing now? Well it's the sound of rain thundering all around me and not much else, to be honest.

I look up and I look down. I have to make a decision and trust it.

Was it all talk, this wish to do a month-long hike one day? Did I just tell myself I wanted to do that because I never thought I would actually have to, thanks to Matt and my planned out, structured life together? What, am I just going to chicken out because it's got a little tough?

If I can do this, and enjoy this, it will prove to me that I'm what I think I am. An adventurer.

I reach my hand back under my poncho and grip hold of my *onomari*, my good luck charm that the kimono maker gave me in Kyoto that hangs off my rucksack. I feel it, damp and gritty but still there and I make my decision. I'm going up.

I face the rocks with determinism and I use my new-found forest bathing skills to make sure I'm really focusing on what they look like and what they feel like under my fingers and how my trainers are wedged in them to help my balance in pulling me up. It's okay, it wasn't forecast for rain today so this has got to be a passing shower, there's no need to give up.

The rocks are slimy underfoot, the moss squelching under my step and cold on my fingertips. More than once I have to just grip hold of the foliage to haul myself up to the next stone.

I make it to the top of this mound of rocks and, as expected, there is more uphill to come. I trudge forward and at one point my foot slips in the mud and I grab for a nearby branch that slaps me in the face with its wet leaves. Hmph.

Another wet and slow ten minutes of walking later and I realise the drum-like pounding of the rain has lessened, like a marching band at a carnival parade turning the corner at the end of the street. I look up, just for a moment.

'*Oooohhmygod*!' A tree root, wet and slick, is exposed and my foot slips right off it, my ankle twisting painfully, and I crash to the ground, sliding a little way down the muddy bank, my leg under me and the stones ripping a hole in my leggings.

I come to a stop and sit up, panting, and tears of shock spring out of my eyes, cutting through the mud on my face and, 'Fuuuuuucckkkkkkkkkkkkkkkkkkkk.' I grip my ankle while unbearable pain pulsates from my toes right up to my knee.

Chapter 15

Japanese proverb:
'Fall seven times, stand up eight'
Nevertheless, ouch.

I can't calm my shallow breathing and I sit there in the cold, my knees up to my chest, my hands, though they sting, holding on tight to my poor foot and I feel stupid.

Stupid stupid me for carrying on going up. Stupid me for not looking where I was going. Stupid me for being out here on my own in nothing but trainers and grandiose ideas of being a mountain goat. Stupid me.

The shock very slowly subsides, though the pain is still intense.

'*Now* what am I going to do?' I whisper. 'I guess I could blow my whistle, or I could try and call someone.' Strangely, talking out loud is helping a small amount. I begin to get my breathing under control and I dare to unclench one of my hands and wipe my face. 'Oh God, it hurts so much.'

I gingerly untie my laces, which are also dripping wet, and they slide from my trembling grip. Slowly slowly I pull my trainer off my foot and I wonder, if an injured hiker falls in the woods, does anyone hear them?

My trainer off to the side, I nudge my sock down from my calf and pull it wide over my ankle, trying not to touch it, even the slightest graze stinging me. With my sock off and also flung to the side in a puddle of mud because who cares, my trainers were soaked through anyway, I can see the damage. One big, bulbous, swollen, sprained ankle. I wriggle my toes. Well, at least it isn't broken, so there's my silver lining. But it's still swollen fast, and I can't imagine walking on it right now.

I flop about like a beached whale, trying not to move my foot, until I can get my poncho and my rucksack off. At least the rain has now stopped and the brightness in the sky is back.

'Where are you, first-aid kit?'

Because I'm actually not stupid, despite what I scolded myself on a few minutes ago, I do have a bandage somewhere in here. It's not ideal, and I'm sure it won't feel very comfy, but if I wrap it around my ankle tightly then at least it'll be compressed until someone comes past or I feel ready to walk again.

'Ouch ouch ouch ouch ouch,' I mutter, wrapping the bandage around my foot and ankle. I wrap tightly, to the point it would be hard to flex my foot at all, but that's the point.

'So what to do now ...' I ask nobody. 'I don't think I need to be rescued. Maybe if I can't walk in a little while but it seems a bit too dramatic.' I decide to eat a snack, take some ibuprofen and sit here until the next person comes past, then maybe I can try walking with them, if they don't mind taking it a little slowly. Then I won't be on my own any more.

I wait a while, looking at the scenery, calming down, and peering down at my foot to check it's still there. Nobody comes past.

I film a little video, because maybe this will be funny to look back on one day, and when I'm done, still nobody has come past.

At this point I'm getting cold, and I feel like it might be getting darker. Checking my watch, though, it's only mid-afternoon – I'm imagining it. But ... I really don't want to be out here in the dark, especially with only one working foot. If I had to run from anything it would be in circles.

'All right,' I say, standing up, wincing but holding in the swears when I put pressure on my foot. It still really bloody hurts, but it's okay, I'm okay, the bandage has helped. I can do this.

With my things packed up and my wet sock and shoe back on, I continue my walk. I'm now determined to make it to the top, one: to show my ankle who's boss, but two: because I truly think it's the right decision at the moment. It would take too long to walk back down, and it's going to be slippery and difficult whichever way I go.

I am not going back. I am only going forward. I can do this.

I've never been so pleased to see a crowded, steamy dining hall. The room is filled with people in muted-colour fleeces and mud-flecked headbands sitting pressed together on wooden benches, trays full of hot food slotted in front of them. I limped into the Karasawa Hyutte mountain hut shortly before dark, cold, tired, in pain, soaked through, but now I'm beyond happy. I made it! I flippin' made it.

I check in and am shown to my bed, a futon among the wooden beams, numbered in a manner similar to the capsule beds in Kyoto. I'd have some futon neighbours tonight but that was absolutely fine with me. The more people the better, for a change!

Dinner is an array of warming dishes that taste like heaven, and when I accept a miso soup refill the pair of women opposite me get chatting.

'Are you hiking on your own?' one of them asks me and I'm surprised to hear a British accent.

'Yes, I am, all on my own but only for one night. Luckily, since I bust my ankle up on day one.'

'Oh, you poor bugger,' she says and sticks her head under the table to try and have a look.

Her friend pipes up, 'That rain can be such a bugger, can't it, Noush?'

'Noush' brings her head back up. 'A right bugger,' she confirms. 'I'm Noush, this is Tils. Anoushka and Tilly. We've come to Japan together because our old bugger husbands didn't want to do another hiking holiday.'

'Stupid old buggers,' says Tils.

'What brings you here?' asks Noush, and the two of them look at me, awaiting an answer.

'Well,' I reply. 'I called off my wedding, came on honeymoon on my own, and left that stupid old bugger of mine in England.'

Noush and Tils are great company but we're all pretty shattered, so everybody in the whole hut seems to drift off to their futons not long after the food is cleared away.

'Lights off at nine o'clock,' Noush advises me with the wisdom of someone who's been here before, or quizzed the reception staff on her way in. 'Drying room over there.'

I change into my PJs, a job while hobbling about, and am hanging my damp hiking clothes and socks out in the drying room, balanced on one leg, when she reappears again.

'Right, missy, hold on to my arm and up in to bed with you,' she instructs. 'That ankle needs to stay elevated and you aren't to let it touch the floor again tonight.'

'Oh but—'

'You have a she-wee with you?'

'No ...' Who knew I'd one day feel she-wee shamed?

'You can borrow Tils' for the night.' Noush marches away and returns, having thankfully forgotten the she-wee but holding a cup of tea for me.

'For me?' I ask. 'You didn't have to do that!'

'Oh don't be a silly bugger, it's free.' She gives me a smile and a wave and disappears between the beams to an unknown futon of her own. And I drop instantly into a deep sleep, the tea going cold beside me.

Come morning, my bladder is practically screaming and my whole body aches. I'm not sure if that's from my inexperience sleeping on a futon, the fall, or the act of waking up with a jolt of pain every time I rolled over or knocked my ankle against one of the beams. Either way, it was a quiet and comfortable sleep if it wasn't for my own decrepit body and I'd give the mountain hut with its free tea and hot food a five-star TripAdvisor review.

My ankle doesn't feel any better today, but it doesn't feel any worse, so I think I'm going to just grin and bear it and make the climb down and walk back to Kamikochi. I'll leave early today, after a massive wee, and then I can take it slow without any worry.

After weeing and after slapping on my fleece and grabbing my woolly socks from the drying room, plus a mug of tea on route, I hobble outside and am wowed.

Directly in front of the hut is a sea of colourful tents pitched among the grass and stones. Mountain peaks sweep upwards all around us, craggy like meringue but mottled grey and green in the spring weather, with just white tips remaining right up near the blue dawn sky. Sunlight is coming up and spilling over into the basin and I drink it all in.

I feel more attune to the colours and the sounds and the feel of the chilly shade on my skin since my forest bathing experience yesterday. I guess I've learnt something about myself on this part of the trip:

1. Even if it rains and pours and I fall, I can get back up again.
2. I enjoy, *really* enjoy, being in the big outdoors.
3. I can do this.

My journey back down towards Kamikochi is slow, the ground still wet and churned from yesterday in some places, so I end up shuffling on my bottom, tears falling when my ankle hits anything solid and more than once I just have to stop and put my head in my arms and cry it out for a while before picking myself up and carrying on.

But by the time I'm back on flat ground, taking in the last half hour of bends in the river before I know we're going to hit the Kappa Bridge, the joy is back and my steps, even on my bad ankle, are lighter.

I did it. And I could do it again.

That night I collapse onto my camping mat in my pyjamas, extra socks and a clean jumper, and leave all my muddy clothes in a heap outside the tent ready to sort and re-pack tomorrow. My body aches, my skin feels tinged by the sun, my hair is a mess and I do not smell good, but I can't stop smiling.

Chapter 16

A few days to rest
Moments to learn to let the
Sunset soak your soul

If you ever find yourself with an ankle injury in rural Japan and undefined plans for a few days, may I suggest a *shukubo* monastery stay? Well, I am suggesting it. I'm on my way there now, my train edging further away from the Alps, where I'll be spending three nights at a Buddhist temple. A little last chance to spend some quality time with me, searching my soul and saying goodbye to the past, before my final destination of Mount Fuji.

I flex my ankle, just a little, where it's propped up on the seat opposite on top of my coat. It's still pretty painful, but it is just a sprain so I'm glad I didn't start hollering for mountain rescue. And of course it still smarts after my six-hour hike back down the mountain yesterday followed by another, final, night of camping. But it's okay. It's my battle scar.

The *shukubo* I'm heading to is between the Alps and Mount Fuji, not far from a National Park. It isn't the same one Ariel Cortez visited all those years ago for her article, but she sparked the idea in me when I was plotting out the next sections of my journey, back in Nagano and I was flitting between map print-outs, holiday brochures, magazines and web pages like a homicide cop on a TV show. All I needed was some red string to lace it all together. And a homicide, I guess.

It's quite a popular thing to do now, if you're into adventure travel. Not homicide, *shukubo* stays. This one is, like many, run by monks and they have some English-language guided meditations and classes that I can take while I'm there, though I'd be really happy to just try and get the gist from the Japanese ones. I'll have my own room, the weather will be rainy, which sounds fine to me, because meditating with the rain outside sounds like being able to step right inside my Calm app, and it's going to be a real adventure. An adventure worthy of a real, paid job at a magazine? I hope so.

My phone rings and I quickly answer it without looking, to avoid disturbing the peaceful train ride, and I hear a sigh on the other end, followed by, 'Charlie?'

I gasp. 'Matt?'

He sighs again. The line is crackly and I can't tell if he has a bad connection or is shuffling around, but it must be about three or four in the morning in the UK. 'I jusht wanted ... I just want to ...'

'Are you drunk?' I hiss. 'Where are you?'

'In bed. But you aren't here. Where are you?'

I shake my head. I'm not dealing with this. I don't know what's going on but if he's in his own bed he's not in any danger, so I'm outta here. 'Matt, I have to go, I'm on a train.'

He just breathes down the phone at me.

'Bye then,' I say.

More breathing. Pretty sure he's gone to sleep now.

I hang up the phone and shake my head. Shouldn't I be the one making calls like this, begging him to come back to me and leave his new girlfriend? Telling him I miss having him here with me in Japan? Right now, I wouldn't do either.

The street is empty, and the train has pulled away. I stand in the centre of the road, dense greenery and squat palms lining either side creating a long jade tunnel. The only sound is the rain pattering heavily upon all the leaves, and my own breathing as I look up and down, up and down.

I thought the temple was going to be here, right by the station. Did I get off at the right place?

I hold my coat over my phone and peer at the booking confirmation. 'Steps from the train station', it says, and I'm checking every Japanese character as well as the English translation – this is the right station.

Of course, I can't find any mobile signal to call them or look it up on Google Maps, so I guess I'm going on a temple treasure hunt.

I go left, because why not? And follow the road as it curves until the train station is out of sight. I'm still walking pretty slow on this smarting foot, but it's all flat so I'm getting away with not a lot of flexing. Plus the rain is pummelling my face and making my nose run, so my ankle is the least of my grumbles right now.

'Steps from the train station, as if,' I mutter, feeling less zen with every bend in the road that reveals nothing. No wait – there's a building! I see a flat roof poking out above the trees, just around this left turn, *sonofabitch* it's the train station. I've circled the damned train station. I blame the rain in my eyes for not spotting the track I must have taken a bridge over … twice.

Just as I'm getting to my starting point again, and beginning to have just a teeny tiny sense of impending doom, something catches my eye on the other side of the path. It's an opening in the hedgerow, a narrow, discreet gap with a line of steps – yep – leading up away from the road.

I poke my head through and walk up, just a little, and sure enough, there is my temple lodging, hidden from the road but very much where it was supposed to be.

I walk up the steps, which are like stepping stones up a hill, into this secret garden, until I reach a modest red *torii* archway standing before a small, matching bride, curved over a dip in the hill before the temple. The rain on the leaves is still the only sound I hear, but hopefully someone's home …

Bowing first, I enter through the *torii* and walk the bridge, looking down at the bed of green foliage beneath me. It may be grey and drizzly here today but the emeralds and limes of the vegetation shine bright.

I reach the entrance, a small temple atop a small hill, but with paths that wind in intriguing directions off around the side of the building. Rain runs off the roof and drips onto the tarmac, and the red entranceway welcomes me to step onto the wooden decking and under the cover. To my left is a rack of cubby holes, filled with shoes paired neatly, at least fifteen pairs, with several more gaps. I see ballet flats, flip-flops, walking shoes, and so I add my own trainers to the mix, and walk in just my socks to the door.

Do you knock at a temple door? I'm not sure whether this should be treated more like a house or a hotel, but while I'm still weighing this up, the door opens and a monk, short and with a shaved head, wearing the same black robes as those in the Kiyomizu-dera Temple back in Kyoto. He smiles at me, and we bow, and then he points to some black sliders by the door that I hope he said I can use, and he wasn't just showing off his nice footwear collection to me, because they're now on my feet.

As he leads me through the door he stops and points towards my ankle and says 'Oh!' in a concerned manner.

'Yes, I was walking, *aruku*, near Kamikochi, and ...' I use my fingers as legs again and mime falling over.

He nods with understanding and leads me towards a little reception desk where he asks me to fill out a form and then gives me a map of the temple. He moves his fingers along the little pathways in the map and says to me, 'You go anywhere, night and day, it is yours now.'

I don't think he means I've accidentally bought the temple or anything, but I did read on the website that visitor access restrictions are lifted for overnight guests and that we should explore the grounds and the few buildings all we want as if it were just as much ours, as long as we respect the quiet and observe the timings for prayer and meditation.

As he leads me to my room, I spot other people, visitors, dotted about the temple grounds, taking their time and enjoying the peace and quiet. My room is simple and small (but not as small as my tent was!) and it has tatami flooring and sliding doors painted with delicate murals of cherry blossoms and willow trees. After he points out the shared bathroom facilities at the end of the corridor, he turns the map over in my hand, where there's a schedule listed in English for the next seven days, not that I'll be here quite that long, unless I decide my life's purpose is to take up Buddhism and not go home at all.

Gah! I can't believe I'll be flying home in seven days' time!

'Please, do here what makes you happy,' he says and then he leaves me to it, departing with a bow, and I make myself at home in my little room, sitting on the floor and stretching my leg out in front of me, and looking at my schedule.

Tonight at 6.30pm we have '*Nissokan*, sunset', so I'll need to look into what that is. Morning prayers are at 6am, and I think it's expected that guests do join in with those. Tomorrow there's a free *ikebana* class which I think is to do with flower arrangements if I'm remembering that correctly. That could be fun. Maybe I'll find that all along I'm meant to be a florist, it could be an undiscovered talent.

It looks like dinner will be in my room at five thirty, so since I have a couple of hours I think I'll warm up from my walk in the drizzle and soothe my achy foot by relaxing in the bath. The shared bath.

I gather my washbag and change into a robe that's been left for me, and shuffle my way down the corridor to the women's washroom. The door opens into a pretty tiled room with cubby holes and loos on one side and a large bath, similar to the size of a hot-tub, and some showers, on the other side. There's instructions on the wall which I'm peering at and memorising as I take my robe off when somebody says, 'Hello, would you like any help?'

My robe drops and I let out a whisper of a shriek as I whip around to face a woman already submerged in the bath. My bazoongas face hers and although I'm all British and mortified she doesn't even flicker beyond moving a stray lock of glossy black hair from her face that's fallen down from its bun.

'Sorry, *sumimasen*, I've not done one of these before. *Nihon jin desu ka*?' There is literally no reason I needed to ask if she was Japanese – what difference was it going to make to me and my nakedness right now? – but for some reason it's like I wanted to add to my embarrassment by throwing out a phrase I'd learnt in an attempt to prove I wasn't just a bumbling tourist in the buff.

'Yes,' she smiles. 'But I speak a little English. You use showers and wash and then in bath. Sitting down.' She points to the little wooden stool, clearly wary that I might try and crouch under that shower attachment that isn't far off the ground.

Yes, it's coming back to me now, I did read up on this way of using public baths and it's similar to how the Japanese sometimes wash in their homes, except that you're sharing with other women. It's perfectly normal, at least for her, I'm still blushing and struggling to wash my lady bits with my washcloth without drawing too much attention to myself.

I take my wet bandage off my ankle and leave it in my cubby hole, and then head over to the bath to join my new friend for a soak. Chin up, I tell myself. No need to be shy now I suppose.

And it does feel amazing, the warm water, the steam caressing my pores. I move my ankle in small circles under the surface and it feels heavenly.

A while later my friend leaves with an elegance I don't think I'll ever possess, and I wallow for a little bit longer before heading out as well and back to my room, where dinner will be brought in a while. I can't wait! I love Japanese food. But first, since I have a smidgen of phone signal, I'll make a short IGTV video.

'Hi adventurers,' I start, having set the camera up at the far side of the room while I sit in front of my painted doors, and I'll intertwine a little footage I took of the outside of the temple when I was first arriving to this episode. 'I've arrived at my *shukubo*, my Buddhist temple. It's very peaceful here, a great place to reflect on my journey through Japan and make some decisions about what the future has in store for me. I'll probably switch off while I'm here but I'll tell you all about it afterwards before I get to Mount Fuji.' I look away for a moment towards the window, where the rain still pitter-patters but a stream of sunlight is managing to break through the late afternoon clouds and it hits my face. 'Yep, I'm going to stay a few nights.' I smile at the camera, upload it to Instagram, and switch off.

I sit on the floor of my room while a monk brings in a large, lacquered black tray filled with tiny plates of food morsels. I'm doing my best to smile my face off to show my gratitude, because I'm not sure I should be babbling a million thank yous while he's so quiet and careful.

When he's laid everything out on my table he says, 'All vegetarian, this is what Buddhist monks like to eat.'

And with that he bows and leaves and I'm left to devour this all on my own. It's odd not having a TV or other people to stare at, but it does keep my focus on the crunch of the bamboo shoots, the zing of the ginger on the spongy tofu, the crisp of tempura sugar snap peas, the vinegary heat of udon soup and the salty, slimy squish of grilled aubergine.

My tummy is full and happy and it gurgles with thanks for all the fresh, healthy grub. And since the light is fading, I slide open the door to my room and pad back towards the reception desk area. On the way I pass a couple heading the opposite direction down a corridor.

'*Konbanwa, sumimasen*,' I stop them. 'Do you speak English?'

'Sure,' answers the guy, his accent North American and his muscly arms looking well … let's just say I was looking. 'Can we help you with something?'

'Oh, great. Do you know what *Nissokan* is? It was on the schedule for tonight at sunset but I'm not sure where to go. Or what to do.'

'I can help you with that,' says a voice behind me, and I turn to see the monk from earlier, the one that brought in my dinner. He is young, but a little older than me, maybe early thirties? His head is shaved, his jawline strong, and his mouth curved into a smile.

The couple continue on their way and the monk bows to them. 'I will see you in there,' he says to them.

'You speak good English,' I say, in bad English.

'Only a little, and only when it is important.'

'I'm Charlotte,' I bow, which he returns.

'Follow me, Charlotte, I will show you *Nissokan*.'

He leads me through a doorway and into a large open room, tatami-matted floor, and a handful of other guests and monks finding a spot to sit on the ground, adjusting their bottoms to be comfortable, rolling their shoulders. They're all facing west, where the entire length of the room has been opened up via sliding *shoji* panels. Outside, the sun has broken under the clouds and shines directly towards the temple, giving everybody a beautiful golden glow on their face. Under the peach sky, the trees and bushes follow the hill down and are a copper-tipped jade in the evening light.

'Take a seat,' the monk tells me with a smile. 'This is the practice of *Nissokan*. We will meditate as we watch the setting sun and you can imagine the paradise of the Pure Land.'

'How do I do that?' I whisper, out of my depth.

'However you want to. There are no rules, this is a calm meditation anybody can do anywhere. No experience or knowledge is necessary. It is good for the soul.'

He steps back away from me and I settle in, but the minute I close my eyes I'm aware of how uncomfortable my ankle is, twisted under me. I quietly poke one leg out so it's straight and turn my head to look at the monk. He catches my eye and I point to my bandaged ankle, and he simply nods and smiles and shuts his eyes, so I think it really is okay.

Mmmm, this is nice. I alternate between eyes closed, just aware of the glow and warmth on my face as the sun sinks in the sky, and opening my eyes to watch it fall asleep. I watch the sky change from honey to lavender and search my soul for the answers I've been looking for. Who am I? What do I need? What should I do?

They're big questions to come up with all the answers for right now, and I feel a chill coming to shelter in the room once the sun has gone, which causes the guests and the monks alike to stretch and stand up, bowing to each other before silently leaving the room.

'What did you think?' the monk asks me.

'That was ...' I look back out at the view. 'Can I do that every night?'

'You can do it as often as you need to do it. Of course you can come back and practise tomorrow night.'

I notice that, even though darkness is settling in outside, the pathways of the temples are visible still. 'Can I take a walk in the temple grounds?'

He nods. 'Of course, it's a very pleasant thing to do.'

I stop back at my room to layer up a little, and then make my way to the entrance I came into. I presume I can put my trainers back on for the outside walking ... I look around. Oh bugger, I really don't want to make a knob out of myself by doing the wrong thing here. So I loiter on the steps until a family of other guests return from, presumably, their evening stroll, and when I clock that they're all in their 'outdoor shoes', I quickly change into mine.

When I step down onto the gravelly pathway it's clear how the routes were all still illuminated after the sun had gone down. Leading me left and right, up steps and down steps and over bridges, is lantern after lantern. Paper lanterns that hang from trees, glowing reds and whites and each with carefully stencilled Japanese calligraphy on them. Stone lanterns that stand tall in the ground like bird houses that have a reading light on inside them. It's like being back in Borderless, inside the 'forest of resonating lamps', only this is art outside in real life.

I walk along paths, over bridges, under gateways, through the zen garden, all the while keeping my pace slow and the techniques of *shinrin-yoku*, forest bathing, to mind to make sure I'm really concentrating and capturing all this. The sounds of the wet gravel under my feet, the crickets chirruping, the water babbling through the stream, a faraway whoosh of a train, it all seeps into me, so that by the time I've done a full loop it's like I've been listening to one of those eight-hour 'night sounds' tracks on YouTube and I think I'm ready to climb into bed. Even if it is only about seven thirty in the evening.

As I lie on my futon, snuggled under my soft duvet, and listen to the discreet sounds of night wildlife beyond my window, my soul relishes this alone time.

It's funny … when I first arrived in Tokyo, I felt free and excited to be going solo, but the second I stopped being busy and was left to my thoughts the loneliness kicked in. I remember, what, three and a half weeks ago, I guess, sitting in my room in the Park Hyatt and feeling lost. Then the tour started and I had company again, and an itinerary, and people to tell me where to go and what to do, lovely people, but it was a plaster, a band aid over the problem and I'd then craved to be alone again, to feel that loneliness and experience being lost.

And now, I'm enjoying being alone. Here I'm eating alone, sleeping alone, walking alone, but it isn't lonely.

DONG.

DONG.

DONG.

All right already, I'm awake! I reach to switch off my alarm only to realise it's coming from outside the room. A moment later I clock the time.

Jumping out of bed and cursing under my breath because I forgot about my ankle, I throw on my clothes as quickly as I can and slide out of the door. It's 6am, morning prayer time, and I expect it would be super-disrespectful if I was late. In the corridor I whirl about because in the rush I don't actually know where to go, so now I'm twirling about like there's a fire drill and I can't find the emergency exit.

'Ah-ha!' I whisper, looking out of a window and spotting other guests, their hair dishevelled and rubbing their eyes, making their way towards a separate building behind this one.

I race out of the entranceway and then slow to a zen-like pace as I catch up with the others, just managing to join at the back before the doors are closed.

Inside, the prayer hall is dim, and candles burn while incense drifts up towards the ceiling. I take the lead from the other guests, who sit and watch with respectful interest as the monks chant and move around the hall, but don't actively join in the hour-long ceremony.

Can you believe I would never have done this if I'd stayed on my tour? What an experience.

And afterwards, thankfully, is when my tummy lets off the most massive growl.

Back in my room and over a scrumptious veggie breakfast I decide to give Benny a FaceTime.

'Hey bro! First of all – I don't have a lot of signal here so sorry if we cut out. Are you okay?' I notice that his face, usually so smiley and carefree, appears sallow, his smile forced.

'Yeah, I'm fine, where are you at the moment?'

'I'm in a monastery, a Buddhist temple, I'm staying here for a few days. Are you in bed already? Very well behaved, B, to not be out partying tonight.'

He smiles into the camera.

'Benny, what's up, you don't seem yourself?'

'I'm fine, tell me about your temple.'

I ignore him. 'How's the studying going? You said you weren't feeling very motivated before ...'

He sighs and is quiet for a while, before simply saying, 'Yeah.'

'Do you want to talk about it?'

'I don't know.'

I channel my inner-Mara. 'Okay then, I think we should talk about it. What's on your mind?'

'I just feel really … confused.' He puts a hand over his eyes and my heart breaks. My brother.

'Please don't cry, B, it's okay. I can help. I can help.' Oh but what if I can't, I'm so far away. 'Just breathe, breathe with me, in-two-three-four, out-two-three-four.'

He lifts his head. 'I'm doing all this work and I don't feel at all interested in it.'

'What's changed?'

'I don't know. Me. I don't think I'm who I always thought I was any more.'

Well that's a familiar feeling. 'It's okay to change and grow, you know, and you're under so much pressure at the moment.'

'It's not just that,' he rubs his eyes again, the tears falling, and all I want to do is be there with him.

'What is it?' I whisper.

'It's me. I don't know who I am any more and I don't know what to do. You're out there finding yourself and all I'm doing is losing myself.'

'You're not losing yourself, Benny, I promise. I don't know everything that's going on in your head but I can promise you that if it feels like you're lost at the moment it's just because your brain is figuring out what to put in the next chapter.'

He seems to let this sink in, but his little face still looks sad and distant.

'Benny?' I say, and he looks up and into the camera. 'I'm sorry I said you shouldn't come out to Japan. I didn't realise you were going through this.'

'It's fine, it would have just been running away anyway.'

'Sometimes it's okay to run away.'

'But running away to try and copy you probably wouldn't help me with *me*. It's okay, really. I couldn't afford to come to Japan anyway at the moment, you must be broke AF.'

I smile. 'I am a bit. But even so, you don't have to go through this alone you know. Alone is working for me but I'm only alone in the sense of having time away from other people. I'm actually getting so much help from being around nature and new scenery and different experiences. Maybe you could talk to someone, or maybe you could try some new things? You don't need to fly halfway across the world to do that.'

'I'm scared to try new things,' he says, and I can see he's really struggling with something. He's always been thoughtful, but he seems to have gone into himself more than usual.

'I know,' I comfort him. 'I know. It's not easy, but be kind to yourself, and give yourself the time to think and breathe and take your foot off the accelerator for a while.'

He sniffs and the screen freezes midway through. 'Bugger,' I mutter, and I stand up, walking around the room until it comes back to life again.

'Charlie?' he's saying. 'Oh there you are.'

'Benny, I'm sorry, I'm losing signal.'

'That's okay, I'm just going to go to sleep.'

'Do you need to keep talking though? I can try and call you back?'

'No, go and enjoy your day, I'll speak to you soon.'

'Are you going to be okay though?'

He nods. 'Thanks for listening, sis. Let's chat more when you're home.'

'Okay … Bye, B, take care.'

'You too, C.'

I hang up the phone and pick at a spot on my face for a while, staring out of the window. I wish I knew what he was going through, I wish I knew how to help.

Mara, are you awake? I text my sister.

Yes, are you okay?

Have you spoken to Benny?

My phone rings and I grab it before it cuts out. 'Mara, what's going on?'

'I don't know, that's why I was calling you. What's up with Benny?'

I hear the sound of giggling and squealing in the background and then it goes silent. 'What was that?'

'I was turning the TV off,' Mara answers.

'I recognised the background music ...'

'It was the news.'

'No ... Mara, are you watching *Love Island*?!'

'No,' she cries. But she bloody was. That's so unlike her, or so I thought, but I guess everyone is always on a journey to discovering what they do and don't like, so fair play to her. 'Anyway, tell me about Benny.'

'We just spoke and he's so down,' I say, bringing it back to the reason we're speaking. 'I'm worried about him; he was talking about feeling lost and not knowing what to do. He was crying.'

'He was crying?' My big sister sounded just as surprised as I had been.

'Shall I call Mum and tell her?'

'No, not yet. Marissa mentioned he showed up the other week to stay for a few days without much notice.'

'I think I should come home,' I say.

'Oh, stop with the coming home, he's really going to be fine, Charlie. I'm going to drive over there now and I'll stay with him until he's okay.'

She's always been so self-assured, my sister, and I love that about her.

'But it's the middle of the night.'

'It's barely past ten, and I can be there in a couple of hours.'

'What about work tomorrow?'

'I'm the boss, I can do what I like.'

'You always know what the right thing to do is,' I tell Mara, relaxing a little knowing she's got it in hand.

'No, I don't, nobody does,' she replies briskly, but I know she's saying it to make me feel better, and she'll probably say the same to Benny too. 'Okay, you bugger off and enjoy the last few days of your trip, and I'll text you with updates on our little brother.'

'Thanks Mara, I appreciate it.'

'Bye, love.'

Chapter 17

Delicate flowers
Branching out when a silence
Is interrupted

I stand just inside the doorway of the small, sunlit room, fiddling with the cuff of my jumper. A few other people are standing around as well, admiring the artwork on the wall, or looking out of the window, but keeping an eye on the *shoji* to see who will enter next.

'Have you done this before?' an American girl asks me, the one who's with muscle-man I met in the corridor yesterday, who is currently taking a little meditation break at the side of the room in a beam of sunshine, by himself.

'No,' I answer. 'Have you?'

She shakes her head. 'The monk, the one who speaks English, was telling us that the lady that runs the class is the one who makes the flower arrangements you see in the alcoves around the temple. It isn't normal to have an *ikebana* class somewhere like this but because she comes every few weeks, they decided guests might like to try it out, and that way it gives her a bit of help, I suppose.'

'So will our arrangements end up around the temple?'

She shrugs. 'I guess.'

At that moment we hear someone approaching the door. *'Ohayo!'* calls a muffled voice. *'Ohayo!'*

Oh, I think she wants someone to open the door. I turn and slide open the panel, coming face-to-face with a mass of stems, branches, spring flowers and foliage. A woman pokes her head around the side and grins at me. *'Arigato!'*

In she comes with all of her garden, and spends the next few minutes coming in and out with pots, dishes, scissors, etc. At one point I try to follow and help her but she waves me back into the room, so instead I check my phone for news from Mara: nothing.

Once she's got everything she needs, she encourages us to all sit in a circle with our legs tucked underneath us. I have to stick one leg out again which makes me feel like a bit of an idiot but she doesn't seem to mind. She then hands out pieces of paper to us all, and pencils.

'English?' she asks as she's handing out the paper, and I see it's a printed guide to Ikebana, translated into English, which is kind of her.

So here's the dealio. *Ikebana* is Japanese flower arranging, and it's quite distinctive. Each arrangement is like a work of art, be it small or large, and there are delicate techniques involved to get the stuff – the flowers and branches and things – the right size but also displaying them at their best. It's an artform. For that reason, I don't fancy my chances all that much.

'*Watashi wa* Mio *desu*,' the woman introduces herself, and then adds, 'Mio means beautiful cherry blossom.' We laugh: how ace to have a name that suits your job.

She gestures to us to choose one of the pots in front of her, all different shapes and sizes, and I go for a small, shallow dish, pale green, about the size of my hand.

She then explains the next steps in Japanese, but slowly, and pointing to the parts of the print-out that she's referring to. She tells us that although we can make our own unique *ikebana*, there are certain skills that should be followed in order for the arrangement, which should end up looking almost like a simple but beautiful work of art, to be representative of the elements.

It's flower-picking time. We should all take whatever we feel drawn to from the collection, but a variety of flowers, branches and stems of varying lengths should be collected.

Jackpot! I've always loved pussy willow so when I spy some long branches with *pink* dangling little blobs instead of grey ones I know my arrangement is going to be perfection.

'Japanese pussy willow, nice,' says the American girl, holding a few irises as she moves down the line.

I pick up some simple green leaves and a couple of daffodils to go with my branches, and head back to my spot, where I stand and flex my foot. Looking at my collection, though, I don't quite see how this is all going to come together to look like a work of art.

Turning my pot over absentmindedly in my hand as I wait for the others to come back to their places, my mind rolls back to Benny. He'll be okay ... right? I go to take my phone out of my pocket again for another quick check, and –

'Oh!' I cry, as my stupid butter fingers let the pot slip from my hand, the ceramic cracking in half when it hits the tatami-mat flooring. 'I'm so sorry,' I say to Mio. '*Gomen-nasai*,' my memory finds the formal way of apologising just in time. 'I was distracted.'

Mio looks unfazed, and comes to take the broken dish from my hands, wrapping it carefully in a square of silk and putting it on the windowsill.

'*Gomen-nasai*,' I say again.

She smiles at me and shrugs. '*Wabi-sabi*.'

'Wa-bi-sa-bi?' I repeat.

Mio nods. *'Wabi-sabi.'*

I'm going to need to look that up. I pick up my pencil and write on the side of the print-out the hiragana characters of what I think she's saying, to make sure I'm getting it right. わ び さ び, I write. Wa-bi-sa-bi.

She nods again and gets me another pot.

If I had to guess, I assume it maybe means something akin to 'shit happens'? But I will look it up as soon as I can.

My new pot is larger, a low stone cylinder (less breakable?) and cool to touch, but I wrap my hands around it tightly nonetheless and sit down on the floor in front of my foliage.

Apparently, we're making *moribana*-style arrangements today, which means we're clustering our flowers in these shallow bowls but with three distinct stems of different lengths to represent heaven (the longy), man (the middley), and earth (the shorty).

First we have to pour water in the bottom of our dish, then put in a thing which looks like the head of a paddle hairbrush, but if I'm reading the pictures correctly it's to stick our flowers into.

Next, I need to choose which of my three pink pussy-willow stems are going to be the big tall heaven one, the cute little earth one, and the man one. A little part of me feels miffed we're referring to it as 'man' but then I decide I'll make this for Benny, so it's okay.

Mio walks around the room helping us cut out stems to the appropriate lengths and stick them into the hairbrush thing once we've considered the best angles and the type of look we want to give our *ikebana*.

More than once, despite the silly mistake I made earlier, I look at my phone and when I finally see a message from Mara, I excuse myself to visit the toilet.

At Benny's, everything fine, my sister writes, oh she of few words.

Is he still upset? Are you staying? I type back, hoping she hasn't already left.

She replies immediately. *I've taken him out to a 24-hour cafe for some food and a chat, and yes, I'm going to stay with him for a few days.*

Then she adds, *He says hi* ☺

I exhale, the tension in my shoulders, the shake in my hands I hadn't even noticed was there, subsiding.

Say hi from me. Thank you.

Of course. We'll be fine xx

I have a quick wee, because I might as well make the most of it, and then head back into the room to continue my arrangement, which looks quite pretty from afar when I walk back in, its pink-droplet branches tall and proud.

Okay, no more phone, no more being distracted and rude. Knowing my brother is in the safest hands, I refocus my mind.

By the time we finish our *ikebana*, I'm feeling quite pleased with mine. Not in comparison to everyone else's. In comparison to everyone else's mine looks like a three-year-old jammed some sticks into a pile of leaves. But I like it. However, I think I need to succumb to the fact that my life's purpose is perhaps not to be a florist. I'm sure I could learn to be a little better at it, to create beautiful artistic centrepieces like the ones around me, but it's also okay to be happy with my straggledy pink stick sculpture exactly as it is.

I take another bath that afternoon, wallowing for a long time in the water, cementing the memory so that when I'm home and can't take baths in the middle of the day any more I can cast my mind back to this moment.

What am I going to do when I get home? Really, I need to decide this.

But first, since it's finally a decent hour in the morning back in the UK, I send Mara another text checking in.

Everything is fine, she says. *I'll tell you if it isn't. Focus on making your own decisions and stop getting sidelined by other people's.*

*

The next day, my last full day at the temple, I'm completely unwound. The serene silences, the warm baths, the light, healthy food, the early mornings and early nights and the wonderful *Nissokan* meditations in front of the evening sun are unfurling me like I was a tightly wound fern.

I'm even walking around with the same slow, chilled pace as the other guests, and after breakfast I head to the small library on the second floor of the main building where I spend a while dipping in and out of books on the history of Japan, anything I can find written in English.

Wabi-sabi.

You remember way back in Kyoto, at the Otowa Waterfall within the Kiyomizu-dera Temple? I drank from one of the streams, but it took me a while to pick which one? Well the one I chose was 'school', because I figured that while I was out here I was going to be using Japan, and learning about Japan, to learn about myself. I guess my wish was along the lines of 'I hope I can learn what I need to know'.

I think about that now, as I drink in morsels from these books, a snippet here and a paragraph there, and the meaning of the phrase that Mio, the teacher, my *sensei*, said to me after I broke the pot becomes clear.

Wabi-sabi seems like a hard thing to define, and the more I read the more I feel I'm just scratching the surface. But essentially what I'm getting is this: Life isn't perfect, it's actually quite unpredictable, but that's not only acceptable – it should be celebrated. So, as tricky as it might seem, it's about enjoying the way things are and not worrying about how they should be. There's also a lot of discussion around accepting the transient nature of life and finding beauty in things even if they don't last. I'm not sure how this relates to my broken pot yet, but that becomes clear a short while later.

Back in my room there is a tap on my *shoji* door, and when I open it, there's the friendly monk. He bows to me, and I bow back.

'Is it time for dinner already?' I ask, thinking that the day can't have drifted by that quickly. Perhaps I fell asleep while I lay on my futon listening to the gentle rain soundscape outside the window.

Sidenote: I have a new appreciation for rain. I might not say that back in England if I'm waiting for a bus and everything's drenched and my bag's let in the water and my sandwich is soaked and it's not even 8am yet, but here in the hills of Japan I'm finding it quite tranquil.

The monk shakes his head. 'This is from Mio-*san*, your *ikebana sensei*,' he says, and he hands me a cloth-wrapped gift. 'She says it is yours, a souvenir of *wabi-sabi.'*

He bows and walks away, and I slide the door closed behind him.

Opening the cloth, I gasp at what's inside. It's the dish I broke yesterday, the shallow, pale-green pot I dropped on the ground. Only now it's whole again, fixed together with gold resin, a stripe of beauty that celebrates the line of the break, the imperfection, rather than considering it broken. It's so much lovelier and more unique than before.

I'm searching my soul with the sunset on my face. This is my final chance at *Nissokan* meditation while I'm here at the temple and I want to make it count, sinking into the silence, the only sound my breath coming in and drifting out.

I was getting the hang of this now, and the monk did say that this type of meditation – gazing towards the setting sun – could be done anytime and anywhere, so maybe it will be something I'll take home with me.

I flitter my eyes open for a moment, paying no attention to the fifteen or twenty other people dotted at personal-space-respecting distances around the vast room, and only looking forward, watching the sky. It's cloudy this evening, the rain still coming down, though not hard. The sun breaks through on the horizon, streaming light towards us, and painting the edges of each cloud a deep pinkish orange.

My eyes close again, and I go back to welcoming the silence.

A noise cuts through the peace somewhere elsewhere in the monastery. I try to ignore it until I hear it: my name, clear as the 6am prayer bell.

'*Something something something* Charlotte? She's staying here.'

For a second I think it's Benny, that he really got on a plane and came here, but before I'd even opened my eyes and turned to look at the door behind me, I knew.

Who would rock up to a Buddhist monastery, still in serene silence, and start yabbering? Who is the one person I can always rely on to pick the worst possible timing for any situation?

Chapter 18

What is happening?
What are you doing here, now?
Seriously ... what?

'Is she in here?' the voice gets louder and then there he is, Matt, in the doorway of the meditation room, grinning. I stare at him. Did I drop off to sleep? I must have, this has to be a dream.

Matt. My Matt. Is here.

'Hello!' he bellows, and starts striding across the room towards me.

I stand as quick as I can while still a bit hobbly, grabbing the shoulder of a nearby monk for balance. 'Sorry,' I whisper but he just looks up at me like this is the least of my worries. 'Shhhh,' I hiss to Matt, as he picks his way between the other guests and the monks, saying 'Sorry, oops, 'scuse me, that looks uncomfortable.'

He reaches me and sticks his arms out. 'Hi, Charlie.'

One of the monks does a discreet cough, and I realise I'm still holding his shoulder. 'Sorry. Sorry for all of this. What the hell is going on?' I ask Matt.

He answers by launching into the chorus of Justin Bieber's 'Sorry' and even the monks look embarrassed to be there.

'*Shut up, shut up, shut up*, this a silent meditation.' I hiss. 'This is a monastery. This is not *Britain's Got Talent*. Why the fuck are you here?'

'I came to win you back. I'm sorry for everything. Will you marry me again?' And he gets down on one knee, holding out the engagement ring I gave back to him a month ago.

I look down at him, in front of me, my Matt. Those familiar eyes, that face I've touched a hundred thousand times, the hair I've run my hands through and the lips I've kissed over and over again. He was my whole world, or at least, he occupied the biggest space within my world. But now ... the world seems bigger.

'Get up,' I say quietly.

'Huh?'

'Get up, we can't talk in here.'

'Are you going to say yes?' asks one of the other guests and his wife shoves him. The monk beside me shakes his head just a little, a small sigh escaping.

'You are, aren't you?' asks Matt, completely unaware of his own inappropriateness. And suddenly I feel really mad.

I push him towards the door, apologising to everybody on my way out.

'What's going on?' he asks, trying to hold my hand, which I shake off. At the door I grab a pair of the sandals for both me and Matt and I march us outside into the fine rain. I don't stop until I reach the monastery gate where I give a quick bow, make Matt do the same, and then step onto the deserted road outside the temple grounds.

'You have no respect,' I declare, facing him.

He looks blindsided. 'No respect for what?'

'For the temple, the culture, you can't just barge into a place like that and start shouting. And demanding things and putting unrealistic expectations on other people. It just proves you have no respect at all for any of it. You have no respect for me.'

'I came all the way to Japan for you, to sweep you off your feet.'

'I don't want you here.' My voice cracks because I realise it's true. Many times on this trip I've wished Matt was by my side, that we could be pointing out things to each other, laughing together, doing everything our honeymoon trip promised. But things have changed. I, finally, have changed.

He pushes his wet hair out of his face, vulnerable and confused. 'I just wanted to make a grand gesture for you, show you I mean it.'

'I don't like grand gestures.'

'Yes, you do.'

'No, I don't. I like being given a choice and, and I like making my own decisions and not having someone else make them for me.'

He pauses and looks up and down the road, at the rain pattering on the trees, at the crimson monastery gate behind us. 'You really don't want me here?'

'I don't even understand *why* you're here.'

'I've been watching your Instagram stuff over the past month and with every video I've ... well ... you've just become more relaxed and beautiful and I missed you.' His voice quietens and his breathing slows. 'I realised you were getting further away from me each day and I wanted to win you back.'

'And bring me home? That sounds a little controlling.'

'You know that's not what I mean,' Matt protests, sadness and confusion on his face. He really thought he was doing the right thing this time, didn't he? 'I just realised how much I still loved you. I saw your video saying you were staying at this temple for a few days and I jumped on the next plane. I've not slept for forty-eight hours.'

'How does Katie feel about you coming here?' Oh come on, we were all thinking it.

He blushes a little and tries to hide it from me. 'That's all finished. Wild oats are sown, yay ...'

Ouch. I knew it was happening, of course I did, but still – ouch. Even when it's put in such a pathetic way. I turn my face to the sky, my eyes closed, and I breathe in ... and out ... and in ... and out ... 'I appreciate the effort but we can't go back to how things were, Matt.'

'It can be better than it was, for both of us. Look, this is what I was talking about when I suggested the break – we've both had some new experiences and now, well, nothing needs to change, it's just that now we'll have some new things to talk about.'

'I really don't want to have a big chinwag about your new experiences with Katie. Please don't talk about this whole thing like you did me a favour.'

He shrugs. 'Well ...'

'What?'

'In a way I think I *did* do you a favour.'

Oh, I'm going to kill him, right here in front of this temple and then seek refuge.

Matt continues, more softly this time. 'Charlie, I know that the way I did what I did was ... I know it was bad. It must have been really awful for you, I know that, and I'm sorry, but I don't think you wanted to get married either. I think you wanted an out.'

'Why on earth do you think that?'

'It's not like you fought for us. At the first sign of me showing doubt you shut the whole thing down. Yes, I wanted a break, but I always wanted to marry you. There was no doubt in my mind. You were the one who called it off.'

I leaned back against the wall, soaking my back but without caring. Was he right? Did I push him away too easily, dismissing his own fears too quickly? I stand like that for a long time, and Matt comes and stands next to me. This wasn't what either of us expected from today.

Eventually I say, 'You didn't say to me, "I'm scared, what if we regret never being with other people?" You said you *wanted* to be with other people. That's very different, Matt, and that's not the type of love I wanted to fight for. Do you understand that?'

He nods, slowly, and he looks like he's about to cry. 'But now that's behind us, can we move forward? Can we try again?' He waits for my reply, but I just stand there, rain on my skin. 'I can put the ring away for a bit if you like.'

'It's not about the ring, though,' I say, my voice barely audible.

Matt steps a little closer into my space. 'We can pretend this whole month never happened. I miss you, Charlie. I love you.'

Matt loves me, and I know deep down that I still love him.

We could go back to being Charlotte and Matt. I could get it all back, everything I thought I'd lost. It could all go back to our happily ever after, all it needs is one little decision.

Chapter 19

We shared some lifetime
I don't regret its broken
lovely memory

I reach out and touch his face with my hand, his skin damp from the rain but familiar, the shape of his jawline just how I remembered it.

'I need a minute,' I whisper.

'Sure,' he replies, and before I can pull my hand away he kisses my palm and then pulls me closer to him where we stand for a moment, lips close, tears mixing with the rain. After so many years, the feeling of his face so close to mine still makes my heartbeat quicken.

He's kissed someone else since me.

I kissed someone else too.

I don't want to pretend this month never happened.

'I need a minute,' I repeat, and pull back. 'Come and wait inside, I need to clear my head.'

'Don't take too long,' he says as I leave him and walk up the stairs to my room.

Don't take too long to decide if I want to spend the rest of my life with him? Should I give myself a week, like he wanted, back when we were still due to marry?

I shake that thought from my head. If I'm going to do this, I can't keep being bitter about the past. We were so much more than that one day that changed everything.

My room, my little bedroom in my Buddhist temple. If Matt stayed would he stay in here? No, this is my sanctuary. I slide the doors closed and stand by my window, practising breathing in and out, trying to clear my mind and search my soul.

Should I call my siblings? Brienne? My mum? See what they all think I should do? I hesitate, my phone in my hand, but then I spy my *omamori* dangling from my bag. I have to make this decision. I have to have faith that I *can* make this decision.

I could get back everything I thought I'd lost, and we could be us again. Him and me. Matt and Charlotte. We could finish the latest season of *RuPaul's Drag Race* together. We could laugh in our kitchen over a bottle of wine as we talk about our workdays. We could rent that flat, just like we planned. I could feel the warmth and safety that I always felt when he slung an arm over me in the night.

And eventually we could plan our wedding again together, and we could joke about doing maybe something refundable next time, just in case, ha ha ha.

Only ... that doesn't feel like much of an adventure any more.

I open my eyes to see the last of the sunshine as she's travelling on her way to the other side of the world, and it hits me like a spark.

It's all just fear holding me back, fear of the unknown, but isn't it fear and unknown that makes something an adventure? Would I have experienced Japan in the way I have without that fear of the unknown? Something tells me that I wouldn't.

Fear of the unknown is telling me I can't follow my dream to work at the magazine unless I've figured out everything about myself first.

Fear of the unknown is telling me to play it safe, to go back to Matt, to grasp hold of the life we promised each other now it's back within reach.

'Matt?' I come down the stairs to find him where I left him, sort of, though he's shuffled over to a display case near the reception desk and seems to be trying to put back together an ornament he's knocked over.

'Hello,' he says, managing to save it and turning to me. 'Uh-oh. That's not a good face. I mean, it's a lovely face, lovelier than ever, actually, but you don't look like someone who's just got engaged. Again.'

I shake my head. 'I'm sorry,' I say, with a softness that I know I'll always feel for him.

'We can't try again? Just one more time?

'That wouldn't be moving forward, that would be going back. I'm not happy about how it ended, Matt, but it's okay that it ended, and that we aren't the same people we once were.' I pause, and he nods. He's scared to be without me, and I get that, of course I do, I was scared to be without him and I'm sure they'll be times I'll regret not just saying yes. But ...

'My goal right now,' I continue, 'is not to get you back or replace you, in fact, it's not even to get over you. It's not about you at all. My goal right now is simply to get to know me. Be my own best friend. Be happy.'

I'm sure a time would have come where Matt and I could have been happy again if that's the road I'd followed. And if none of this had ever happened, if we'd been on that same page, we would have been so happy together, I'm sure. But it did happen, we *were* on different pages. I've read the book of him and me. For the first time I feel like I'm writing my own book now, and I know what I want to write.

Outside the sky cries for us and Matt, hearing me, accepting what I'm saying, pulls me to him and we hold each other, for what I know for sure now will be the last time as anything other than friends. 'It's been a hell of a ride,' I whisper to him. 'Thanks for growing up with me.'

'Thank you for being everything I needed, even when I didn't know it.' He pulls back and looks at me one more time, really looks at me. 'Good luck with your next chapter, I think it's going to be amazing.'

'Yours too.'

We break apart, our fingers lingering together until the end, when Matt puts his hands in his pockets and looks back at the temple. 'So, you don't think I should ask them if they have a room for the night for me or will I be banned for life?'

I chuckle. 'I'll be surprised if they even keep my room open for me.'

'Was it really that bad?'

'It really was, Matt.'

We say goodbye and I watch him leave, drifting out of my life like the last petal on a cherry blossom. But I don't feel sad any more, I appreciate what we had. Life is transient, and that's okay.

Later I text him to check he's found somewhere in Tokyo for the night, and he has. He's going to stay for a week and have an explore around, since he's made the journey, before heading back to the UK. I won't try and meet up with him before I get on my flight, but when he asks for my top tips I suggest he goes to Borderless, like we had planned to do together all those months ago. He could do with a bit of headspace. I also suggest a day at Disneyland ...

That evening, I email Amanda at *Adventure Awaits*, and I ask her: am I allowed to apply for the junior travel writer role so soon after starting the internship? I need to know. I'm going to work there one way or another, and I need to know if I have to give up the internship first and then pray to everything and everyone that I get the job, or if I can do both without being seen as the most fickle employee ever.

The second I hit send I worry about what her answer will be. But you know what? Life isn't perfect, sometimes you just gotta try.

I call Mara from my room afterwards, to tell her what happened, and to check in about Benny.

'Yes, he's okay for now, he's looking forward to a chinwag with you when you get back but really, Charlie, you don't need to worry about him.' I'm not sure if 'for now' is good enough, but I do know where she's coming from. It can be tough for young people, or anyone, when they lose sight of why they're doing what they're doing. 'How about you? How did it feel seeing Matt again, you know, after the mad dash to extract him from bellowing his heart out in the middle of the silent meditation?'

'It was okay,' I reply. 'Well actually it was heart-breaking all over again, but *I'm* okay. I think. It's just been kind of exhausting navigating life after a break-up.'

'Right, he was your first boyfriend, so he was also your first break-up,' says Mara.

I sigh. 'It's not fun, I don't know how you've got through hundreds of break-ups.'

'Thank you,' she deadpans.

'I don't mean like that, just … how do you keep picking the pieces back up?'

'You just do, honey,' she says.

I guess even Mara doesn't have all the answers, all the time, and in a way that makes me feel better.

'It's funny, really,' I say with a yawn. 'I felt so lost when I first flew all the way here to the other side of the world. But now I'm still here and I can't put my finger on what's changed because I still feel like me, the person I always was.'

'Just because you lost yourself doesn't mean you had to find someone completely different. You're still *you*, now you're just getting to know you better. You're like

Charlotte, two-point-oh. Charlotte, with the saturation turned up.'

Lightbulb moment. I say to Mara, 'Wait. *I'm wabi-sabi ...'*

'Well, darling, don't say that, everyone puts on a little holiday weight.'

'No.' For God's sake. With Matt being part of my life and identity for so long, when my heart broke it felt like all of me broke. Crack. Right in half. But, *'Wabi-sabi* is ... it's like when something is broken, like in my case my heart, it's not viewing it as finite, or even as a bad thing. It's about putting it back together into something beautiful.'

After my call with Mara, I can feel a tiredness beginning to soak me, like I'm sinking into the warm waters of the hot springs, right up to my ears. But there's one more video I feel I need to shoot before I go to bed.

I set my phone up on my windowsill, so I'm facing the moonlight, which creates a calm, blue filter on my video. I pull my hair into a ponytail and settle down on the floor.

'Hi, adventurers,' I smile. 'I'm nearing the end of my time in Japan now and after a very ... unexpected day I wanted to talk to you about something I've just learnt, but have also unknowingly been learning about all along.

'You might remember from way back in episode one that this whole solo honeymoon thing came about because something happened between me and my fiancé and we called off the wedding. Coming to Japan on my own wasn't planned, it wasn't perfect, but that was my only option. That or stay home.

'But if I'd stayed home, if I'd refused to take a chance on the plan that wasn't perfect, I wouldn't have swum in a rooftop swimming pool over Tokyo. I wouldn't have walked among an entire forest of bamboo. I wouldn't have even tried kayaking on a tropical island, let alone fallen out of one and discovering I quite like the salt water on my skin. I wouldn't have seen the paper cranes in Hiroshima or the monkeys bathing in Nagano. I wouldn't have completed my first-ever overnight hike and known that I want to do more. I would never have tried forest bathing and if I had I probably would have done it wrong and have been arrested for indecent exposure. I wouldn't have spent the night in a Buddhist temple. And I probably wouldn't have said no when the opportunity to pick my marriage up again was presented to me.

'There's a concept in Japan called *wabi-sabi*, which I won't do any justice trying to explain without adding in a lot of "um"s and "err"s. But in a nutshell, at least partly, it's about the beauty of imperfection.

'When I left England, my heart was so broken. Not just in a romantic sense but the broken dream of the perfect wedding, the perfect marriage, the perfect home, the perfect life. And now I feel ...'

I pause, shifting my gaze from the camera and looking out of the window for a moment.

'Yes, that was all broken, but it doesn't mean it wasn't beautiful before, and it can still be beautiful after, because of what you do next.

'I think what I'm saying is, if you're broken it's never really the end, you're never really lost, you can always put yourself back together. You bind yourself with the threads of the new experiences that you make, and what you come out with can be more beautiful and more unique and more fun than before.

'And if you break again, you put yourself together again. It's not easy, but it's not bad. And I certainly feel happier accepting that.'

I look into the camera for another few moments, digesting my own words, and then smile, place my hands together, bow my head and say, '*Konbanwa*.'

Chapter 20

So now, like this land
My sun will keep on rising
day after day ...

I'm happy.

My face is turned towards the morning sun, flashing against the window of the train, my journey to my final destination for two nights before returning to Tokyo and boarding my flight back to my new life. In London. Following the dreams my *ikigai* wouldn't allow me to let go of.

I had the best night's sleep I've had in years last night. I think I've finally cracked the art of snoozing on a futon and every part of me feels rested and ready to move forward.

On the other side of the glass, Mount Fuji sweeps up into the azure sky. She's topped with snow and surrounded by a petticoat of miles of fuchsia pink phlox moss which blooms every year and is knows as the

Shiba-sakura Festival. It's breathtaking, and it captures everything I'm feeling.

Tonight I'm sleeping in a *ryokan*, a traditional Japanese inn, which has its own *onsen* to bathe in with views towards Fuji. I'll be rejoining my Honeymoon Highlights friends there, and I smile thinking of them. What have they seen, compared with what I've seen? Has Japan changed them as much as it changed me?

Actually, 'change' isn't the right word …

With my eyes closed, I can still sense the bright light of daytime seeping in thanks to the rice paper sliding doors, the *shoji*, that divide my room from the rest of the *ryokan*. The tatami mat flooring squidges under my bare legs as I shift position. I'm sitting on the floor with one leg outstretched, giving my ankle some TLC, and taking a moment to appreciate the room for its simplicity. In front of me, on the low table, I'm brewing tea as I was taught in Hiroshima, using a ceramic tea set of pale green, the colour of the river running through Kamikochi. An alcove on one wall contains an *ikebana* flower arrangement, pink, to reflect the colours of the season so associated with Japan. And in a closet is a futon which will come out in the evening to be placed directly on the tatami mat.

And after last night's sleep, bring it on.

'Excuse me, Ito-san?' A familiar Australian accent rings out in the corridor outside my room, asking for help from the *ryokan* host, Mrs Ito. Lucas adds, 'Am I really allowed to wear this even to dinner? My wife isn't so sure.'

'Yes, please do,' replies Mrs Ito, *Ito-san*.

I hear another *shoji* slide open and Kaori's voice sings out. 'This is the *yukata*,' she explains, and I know they're talking about the cotton robes that are provided free and act as loungewear for around the *ryokan*. 'Would you like help putting it on?'

I open my door quietly and stand watching them.

'Thanks, Kaori, that would be ace, Flo hasn't got a clue,' Lucas guffaws back at his wife who comes out with hers on perfectly.

'Kaori doesn't want to see your undercrackers,' Flo laughs. 'Come in here and I'll do it.'

Further down the corridor Jack pokes his head out of his own room. 'Did someone say Lucas was in his underwear?' And that's when he spots me. 'Charlotte!'

They all turn to face me, at the end of the corridor, and I'm walloped with a chorus of 'Hello! *Konnichiwa!* Welcome back! How are you? What time did you get here? Is your room the same as ours?'

I'm about to invite them all into my room for tea when Mrs Ito reappears and beckons for us all to follow her onto the veranda at the back of the *ryokan*, which looks out onto a beautiful sloped zen garden complete with mossy rocks and a tiny waterfall. She instructs us to sit, and she brings the tea to us.

'So tell me,' I address the others. 'How was Shirakawa?' That's one place I would have liked to have made it to had I remained on the tour. It's a small traditional Japanese village, and World Heritage Site, up in the mountains.

'Oh it was beautiful,' enthuses Cliff. 'Reminded me of where I grew up, actually.'

'We spent a couple days there,' adds Jack, 'and it was definitely a highlight. The food was incredible, and the views stunning. Did you see anything of the mountains?'

'I did do a hike in the Japanese Alps,' I say. 'And I fell over and sprained my ankle, but it was possibly one of the best bits of the whole trip. I felt ...'

'Alive?' asked Lucas. 'That's how hiking makes me feel.'

'Alive.' I agree.

'What did you think of Ishigaki?' Kaori asks me.

I smile at the memory, at all the memories. 'I tried the snorkelling, like you recommended. Did you know there are things called parrot fish that are all the colours of the rainbow? But they aren't rainbow fish, those are something different.'

Flo clapped her hands together. 'Talking of fish! We did a sushi-making class and it turns out Jack is an absolute legend at sushi-making!'

'It's true,' Jack nods. 'Apparently I can roll seaweed as tightly as a professional.'

'Will you have a go at it when you're back home?' I ask.

Cliff answers, 'I'll make sure of it.'

'So come on, tell me,' I pour myself some more tea. 'And I mean it this time. What was the most romantic part of your honeymoon?'

They lapse into silence for a moment, thinking, murmuring things about how it was all so special, they loved every minute of it, and I spy Kaori looking genuinely chuffed.

Jack reached over and held Cliff's hand. 'For me it was staying in our own private little farmhouse up in Shirakawa. Just being together, being ourselves, and it was so peaceful.'

Cliff nods, holding his husband's gaze, and then Jack continues. 'It was like where you grew up, huh? Maybe we should find somewhere like that together back home.'

'A farm?' asks Cliff, a smile working its way onto his face.

'At least a farmhouse, or a small ranch. Somewhere in the mountains. Maybe the Rockies.'

God, they are just so luscious, those two.

So that we aren't all just staring at them, I ask the same question to Flo and Lucas, and Lucas right away says, 'Smooching my wife at the top of the Tokyo Skytree. That was just awesome. I literally felt on top of the world, in all the ways.'

'Aw,' Flo blushes, and clocks him softly on the arm. After a little more contemplating, Flo says, 'I know it sounds a little obvious, but for me it was a shrine we went to, north of Hiroshima: Izumo Taisha. Did you go there, Charlotte?'

I shake my head. 'I went to Hiroshima but didn't get north, only stayed in the city and to Miyajima.'

'Miyajima is so beautiful,' says Kaori. 'And the famous *torii* gate has been under renovation for the past year so we were lucky to all see it in full glory.'

'It was?' I ask. 'I didn't realise that. So what made Izumo Taisha so romantic?'

Flo continues. 'Well, one of the deities that are worshipped at the shrine is the god of happy marriage, so there were rituals and things already associated with it, which was fun and interesting. But it's also a really popular place to get married, and seeing couples posing for wedding photos made me think of our day and, I don't know, it just seemed really special.'

Lucas nudges his wife and raises his eyebrows towards me. 'Flo, *ix-nay* on the *arriage-nay* talk.'

I laugh. 'No, really, it's fine, I'm in a much better place than I was when you all last saw me. No need to treat "wedding" like a dirty word. In fact,' I throw in, because why not. I may have only known these people for a total of six days but they feel like old friends, now that we're all sat together in our cotton kimono loungewear, slurping on tea. 'You aren't the only ones who have been doing some kissing on this trip.'

Cue the communal squeal. Even Cliff, Mr Cool Cowboy, joins in with a whoop.

'Tell. Us. Everything.' Lucas demands.

'What can I say, I'm a sucker for a boy serenading me ...' I tell them about my tipsy karaoke night in Hiroshima and how Riku and I tasted sake after sake, and then sang to each other, and we got cosy and his lips were soft and I, the alluring foreign stranger, had to walk away after the last song. Or, at least, the morning after the last song ...

'What song did he sing? What song did you sing? What did he look like?' Lucas wants to know all the details. 'Do you have a photo of him?'

I show them the snap I took of the two of us cheersing over our sake cups. I don't show him the one Moko took and sent me later on, of us kissing under the lights of the karaoke.

'He's cute,' says Kaori.

'He's young,' says Flo. 'Not in a creepy way, just like, nice one.'

'He is a little younger than me,' I concur. 'But he was *allllll maaaaaan*.'

I look back at the picture of the two of us. Ah, Riku. You were fun and kind and happy not to attach any strings. You don't know how much of a breath of fresh air you were, right when I needed it. Or maybe you did, which makes you an even better lasting memory.

'So the love stones in Kyoto worked after all?' Kaori cheered, and we laughed. But maybe she had a point. Not about Riku, as *fine* as he is, but I have fallen in love with Japan. And I have got to know somebody else in the past month that I'm pretty fond of: me.

My last day in Japan is exactly how I could have hoped it would be: good food, interesting company, some alone time, outstanding vistas, and a whole lot of relaxing (plus more good food, mmmmm).

It's early afternoon and all of us are back at the *ryokan*, whiling away a couple of hours before Mrs Ito puts on her wonderful *kaiseki* meal for us. If it's anything like yesterday's, I know it's going to be a delicious and plentiful feast of sticky soba noodles, fat strawberries, bamboo shoots tenderised to perfection, local pork, salty soy broths, miso-flavoured pumpkin, fresh salted fish, sweetly marinated tofu sponges, and so much more.

I have one last video I want to put together while I'm feeling like this, and that's my submission video for the junior travel writer job. I haven't heard back from Amanda, and I hope I didn't ruin my relationship with her, but I can't keep living in fear of the maybes again.

I've already been tinkering, finding my favourite clips, my favourite soundbites, my favourite things I've done and I know how I want to weave them together into my five-minute story of my time in Japan. And if I don't get the job, at least I've got a memento.

When I'm done, I feel proud of myself, not just for the video, but for me, for the things I've done and the person I've let myself become. As I said in the closing seconds of my hopefully job-winning vlog, I was an adventurer. It was adventure all along that was telling me to move forward, dive in, snorkel with my eyes open, climb the mountain, feel the sunset, kiss the stranger in the foreign land and find my happy today, tomorrow and every day.

I'll send it off properly at home, when I can add my CV and write a proper cover letter from my computer, but for now I'll upload my submission to IGTV, add it to the pool of #AdventureAwaitsJob-tagged clips and see what happens. Just before I do, I see another sweet comment from Thomas on one of my pictures. He's been really engaged with my content over the past couple of weeks, and I with his – I look forward to seeing his latest creative works and make sure to always like and comment back.

My heart flutters a little when I think about seeing him soon.

Some people are packing their bags ready to go straight to the airport tomorrow, some are relaxing, but Kaori, Flo and I are enjoying the women's *onsen*. And we're *nakedddd* but that's because of the rules, not because we're all smashed on sake or anything.

Let me tell you a little about the outdoor *onsen* quickly, in case you're wondering why we're in the buff. *Onsen*s use natural hot spring water and you have to go in clean, which means having a scrub-a-dub-dub before you get in. Same as spa etiquette really, or like the indoor shower/bath situation at the temple. Only here, nothing should touch the water except your sparkling clean birthday suit. No swimsuit. You can bring a small towel with you, which is really just a big flannel, and generally people keep it on top of their head while they're in the water, rather than getting it mixed up with other people's on the side, but when there's only three of you – like now – it's not really a problem, so we scamper into the water and plop our towels a good distance apart from each other.

Flo floats past me. 'I don't want to go home,' she sighs. 'That means it's really over.'

Kaori, a vision of loveliness sitting with her back to the mountains, the loose tendrils of her tied-up hair tickling her face in the breeze, says, 'No, it's just beginning, your new life with your husband. And Japan will have you back anytime. And you, Charlotte, of course.'

'Thank you. And you should let me know if you ever come to England and I'll be your tour guide.'

'If your magazine sends you to Australia, Charlotte, look me up,' Flo adds.

I laugh. 'That would be nice, but I'll be on an internship, so no more big adventures for me for a while.'

Kaori turns to me and asks, 'Do you feel sad that you didn't get to experience Japan as a honeymooner?'

I slide through the water to the other side of the hot spring and rest my arms on the cool stone. Mount Fuji rises up ahead of me, her pink gown of flowers beneath her, and I think about the question.

'I don't view it like that,' I say, breathing in the clean air, along with everything I've learnt and seen, and then breathing out any doubt. 'I did go on a honeymoon over the past month. I just went with myself.'

It turns out, my *ikigai* was pretty clear all along. My life's purpose – at least for now, in this point in my life – is to be me. To get to know who I am.

To be happy with me, myself, and *ikigai*.

The End
Or the beginning …

From: Amanda <AmandaB001@AdventureAwaits.com>
To: Charlotte
Date: 5 May, 15.00

Hi Charlotte,

I hope you're well and sorry for the late reply. I want to tell you that we've all been really enjoying following your adventures in Japan through the vlogs on your Instagram channel. You have a natural warmth with your audience, a fearless way of showing your true self, great goals you worked towards and shared, and clearly, from the places you've gone and the things you've seen (and shown us) a passion for adventure. Very impressive. So to answer your question, yes, you very much can apply for the Junior Travel Writer role even though you'll have only just begun the internship. In fact, I strongly encourage it!

Congratulations on finding your ikigai, *can't wait to hear more about it, and safe return travels.*

Best wishes,
Amanda Sakerson
Editor, Adventure Awaits

From: ArielMBCortez
To: Charlotte
Date: 7 May, 9.42

Hey Charlotte,

I think you might remember me! I certainly remember you, from way back when you came to my talk at Stanfords bookshop, what, ten years ago?

As you may know, I don't work at Adventure Awaits *any more, but I'm still so close with the team there. One of the editors, Amanda, sent me a link to your video in Instagram where you talked about your inspiration for heading to Japan and how my article had a little something to do with it. I am so pleased! And I ended up watching all the rest of your videos while I was there too, and I have to say, you're now <u>my</u> inspiration, because it makes me want to go back to Japan!*

I hear you'll be starting at the magazine soon and I wanted to congratulate you on following your dream, and catching those adventures.

Best of luck with everything,
Ariel (Cortez)

From: Thomas <ThomasD006@EcoAdventure.com>
To: Charlotte <CharlotteA002@AdventureAwaits.com>
Date: 1st June, 11.05

CONGRATULATIONS!!!!!!!!!!!!

Lunch? On me ☺

xx

Acknowledgements

Hey readers, I hope you've enjoyed an adventure overseas within the pages of *The Broken Hearts Honeymoon*. My first and foremost dollop of gratitude needs to go to the country that inspired this whole story: Japan. The setting, the people, the *ikigai* and the *wabi-sabi*: thank you.

Huge thank you to Sonny Marr at Penguin Random House for taking me on and guiding the novel from start to finish. Your enthusiasm and sparkle are limitless! And to the rest of the team at Arrow, and Justine – a big, big thank you to you too.

Thank you, always, to Hannah Ferguson, my lovely literary agent. I couldn't do this without ya, you gorgeous-haired superwoman! And *arigato* to the Harman & Swainson crew too!

A big thank you to my favourite author and fabulous friend, Belinda Jones, for cheerleading and championing this project. You inspired me to travel and write from day one and still do. And to Holly Martin, whose talent, dedication and fantastic sense of humour keep me motivated daily. Big love to you both!

Phil, Kodi, Mum, Dad, family and friends: as always, thank you for your support, your help, your patience, and your excitement, even as I regaled you with Japan facts daily over the past few months, and practised my Japanese on you. Chloe, thank you for helping my IGTV-clueless self!

Finally, thanks to the fictional Charlotte, for not going on honeymoon completely alone, but letting me, and you guys, join her for the ride.

Sayonara, sunshines,
Lucy x